T0285833

# Elaine

Also by Will Self

NOVELS

# Elaine

### A Novel

# will
# self

Grove Press
*New York*

This book is set in 11-pt. Sabon by Alpha Design & Composition

First published in Great Britain in 2024 by Grove Atlantic UK
First Grove Atlantic US hardcover edition: September 2024

*Published simultaneously in Canada*
*Printed in the United States of America*

Library of Congress Cataloging-in-Publication data is available for this
title.

ISBN 978-0-8021-6353-0
eISBN 978-0-8021-6354-7

Grove Press
an imprint of Grove Atlantic
154 West 14th Street
New York, NY 10011

Distributed by Publishers Group West

groveatlantic.com

24 25 26 27  10 9 8 7 6 5 4 3 2 1

Pour Nelly . . .

A woman who cannot, or will not, accept the conditions of her servitude naturally and gracefully, deserves what has happened to me.

*Entry from Elaine's diary, February 1956*

# Elaine

# .1.

## November 1955

Standing in the roadway outside 1100 Hemlock Street, Elaine thinks to herself: I'm standing in the road outside my home—our home, one that I make lovingly brand-new every day for the husband and son I love . . . But is this . . . it? Her eyes travel from the buff envelope in her hand to the open mailbox she's just retrieved it from—then drop: What's the point in opening one or closing the other, there's no money to pay the bill, or any of the others already winging in in its wake.

She doesn't dare look up—yet even the immediate surroundings seem to Elaine an aching void: the vacant lot across the road *seethes with ever-greenery*—a sinister undulation. An overhead cable, long, low, and swinging between two far-flung posts, soughs in the freshening breeze. Beyond the sparse shrubbery and some isolate trees, the ground falls away, and she senses—rather than sees—the lake below.

Billy delights in telling her just how deep Lake Cayuga is, and how many millions of gallons of fresh water it contains. His mother wishes he wouldn't—to her it's only cold . . . *and fathomless*: an Aegean from which no Odysseus will ever return to claim his Ithaca . . . *and his Penelope*. While up above? Not *only sky*, but a metaphysical realm in which man's fall is inverted so as to become . . . *woman's rise*. She seeks the joints of the bricks the road is paved with through the soles of her slippers—and summons the silky touch of riverside sands from summer camps long since struck: *With a step that is steady and strong, the Campfire Girls march alo-ong . . .*

If only—if only she had skinny, prehensile toes, could cling securely to the earth. But she doesn't—and she can't, because the sky is sucking her up: she can feel her body twisting, as, with the assistance of her own whirling mind, she's helicoptered into the chilly heavens.

You're not playing in a cloudy playground anymore, she admonishes herself: you're not in Ohio—and not in New York or Vermont, either, but buried alive here in upstate suburbia—from which the only way out is . . . *further up*.

Maybe the little house will ascend with her—the wooden cell within which she's imprisoned. It's a nice enough cell, at least from the outside—but what difference does that make? You can't see what color it is when you spend all day inside. Suddenly, she howls aloud: Is this it? Is this fucking it?!

The obscenity is, she thinks, the hairy leg her husband inserted between hers the last time he wanted . . . *to take me*. And afterwards, he clung to her—although patently not for security, for there's none of this to be found in the quicksand of her troubled being. *Is this it . . . ?* Moreover, do it and this refer to the same object: her life, which is full of things that must be wiped, dusted, and ordered. Plaited, plumped, and *put out* . . . ?

It doesn't help to say it—but she does anyway, this time aloud, the full pack she smoked yesterday, plus the four or five cigarettes she's already smoked this morning, muting her voice so it's halfway between a wheeze and a scream: Can it be . . . that the acme of success . . . for me . . . is being able to do my job as a . . . a . . . housekeeper?

Her words—already *damp and decaying*—fly up into the fall sky. Evelyn Tate, who lives fifty yards along the street, and who—on no basis whatsoever, apart from her bottle-blondeness and her blousy looks—Elaine has decided is a slattern, has at this very moment arrived beside her own mailbox. She opens it and withdraws a manilla envelope with a glassine window: . . . *her own overdue bill*, then inclines a little in Elaine's direction, her pale lips forming the shape associated with the sound *hi*.

Clearly, she didn't hear me.

So, Elaine says it again: Can . . . it . . . be . . . that the acme of success for me . . . is being able . . . a-ble . . . to do m-my job as a housekeeper?

Her hysteria is mounting—and as Evelyn Tate's screen door snaps shut, Elaine says it a third time: Can it be . . . that the acme of success . . . for me . . . is being able . . . to do my job as a housekeeper? Each phrase is separated by a troubled gasp—but it doesn't matter how fast she babbles or deeply she breathes, the panic has the better of her: I'm going to collapse, she thinks, then be swept up into the sky with my goddamn nightie up around my shoulders . . . The last anyone will ever see of me is the first anyone did: my bare behind, waiting to be smacked.

From some studious and irrelevant part of her brain this spidery thought comes a-creeping: *The great complex of associations that are meant to dissolve trauma no longer obtains . . .*

And when it's retreated to a crevice inside her, Elaine rediscovers herself standing in what they call the front room, thinking for the thousandth time, it'd be the drawing one if they could manage that degree of pretension, or the living one if they gave up any ambitions to better themselves.

She stares wildly about at the shopworn props among which they play out their senseless scenes: Billy's beading lies on top of the pink leather pouf they've carried with them since Madison. Elaine remembers buying it in the little secondhand store next to the zoo, where she and John had gone to visit the badgers—because neither of them had ever seen these creatures before, or even knew what they looked like, and since the University's mascot was a badger . . .

Anyway, they'd looked pretty damn miserable in their empty, cold cage—while the pouf, which John bought to cheer her up, had soon enough become a repository for his notes, when he sat beside it in an armchair, working. It still is—and peering at his crabbed handwriting, she thinks how funny it is he's been preoccupied for so long, now, with an epic poem written three hundred years ago—one whose subject is a grand battle, fought clear across the cosmos

between God and Satan, for the very soul of humanity—
while down here in his own backyard . . . *the serpent has
come a-slithering.*

Creatures slimy . . . small . . . hairy—quick and erratic
in their movements. At best blundering—at worst quite
determinedly aiming for eyes, mouth, hair . . . *down there.*
If metaphors are inventions, *poetry is delirium . . .*

Which is funny, yes—but funny peculiar, not ha-ha.

Ha, ha! Elaine barks—bitter laughter, *bitter as the
cud* . . . the poor housebound cow chews on as she does
the housework.

She picks up the beadwork and puts it in a colorful
Mexican bowl John bought for her in Poughkeepsie, the
day when they were driving back from New York, and she
had a crise de nerfs so bad, he had to stop the car in the
main street and, badly panicked himself, ask first one pass-
erby then several more before he could get the name and
address of a local doctor.

Elaine remembers how she was curled up sobbing in the
hollow beneath the dashboard, and her husband had to labo-
riously extract her. She recalls, also, the doctor's waiting
room, which had been the family's parlor . . . *for longer than
a generation*: a grandfather clock tut-tutted crisply in the
corner—there were yellowing mezzotints on the striped flock
wallpaper and cat hairs woven into the balding pile of the
divan's velvet upholstery. A detail she'd found reassuring—it
takes a slattern's husband to treat a slut.

When the doctor appeared a few minutes later, having
interrupted his luncheon, he was carefully wiping his pudgy

hands on a monogrammed linen napkin—and Elaine was already disposed to like him. Rosenbloom had been his name . . .

. . . and her tall frame folded into a little leather-covered easy chair, she'd choked and sobbed it all out to him—from time to time lifting her ugly face up from her ugly fists, tearing her ugly brown curls—until the doctor firmly but forcefully clasped her hands, and . . . *the fight went out of me.*

Kids had been playing ball in the empty lot behind the house, which was an impressive old pile of a place: its finials and a rooster-shaped weathervane surmounting turrets surmounting bay windows surmounting verandas. On any other occasion, Elaine might've made a sally along the lines of, say, The good folks of Poughkeepsie must be sick enough to require your services—but not so sick they can't afford to pay for them!

Which is the sort of thing people do say, when they're normal and normally sociable.

She remembers a sterilizer wheezing beneath the open window, and sending out puffs of steam to mingle with the kids' cries. When Doctor Rosenbloom rolled up the sleeve of her blouse to give Elaine the shot, she swooned again from the very tenderness of his touch.

He'd said, You're taking Miltown regularly, are you, Mrs. Hancock? In which case, it's probably best you don't take any more for a day or two—this is a pretty strong preparation . . .

Calmed, somnolent, Elaine slouched along behind her husband as they went in search of some memento of this queer episode: *The red-and-yellow Mexican bowl? Oh, my parents bought that to celebrate the end of an attack of hysteria my mother had . . .*

Doctor Rosenbloom's fee had been four dollars—the bowl another two fifty. With a couple of coffees and sandwiches the unscheduled stop had cost them close to ten bucks . . . *and as usual we couldn't afford it,* which was why when they were getting back into the Buick, John had snarled: Next time you bring the goddamn pills with you, right?

Standing in their sitting room, eighteen months later, Elaine looks at her son's beadwork in the bowl and ruminates bitterly: I have an undistinguished family, and I doubt anything I'll do will confer distinction upon it. As for my parents, whatever extra energy they've had to expend has gone into eradicating their distinctiveness, along with their Jewishness, as a housewife goes after brown and scummy patches in a goddamn pot . . .

*Brown and scummy patches in a pot.* There are pots waiting for her in the kitchen—ones that'll have brown and scummy patches in them. And there'll be bowls with cornflakes cemented to their sides with sugar—not forgetting the coffee cups, each with its staling, stinking residue. Is it the curse? Elaine muses—then, after a brief calculation: If it is, it's far too early . . . *red and scummy patches in a stainless steel kidney dish.*

Karma the cat comes smarming from somewhere else— and panicky as she is, Elaine's able to recognize the creature's ineffable beauty. Because that's the point, isn't it: she may see it, but how can she possibly describe it? How can she describe anything but the self she's sick of?

The cat is a small tortoiseshell, and caught in the
low-angled autumn-morning sunlight streaming through
the east-facing window, she's finely etched: every hair of her
fur can be distinguished. *Finely etched* . . . Elaine's besetting problem is this: she can find a phrase quite as readily
as she cracks wise, but it's putting these phrases together
into a passage of euphonious prose that altogether defeats
her: the instant she sits down, pen in hand, some ghostly
colleague of Doctor Rosenbloom's shoots her brain full of
novocaine, so everything becomes numbly mumbling and
dumb.

There's this—and also these vulgar scenes from her
childhood that mock her pretensions, sliding between her
smarting eyes and the page: At the age of two . . . *maybe
three*, Elaine had taken to making watery protests by
lifting up the rag rug in her bedroom, and peeing underneath it. She did it quite often, she thinks—which was
completely crazy. Although she doesn't, of course, do it
anymore . . . *that's Karma's job* . . . and maybe the kitten's,
too.

After the Hucksackers' party on Saturday night, they'd
been so tight they went to bed with an old, half-full wine
jug that had been moldering away in the back of the food
cupboard for months. In the morning, Elaine's bare foot,
feeling for a slipper, knocked it over and the remains of
these dregs spread under the bed. When she got down on
hands and knees to mop the mess up, she discovered a clus-
ter of the cat's turds positioned in the exact center, as if the
cunning little bitch had set out deliberately to show just
how cursory her mistress's housecleaning was.

During the night, Elaine had cried Ted's name out—and also during that night, with dumb, drunken collusion on her part, John had taken her—but it wasn't because of the latter that the former had occurred. She'd been far too tight for any fakery—and fakery it would've been to've pretended his caresses had undone her to this extent. No, there'd been no orgasm—there never is: only a crude animal relief.

What's wrong with that? They are animals—they do need relief, and they're practiced, if not at pleasuring each other, at least at providing this precious sort of balm. There have been rows and spats, cemented together with bickering so continuous it's smooth—but on balance, she thinks, they've done well to stick together—and who knows, whatever the significance of her thing for Ted, without any actual adultery having taken place, surely they're both capable of remaining that way—for Billy's sake, if not their own.

This was waking wisdom, though: it was while asleep that she'd betrayed herself as much as her husband—who was sitting up in bed when she returned from flushing Karma's turds down the can. Sitting up, and wearing the sleeveless undershirt that proves he's quite as much a slut as . . . *me.* He puts on his pyjama bottoms no matter how far gone he is, but he doesn't bother with his top half. And it was unshaven, reeking of stale sweat and staler booze, yet evincing a certain sly satisfaction—that he'd told her of her own . . . *involuntary ejaculation.*

Elaine knows he feels humiliated by the fact of Ted quite as much as by Elaine's passion for him. She assumes John's heavier-than-usual drinking, together with this dishevel-ment, is part of some blue-collar fantasy—a he-mannish pose that will make him a bigger, tougher fellow than Ted—and also explains why he'd screwed her through his pyjama bottom fly. Which explains, in turn, why she hadn't detected any ardor—drunk as she'd been—only a desire to be workmanlike: *get it out—stick it in . . .* After all, since he'd been screwing her, it made sense to use . . . *a screwdriver*—or some other tool often employed for the practical jobs needing doing around the house, which *he usually very much enjoys . . .*

Not for the first time, figuring herself as only her hus-band's vessel, Elaine is first revulsed—then convulsed: she lets her legs fold and collapses into a kneeling position, knees pressed deep in the pouf. She sees herself equipped with an erect penis that spurts obscenities all over the cream-painted walls of the sitting room: *fucks and shits and dicks and cunts . . .* because these are the only words . . . *I have to freely give.*

Whereas when she makes the necessary preparations—settling on an idea, devising an outline of the narrative, jotting down notes on characterization—and assembles the necessary equipment—pens and pencils, notebook and typewriter, paper and carbon—once she begins, everything becomes hopelessly hazy, as if thick smoke or gas were being pumped into both her eyes and the room, so the blank page is blanked out.

And if she persists? There are no better words to express how worthless and banal her writing is . . . *than my own.* Only in the past week she'd tried yet again, beginning a short story about a girl having an affair with a mysterious man in Manhattan . . . But when she'd read back the first couple of pages she was appalled: the prose so very much worse than clichéd—while there was no plot, as such, only a feeble gesture to her own . . . *pitiful and self-pitying past.*

Before that, a month or so ago, she'd been full of the brave intention to write something based on the biography of the composer Telemann, because she'd heard a beautiful piece by him played on WQXR. But what did Elaine know about Telemann and his times? Next to nothing—and now, remembering the dumb hash she'd made of describing Hamburg in the eighteen hundreds, she thinks: Why didn't I go the whole way and show him *screwing through his fly* . . .

A dumb hash? No, an abortion—such that the poor cow who's miscarried it looks blearily down at the fetus and its placenta, coiled slimily together . . . *in the meadow grass.* Perhaps it's that she should've described—because she has at least witnessed this doleful sight. That summer in East Jamaica, when they were staying with Ken Durant, and she and John had taken turns having hushed conversations—albeit on quite different matters—with the much older man.

On the hottest day of August, Durant took her for a drive to see the overgrown plot and accompanying tumbledown buildings he was intending to turn into a summer camp for juvenile delinquents from the Boston slums. Standing, with the sweat trickling down between her thighs, her arms crossed to hide the damp patches spreading from her

armpits into the red gingham of her blouse, Elaine had
been as certain as she could be that he was about to make
a pass at her—but he hadn't.

He'd only stood there, in the tawny, thigh-high grass, a
living frill of cabbage-white butterflies rippling about the
neck and armpits of his own sweat-stained T-shirt. Stood
there stock-still—even though there must've been scads
of flies, because there, only a few paces away, *in a chill
cold blast of sunlight* were the cow and its slunk. Ken had
explained to her how unusual it was for a cow to miscarry
at this time of the year—and Elaine had thought, *Poor
cow.*

It had been an unusual sort of summer for the Hancocks
anyway—Elaine was surging with all manner of unrealized
passions, ones that affected her suddenly and physically—
like cramps *in my belly . . . my breasts . . .* Billy had been
a towheaded two-year-old, lithe as a monkey, who, during
those interminable sizzling afternoons, lay alongside her
on the couch where Genevieve Taggard had died only eight
months before, while she listened to John and Ken's two-
power summit meeting in the next room.

They'd been talking—in a highfalutin fashion—about
what could be said and what could be written, now that the
jackboots were stamping on the faces of American activists.
Even then—and even talking to someone like Durant, who
was so much older, so much more of a man of the world,
John's tone—which Elaine reads pitch-perfectly, although,
*like Telemann, I'm self-taught*—had been caustic, almost
mocking. A manner that was also belied by his curiously

baffled expression—which his wife also knows . . . *all too well*.

It'd been near impossible to persuade Billy to nap. He kept squirming about in her arms, breaking free to confront her with his bluer-than-blue eyes. Then, one afternoon when he'd at last fallen into an uneasy slumber, she'd disentangled herself from him, unstuck herself from the leather skin of the old chaise longue, and retrieved the grocery sack she'd hidden behind the row of city directories on one of the library shelves—for this had also been Genevieve's study.

She'd make-believed . . . *I made believe*, that the sack's contents, these quite dull, buff-card-covered exercise books, *were hers* . . . their host's dead wife's: the celebrated poetess. Clutching this trove of writings, her posthumous guest had then gone quietly upstairs in her bare feet, and entered a musty and unused bedroom, where flies lay dead on their backs on the windowsills. Kneeling on the warm floorboards before a cool iron fireplace, she'd first torn out, then fed into the flickery little fire she'd lit, page after page of her own clear cursive handwriting, trying to maintain that illusion—and with it the conviction that in destroying the record of her adolescence and young womanhood, she was somehow releasing her own muse . . .

But the truth was . . . *I was all bitched up inside*. Bitched up, and struck by this not particularly original observation, albeit one that's remained revolving around her—a buzzing insistence that *one is only a collection of mutinous selves*, the coherence of which—if any—is made possible by skin alone, that singular organ at once thick and thin, smooth and dry to the touch—yet from which can be rendered . . . *a quart or more of yellowy tallow.* Skin . . . *the thing we're all in* . . . because we're wearing coveralls . . . *made of ourselves.*

Sometimes, when she's transcribing one of John's manuscripts—which he composes, insufferably, in pencil—Elaine picks up her own pen and traces outlines of his words, and as she does so, it feels as if she were wearing gloves made from the skin flayed from his hands, by this perverse act taking control of his writerly being: it isn't he who came up with this sparkling little aperçu, linking the Areopagitica to Rousseau's Social Contract, *but moi* . . .

The dead calf had been such a self, spontaneously aborted—and Elaine's writings were also *nonviable* . . . as some obstetrician might say of an embryo. Whereas Genevieve's poetry was of another order: she'd shelled out fresh selves for decades—they'd appeared in the little magazines and the larger journals—there'd been collections of them and some had made it into prestigious anthologies. Latterly, her several selves had been gathered together into the musty embrace of the Library of Congress. They were whispering there still in the stilled stacks: *Over you, over you, over . . . I hang like a wave, like a lover* . . .

At least some of them were—there'd been other Genevieves, who, as Elaine had burnt her own girlish journals, full of lousy poetry, screamed out loud and clear: What are you doing in my house? And with my husband?

Perfectly reasonable, if shrill, inquiries—because she hadn't only been napping with her kid on Genevieve's couch, she'd been cooking in her kitchen as well, and the poetess wasn't yet dead a full year, although . . . *the last few months it was as if she'd left us already*, her widower had said in that poisoned paddock, with the aborted fetus and the ruffs of butterflies . . . *she turned her face from everything in the world, me included.*

A line Elaine had felt was at best disingenuous, and at worst: *a line* . . . not that he'd require any skill to reel her in, because Ken was one of those screwy, difficult guys she found it tremendously hard—if not impossible—to resist. So, she'd bobbed about in his wake that long, hot afternoon, as he'd driven hither and thither in his station wagon, so indifferent to her presence it'd been as if he were taking the automobile rather than her to these places.

Seven years later, standing still in her own sitting room, Elaine, savoring her *gone mood*, stares sightlessly at a meagre bookcase overflowing with this—for the most part—sterile congress: her and John's poetry books, each volume . . . *a leg* wedged between two of its concupiscent companions. She stares sightlessly, remembering all those other captious selves, going to their deaths in the Durants' fireplace.

In one respect at least, Elaine is indisputably a writer, since she diarizes compulsively—and even that terrible purge had failed to cure her of the habit: within days she'd begun again, summoning still more selves into existence by setting down the truth about her tumultuous feelings pell-mell, without troubling to dress them up in rhyme, or teach them a rhythm.

So, over the months and years, an undisciplined gang of them has been spawned—tens . . . scores . . . hundreds of little Elaines, all ranged in time the way the reflections of mirrors positioned opposite to one another are ranged in space, so: infinite Elaines, all of them falling for difficult, screwy guys—all of them being rebuffed, but still dogging these men's footsteps as they try to escape her clutches. Now, she wrestles with her latest passions—which are a mere shadow play if she considers the stark ratio of touch to imagined touch. Yes—she has made an even more colossal fool of herself than ever.

How long had their troika of a family freeloaded at Durants' place that summer? It had seemed like months— but can only have been a few weeks. Weeks during which John labored away at the paper he convinced her would be a major step towards his establishment as a serious critic, while his wife chased after the dead poetess's widower, and measured herself against . . . *the million reflections of her beauty and wonder.*

There'd been a large, silver-framed studio portrait of the young Genevieve on Ken's desk—one taken when she can only have been a little bit older than Elaine was in 1947. Despite the tubular dress and the lampshade coiffure, young Genevieve appeared simultaneously gamine, nubile . . . *and intelligent.* It'd been hard for Elaine—who'd only met her once, and who'd also had so little experience of death—to believe her truly and irrevocably gone when so much evidence of her remained, right down to the book full of her handwritten recipes that hung from a hook by the old-fashioned range.

Not that Ken had spared them the details—remarking more than once, when he was tight, that while her body wasted away, her once-pretty features had grown first coarse—then horribly swollen. It was, he said, as if her very body had been saying . . . *there's no poetry to be made out of this.*

Stricken, or not, grieving, or not, her widower had taken a lover within weeks—or, quite possibly, had had one waiting in the wings. She came once to the Vermont place. A very feminine person, Elaine had thought—at once pretentious and infantile: I could never have played her role for him—any more than I could've Genevieve's . . . Although back in the spring of that year she'd imagined she might, when Kenneth had written to her, saying he was coming up to New York—and . . . *I waited all that day,* while fantasizing about what it would be like to have him make love to her, with utmost tenderness, on the red plaid rug which Billy curled up on for his afternoon nap.

But he hadn't come—and hadn't even called. When they saw him again—and she got him alone—he'd had the perfect excuse: an unscheduled hospital visit . . . She did realize, didn't she, *the gravity of the situation?*

Still standing—but now staring out the window and across the road to the overgrown lot on the far side, Elaine stops—stops what she's doing, and realizes she's been folding this selfsame rug with her shaking hands. Why the tremor? Is it the feverish alternation between brazen lust and chilly self-mortification—or a genuine malaise creeping up on her, insinuating itself between

one unpalatable thought . . . *and the next*: there's brackish saliva in her mouth, and she's aware of a vein in her
forehead . . . *beating . . . beating . . .*

And the following afternoon, when he'd taken her to
the tumbledown property, what was it he'd said to her?
Ugh. Ugh-upon-ugh—how could she have got herself into
a position where any man could say to her: *I was willing to
take you, but now I see that you're worthless . . .*

*Yes, shame as cold as ice*, so cold she'd been compelled
to burn first all the diaries she'd kept while John had been
overseas . . . *and then all the rest*. In her abject condition
she'd assumed she was entirely readable: a book with a
transparent cover, through which the details of her infi-
delities were dreadfully legible: page after page of neurotic
effusions about Joe . . . about Arty . . . Explicit jottings,
too, about the supervisor at the Newark plant who she
hadn't spotted as any kind of suitor until he shoved her
up against the corrugated wall of the Quonset hut where
the fuses and bulbs were stored and, yanking up her skirt,
grabbed at her vulva, his fingers pulling at the waist of her
elasticized girdle so it peeled away from her sweaty skin
then . . . *snapped back*.

And it's happening again . . . *again and again*.

She'd torn two or three pages at a time from their spiral
binding, then, carefully balling them up, placed each crin-
kly globe atop the velvety, petaline ash of its predecessors.
Multiple immolations—multiple suicides . . . If she did,
and she left behind these vivid accounts of her desperation,
would John feel bad when he read them? Would her parents? Probably not—because if she's entirely honest, it's the

self-pity that *shines through* . . . It's the same now, when
she thinks of the books with which she's replaced them—
more yammering on about the general crumminess of the
human species, and her disaffection from it.

She's seen herself, so many times, prostrate on the cot in
the spare room—an unwanted guest . . . *for all eternity*, the
pots emptied of pills beside her, the spiral-bound exercise
books piled up on the bedside table—and on top of them a
note, apologizing, of course, and also instructing John to
send the books to Doctor Freudenberg, who *has so firmly
cast me off* . . . Does Elaine really imagine he'll make use
of them to assist in his treatment of other poor and tormented souls? Or is it her way of remaining in analysis
forever—a ghostly presence in the corner of his consulting
room . . . *plaguing his conscience?*

In East Jamaica, in the big old creaky colonial, her
motives had been equally idiotic: that by burning her diaries she'd also rid herself of any guilt . . . *and all illusions.*
Henceforth—and for better or worse—she would live in
the cold light of her reason. The men's earnest voices had
resonated in the hardwood body of the house. What had
Kenneth and John been talking about? The same stuff Ted
and John were discussing at the Hucksackers' last Saturday,
where their whispery seriousness—or so they thought—
curtained them off from the other guests.

Why do they hang on to it so, this superior, mocking
one-size-fits-all philosophy? Surely only because it confirms
them in their own superiority . . . That, and because it gives
them something to *sit* beside—the way they'll sit beside a
river, or on Ted's boat, waiting for a bite *or a revelation.*

Because that's what even men like them—smug, superior, above all intelligent—do, in lieu of simply saying what's on their minds.

With a start, Elaine realizes this with complete certainty: despite the conversations their inharmonious quartet have had—stilted to the point of suffocation—concerning their situation, and notwithstanding the hours spent talking and writing and implying—and then talking some more about these involved implications, each with the other . . . and God knows, whatever their terrible derelictions, howsoever their failings, each unto the other, John and she still talk—and talk deeply, she thinks, honest in the admission of how their deceits and disaffections nevertheless betoken respect not grudged but earned . . . Anyway, this she now apprehends with as great and terrible clarity as that with which she apprehends the shade of the woodwork in this room—a beige suggestive of surgical support hose, that has disgusted her on a daily basis for the full four years of their residence—neither man has ever uttered a word to the other about Elaine's consuming passion for Ted.

Which is surely a further superior judgement on her husband's part—and Ted's, for that matter. But hasn't he been as unfaithful to his beloved proletariat as she's ever been to him? In her case, was it truly infidelity at all? With gauche little Joe there'd been more agonizing than lovemaking, although when the latter had occurred, well . . . You've only, Elaine thinks, to be taken somewhere heavenly once to yearn, ever after, for a return: Is it any wonder she maintains a sacrosanct memory of his humble room and the glorious things they did in it?

While with Arty there had been some excellent, if utilitarian, sex experiences—Elaine still feels his weight on her thighs, smells his cologne curdling in the coffee she's only just burned— How can she really have been unfaithful to John, since to do so she would have had to be faithful to him in the first place, which she doesn't believe . . . *I ever was.*

She moans—a guttural bovine sound. She shakes out the plaid rug and swirling it about her shoulders almost succumbs to dizziness . . . vertigo . . . and the suicidal thoughts that are its inevitable accompanists: because if you feel the yawning mouth of the abyss—it can only be because you want to . . . *fill it.*

This is, she thinks, a tremendous effort of will—tearing herself away from the edge of the precipice, pivoting from the sublime . . . *to the ridiculous*: John's left her the Buick today, as Ted gave him a lift in to the campus, and she has to take the kitten, Maya—who she suspects may not be . . . *as she seems*—to the vet for confirmation. She might treat herself to a coffee and a chicken sandwich at the Brush & Palette—perhaps do a little window-shopping at Rothschild's, if, that is, she gets her chores done.

On top of the daily dusting and tidying, the beds and the dishes, there's the *irony* from two washes that's built up—and who knows, it could be that today's the day when Elaine finally empties out the cupboard under the sink and cleans the greasy shelves. She's sworn she'll do it . . . *fucking sworn it*. But first . . . she refolds the rug, lays it on the couch from which she lifts Billy's Mad magazine . . . *what, me worry?* Her laughter is raucous, and bitter as the . . . *burnt coffee* she tastes swilling around in the back of her throat.

The truth is, she does worry—and it's the same worry as it was in East Jamaica: that John will find her hiding place and read all these reams of *girlish gush*—cockeyed and coquettish it may be, but she's carefully set down the particulars of every single one of her and Ted's interactions, even those that occur . . . *in fantasy*. Set them down with such fidelity and attention to detail that this character, at least, leaps vigorously off the page.

Why does the textual corroboration of what she knows he already knows to be true so agitate her? It does, though: her heart beats so strongly it wobbles in her ribcage. He is, above all things, a scholar, a reader, a parser of texts—at times Elaine wonders if he's ever lent any credence to the testimony of his senses at all.

Just as well and as it should be—because Ted is a real, live man: tall, athletic, and with an ugly-beautiful face, dark, beetling brows, and strong, square hands, the backs of which are covered in the same black hair as his head— although not, thank God . . . *as thickly*. She may be a lousy writer—one of the lousiest ever—nevertheless, throughout this long and frenzied year of surreptitious scrawling, she's managed to surpass her limitations. Her evocation of his honking Midwest voice, his—when caught unawares— baffled, little boy's expression, and his air of repressed— but powerful—sexual desire, has affected her only reader to this extent: Elaine has cast pen and exercise book aside on several occasions and . . . *pleasured myself.*

Which sounds better—albeit corny—than . . . *masturbated.* Ted would call it bias blindness rather than prejudice, pure and simple—but when Elaine wrote to Doctor Freudenberg in January and told him what was going on—that she'd fallen for another screwy, brainy guy—she'd admitted as much, and used the technical term favored by the psychoanalyst.

Why? Why does Doctor Freudenberg continue to exert such influence on Elaine? Writing to him months after she'd stopped making her weekly pilgrimage to the dull little office he rents in the nondescript building in downtown Syracuse, she'd transported herself right back to where, for nearly a year and a half, she'd done her best to tell him the truth. Or rather, just as with thinking about the disposal of her writing now, it was sufficient for the syllables of his name to be thought—*Freu-den-berg*—for the man himself to enter the room and take a seat, notebook and pen dandled on his corduroy knee . . .

. . . so summoning—since there's doubting his manifest cleverness, or his latent screwiness—all manner of confessions: I peed under the rug when I was . . . I dunno . . . maybe two or three . . . and now I've masturbated over one of my husband's colleagues aged thirty-four, and I have . . . *sagging breasts* and *lank, thinning hair* . . .

. . . *you'll never be a gamine girl*, her own petite and gamine mother had said to Elaine *a zillion times* . . . near-infinite repetitions of an exasperation with her only daughter that, as Elaine grew older and yet taller, changed from still-hopeful sighs to grunts of a grim finality. At fourteen, Elaine had reached her full adult height of five feet ten inches—if she could be described as willowy, it was only pejoratively so, for her shoulders were permanently rounded, while her scoliosis was the result of her forever bending into the rising wind of social disapprobation.

To be tall was bad enough—to be awkward, worse still, but to be gawky as well, and moreover, to have a nose like a big blob of clay stuck in the middle of her *ugly mug* . . . ? At seventeen, she looked, she thought, like her father in a shirtdress—her father, that even more cut-rate Groucho— no greasepaint mustache, see—who cracked wise the whole time, while remaining, quite simply . . . *vulgar and unfunny.*

Freudenberg had replied to her letter a little too adroitly for Elaine's taste—indeed, *much to my chagrin*: First he reassured her—an obvious finesse—that no, he didn't think she was about to go to pieces, then he gave it to her straight: No, he didn't believe it was the right course of action for her to resume sessions with him—there was no doubt she'd improved during the course of their work together . . . *odious, onerous expression!* but so far as he was concerned, she'd reached a kind of plateau—or impasse—one she'd have to surmount some other way. Besides, her regular Wednesday afternoon appointment time had long since been taken by another. If she found herself in a state of desperation, then yes, he would of course see her, and continue to do so on an ad hoc basis, but if she wanted to resume analysis properly . . .

. . . well, the treatment, having suffered considerable set-backs during the war, was now—rather ironically, because of it—enjoying a steady progress when it came to both training practitioners and attracting patients . . .

. . . Why, he was no longer the only psychoanalyst to be practicing in Syracuse—as he had been when Elaine first came to him—indeed, he was aware there were now two who'd hung up their shingles in Ithaca as well, one of whom—and here he veered closest, Elaine thought, to really revealing his hand—was a woman.

Elaine, as she'd read this self-serving dismissal, had wondered—as she wondered again, now—whether this strange beast, the female shrink, would say the same sorts of things to her as Doctor Freudenberg had about her inability to write being just another instance—pen/penis, *get it?*—of her *all-consuming envy* . . .

Beneath the Mad magazine is the local paper—an advertisement stares up at Elaine, and she peers down at it . . . *why is everything so far away today . . . ?* Three-piece snow suits for girls: $3.90. Two-piece ones for boys: $2.90. Is this something else to envy: the male creature's simpler and cheaper garb, together with his lack not only of adornment but of even seeing the need for it?

Elaine snaps back to Ted with a small shock: the saggy seersucker suit he wore all summer, and which he'll quite likely pack to take on their trip to Cuba. Betty has told Elaine she makes a studied point of not packing for him—it's a demeaning task only movie spouses perform for their husbands. As so often, when she made judgements of this kind, Elaine had inwardly cringed, thinking that whatever else may've happened between them, she still packs John's overnight bag for him—and is that so very wrong? Isn't that a possible way forward for them—if there is any at all—rescreening the silent two-reeler of their intimacy?

Ted had suddenly floated the idea of this winter vacation as the last dying embers of the Hucksackers' party were glowing . . . *with our bourbon breath*, kindling warm hope in Elaine's heart again: In that case let us take Stella again—we so enjoy having her . . .

. . . she'd blurted out—then her bleary eyes cleared, and she saw John's expression of dutiful compliance. A mask, she knows, beneath which burns his own inner conflagration, for a thief will just rob you and take all you save, but *a false-hearted lover will lead you to the grave* . . . such a fearful temper! we both have—and we fight . . . excepting when I've been too ill to.

Fights that begin fugally, as, both being past masters of the verbal put-down, their calls and responses ascend the scale to become full-scale screaming matches, that on more than one shameful occasion have gotten physical. But Elaine doesn't want to dwell on such unpleasantness—not this morning, when right from when she woke everything has seemed *half gone* . . . An actual absence, as if half of the screen door, half of the side door, half of the mailbox, half of the goddamn world has evaporated.

Elaine thrusts down into her jumbled mind the trouble between her and her husband—as she does the Soviets' widely reported detonation of their first hydrogen bomb. After all, she knows this much: her view of the world

closely parallels her feeling about herself—the whole thing
is likely to explode at any moment . . . *and I'm also on the
verge of disintegrating.*

Now, the dishes in the kitchen sink she stands suppliant
before appear not only sunk in cold, greasy water—but
half immersed in an ulterior realm. The same one she sees
when the surface of reality is itself torn, and out swirls dizziness, acute nausea, and a piercing headache—all decked
in kaleidoscopic finery. This, the likely imminence of her
monthly migraine, she ignores as well—which is something
she often does, forgetting that forgetting never works.

Mounting the bare oak treads of the narrow staircase
that rises precipitately from the small hallway, she listens
to the familiar *creaky concerto* . . . as the little old wooden
house stretches and tenses around her. There are all manner of houses in Ithaca—from modern ranch-style affairs
to fretworked fantasias on the Gothic theme, plus quite
a few solid old colonials. They're painted all manner of
colors, too: rusty reds, powdery blues, daffodil yellows. But
the Hancocks' house is pretty nondescript—a kind of half
saltbox, painted a dirty cream color, its gable end-on to the
street, and the single-story extension to the rear with only
wire screens for walls and a concrete floor upon which is
cluttered just about everything from Billy's old stroller to
a couple of cords of firewood in case they run out of coal
for the furnace.

Upon reaching the top landing Elaine keeps her eyes
down—sure, she was outside checking the mailbox only a
quarter of an hour ago, but since then something at once
insignificant and momentous has irretrievably altered: if

she looked up, she'd see through the open door into Billy's bedroom, and through the unshaded window of that room . . . *nothing*, only those invisible elements that, once jammed together in an unholy mush, can fly apart with the force of a million tons of TNT . . . *or more*.

She knows this because Billy also delights in such equations—between the powers of one superhero and those of another, or of this explosive and that one. One million, two million, three million . . . there is, in principle, no limit to the size of the bombs that can now be cooked up as the cold war simmers. When the irrepressible Billy marches about the house, banging his old tin drum and belting out, One million, two million, three million . . . whether it's gallons or kilotons, his mother wants to slap his face—and one time . . . or more . . . *I did*.

So terribly unfair—and damaging, she knows this: he suffers from the same sorts of anxiety as she does, his drumming being surely his own way of pounding it back down into the unconscious. While she detonates hers with a spasmodic swipe, a fusion of *hand and cheek* . . . Elaine shuffles, shamed face heavy and red, across the landing and into the bedroom she still shares *just about* . . . with John.

Then shuffles over to the bureau, which is where she keeps her current diary: in her underwear drawer, under her underwear. If she inveighs against her husband's straitlaced mien—which she does, finding inexhaustible irritation in the way he purses his lips . . . and casts down his chaste gaze––then there's at least this benefit: it's impossible to imagine John so much as looking in here, let alone rummaging around.

The other ones she's already filled are in an old steamer trunk in the attic—together with defunct college textbooks and holey knitwear she has promised herself she'll darn . . . *forever*. Elaine sees side by side the pale pine darning mushroom and the billowing cloud *all flickery within*. She pulls down the shade until there's only a few inches of exposed windowpane, through which the winter light sidles. Seated on the bed, she opens the spiral-bound exercise book at a page full of . . .

. . . spirals and loops coalescing into patterns, some inked in or otherwise embellished. These cockeyed arabesques suggest idle versions of Matisse or Miro, and grow out from the written entries as if they were creepers, choking the life out of shopping and to-do lists—ones of party guests as well, both real and . . . *ideal*.

Fantasizing that takes a more shameful shape when she leafs back a few pages and finds repeated examples of her own signature: Elaine Hancock, Elaine Hancock, Elaine Hancock . . . interspersed with the names bestowed on as yet unborn daughters: Letitia Hancock, Lettice Hancock, Lalage Hancock, Lucy Hancock, Lisa Hancock . . . *and those're just the els!*

Worse yet, bedizening the pages before this wordy birthing are the seals set on an unachieved and impossible union: Elaine Troppmann, Mrs. Elaine Troppmann, Elaine and Edward Troppmann . . . Mrs. Edward Troppmann. Unachieved—and unconsummated. What has been going on between them now for almost a year—twelve full months of drunken fumbles and liquorish kisses? The Troppmanns entered their circle at around the same time, Elaine recalls, as its rather more louche members began with this business of husbands necking with other fellows' wives, and those other fellows' wives necking with . . . well, with other fellows.

*Necking parties* . . . they call them, a childish sobriquet to be sure, and one that diminishes, she thinks, the magnitude and seriousness of her passion. Ted Troppmann, all this long year, has weighed upon her terribly: the fact of him rather less than this phantom man she breathes life into every day, for it's Ted she thinks about on awakening—Ted whose lopsided smile she sees last thing at night.

An obsession? Quite likely—but she has felt his tongue twine with hers, his hands on her hips and her back. A compulsion? Maybe so, but the coffee-and-Camel-smoke smell of the man arouses her . . . *mightily*, and besides, hasn't everything she's ever done been pretty much a result of compulsion rather than choice?

The matter at hand being a perfect example: does she have any choice, truly, when it comes to who she invites to John's birthday party?

She writes John's Party, underlines this heading, then embellishes it with doodles of musical notation—unfurling staves, twisted notes, curled clefs—before adding the first names, Ted & Betty Troppmann, then resting the nib of her pen. Already there's an inky groove in her second finger.

She continues: Pat & Bobbie O'Brien, Bob & Missy Cantor, Phil and Rae Dupré, Digby and Carlotta Henty, Harry and Selma Lemesurier, Caspar and Mona Voss, Daniel and Diane Goldberg, Jimmy Castlemaine . . . *the fairy*, and the Hucksackers, Henry and— She stops again, and pictures them all standing in a necessarily tight grouping in the living room, their glasses raised. She hears herself making the toast for the birthday boy—she's incisive, well aware that nothing ruins an atmosphere quicker than running on. She's witty—and loving.

The applause is rapturous—Ted Troppmann claps the loudest of all, his big hands pounding into their respective palms, his green eyes sparkling . . . *with delight*, while John looks on with his quizzical, half-gone smile—so slight it scarcely adheres to his pale face.

His pale face . . . his pale uncertain face. It can't be thrust away, it looms closer—and Elaine lays her pen down, first massages her temples then curls her fingers into fists and rubs this troubling vision into an afterimage: of course she feels as if she has no choice when it comes to the party—she organized one for him last year, when it was already a gesture rather than something warmly and happily undertaken. What goes around comes around, eh— wholly deadlocked, that's what they are. Will anything ever really change—or, for that matter, truly happen?

Was she ever attracted to John? There'd been that first date, when, flattered by this older and more sophisticated man's interest in her—he'd been to Europe, for Christ's sake!—she'd listened, agog, as he'd sketched for her in the sticky-flock atmosphere of the Chinese joint in the Village the precise trajectory his scholarly career would follow, the books and papers he would write, the positions he would hold, the tenure he'd get.

He'd appeared so very certain of himself—as a twenty-one-year-old woman that's all you really want: a man who knows what he wants, and is preparing himself to get it. In the cab uptown they'd kissed passionately enough that Elaine had to snatch his hand from her breasts more than once. In the booth at the Famous Door, the assault was renewed, as the house lights went down and Wingy Manone, together with his band, took to the stand.

Years later, and completely tight, he'd confessed: Oscar Schaftel, who'd been teaching Elaine at Queens College, had set up the date reluctantly, telling his young Columbia colleague that she was some kind of a *left-wing culture groupie* . . . or words to that effect—because these had been John's own slurred ones, the humiliating implications of which he'd further spelled out: *On that basis alone, I couldn't help but assume you'd be likely to put out . . .*

Outraged then—and if anything, even more so now—Elaine's never seen this as temerity, only weakness: the behavior of a milquetoast man who doesn't know how to make love properly to a woman, to seduce her—let alone take her with true virility, and as of right. John may not exactly be a mother's boy—there's a deep antipathy between him and his Mutti—but he is, Elaine believes, by reason of his father's premature death, a boy who's grown to manhood without being adequately schooled in its ways.

Sure . . . he did the whole street-corner shtick in his time as a grad student: hanging out in poolrooms, collecting anecdotes concerning characters who—the way he'd tell it—were as colorful as anything Runyon ever came up with . . . But Elaine doesn't buy it anymore, seeing only his sex-hungry little simper, which he's immature and selfish enough to believe she finds . . . appealing.

Except that sometimes—in desperation, in objectless lust, and in that mood of near-geographical isolation that grips the irretrievably married, so transports them to a Pacific atoll that is both figurative and real enough to deliriously copulate on—she does.

Which in turn means she's revulsed even in his absence—a spasm that blinds her to the view through the window: the yawning gulf of the empty lot, superimposed with the first, oblique dashes and dots, telegraphing the message that rain is imminent. Instead, Elaine sees John's meagre, hairless chest—his swelling belly and sad, small sack of genitals lurking in its shadow . . .

. . . recently—or, in truth, it's been weeks if not months, he's stopped exposing his body to her, perhaps sensing . . . *my contempt.* No! Not sensing—but experiencing it directly: the rage of a slave who's at long last been freed, and who now sees her master's behavior for what it truly is, not benign paternalism but yet again . . . *weakness.* Each time during the past three or four years when Elaine had one of her crises, it was John who bore the brunt of it—unless he wasn't there, in which case—*Oh, the shame!*—it was Billy.

How long, precisely, had her postpartum neurosis lasted? There'd been episodes not long after Billy's birth—but they hadn't been too bad, and besides, John's own old nurse, Hetty Garcia, had been on hand for the first year. The old woman was about as gentle as a snapping turtle—but she was entirely competent and confident. Then, in his second year, with no help on a regular basis Elaine's condition had begun to deteriorate. Left alone with her child, she felt the one thing she shouldn't have: bereft. Not only that—but quite incapable of ministering to him properly. So incapable, she worried she might do something to him, simply in order to signal more effectively her terrible inability to . . . *love*.

Dr. Spock reassured mothers they knew more than they thought they did about caring for their babies—Elaine felt quite the reverse: the truth was, she knew far less than she'd thought she had when Billy was born, and as he grew, and his demands ramified and grew more insistent, the little she knew dwindled into a stupefying nothing.

Her mother had come with beautifully wrapped and tiny boxes of violet-scented cashews and sugared almonds. She'd sat in the corner of the bedroom and looked at her ungainly daughter struggling to feed her grandson, with a pained expression on her pretty face—quite as if she'd never seen such a thing, and so hadn't the foggiest how to help out.

Which was true enough—because when Elaine was a child, Lilian Rosenthal didn't scruple to tell her that the entire sordid business of baby care revolted her, and that while she may have had her criticisms of Elaine's father,

in this respect at least her gratitude was real and enduring: he'd been earning well enough that she was able to do
precious little of it with either Elaine or her sainted older
brother.

Aza relyef! A rare lapse into her own mother tongue
was Lily's seal of sincerity—and a complementary one, for
when John's Mutti visited them at one or another of the
Brooklyn railroad apartments that they'd endured until he
secured the Cornell position, she, too, would lapse: Mein
Kopfmensch! she'd sigh, with sufficient irony that even her
dozy daughter-in-law understood . . .

Although, with the not-unmixed benefit of hindsight,
she now realizes playing John off against his mother was
never going to work—not, at least, while they remained
married. The old woman spat venom whenever her own
daughter's name was mentioned—and it wasn't until Ginny
finally ditched her hated husband, Reiman, the venal real
estate broker, that old Mrs. Schitz spoke of her with anything other than contempt.

Ach! What does any of it matter? None of these people
are, so to speak, in their lives—but rather, hover in the
middle distance, ineffectual angels in a Renaissance scene
of neglectful motherhood: the foreground littered with
dirty diapers and broken crockery—in the middle distance
the Madonna swoons and the putti bawl, while cigarette
smoke blues the far hills . . . No, Elaine was lonely enough
now—but it'd been far worse then. Now she can—if she
can only summon the required enthusiasm—pick up the
phone that crouches on its little table in the little vestibule
and call Bobbie, say, or Claire—but then there was just an

aching void, from out of which emerged these terrifying compulsions.

Not that Billy had been an intractable or otherwise difficult two-year-old—far from it. When she smacked him and he bawled the transition was so extreme his distraught mother thought, Why . . . whyohwhyohwhy was I so irritated by him? All he'd been was happy and exuberant . . . But on deeper reflection she knew: it was precisely this that summoned her rage: her son could and would be happy so long as she was there to minister to him, but . . .

There was no one there for her. Except his father, who, even when she unleashed on him great flights of bitterness and sarcasm—she could see these darts, mounting swiftly in the dense, shitty atmosphere between them, then descending with sickening alacrity—maintained his thin-lipped, complacent smile. Or at least, that's how she feels about it now, every time another desperate attempt to *get through to him* has foundered: that this smile, whether or not it originated at any particular time in their marriage, has now managed to infest all days and years, hanging in the shadows of diners . . . *and waiting rooms.*

For he'd welcomed it, hadn't he? For, to take up this burden was a foreordained conclusion: it was Providence that had brought him these mountainous tantrums to contain, and these canyons of gibber and drool to drain. Here his materialist conception of history and his manifest destiny conjoined. Moreover, to be martyred in this way fitted his puritanical nature—surely then, it would be cruel to deny him the opportunities her illness provided him for principled self-sacrifice.

When she was well enough to withstand it, he, entirely justifiably, revelled in his fireside talking-tos, and lectured her on prudence and economy.

Hence his prim expression—compounded in equal measure of false and real modesty—when he'd assured her, only a fortnight or so ago, that despite having published only the one book, and although this was his forty-first year, *I still expect to be famous one day* . . . Elaine had regretted the sarcastic laughter that spurted from her pursed *unkissable* lips . . . even as it resounded about John's reddening ears—she regrets it still, and wishes she'd calmly said the words whose sentiment she'd later committed to her diary: It's not that I don't believe him—it's only that I don't care anymore.

Which had been worse? The plain fact of her being a neurotic mess—no complex type but a comic book blob, compounded from phobias and anxieties, a diary keeper and a diary burner, an unfaithful wife and an unloving mother, an angry gouger and a hysterical screamer, chucker, and sobber . . . or this: that he'd borne it all with patience—grace, too: finding the doctors to treat her and earning the money to pay for them as well. And on numerous occasions, walking clear across town at ungodly hours to find the all-night drugstores where he could fill the Rxs for the bromides she'd so sorely needed.

When Freudenberg ended her analysis, it had been time—time for an outpouring of gratitude towards her

long-suffering husband. None had been forthcoming—
instead, there'd been this anger that grew sharper and more
bitter with every month: welling up between them, coating them both in its mix of bile and biliousness. When it
subsides, it leaves behind this vile residue—one that films
Elaine's rotting teeth and sharp tongue, and that looks like
and tastes like resignation.

She'd been so very ill—while he'd been staunch, bully,
batting 100 percent on her team. Now it was her turn to
be the loving one—and most especially, supportive of his
dangerous endeavors in the scholarly coal mine, where he
labors dayuponday, to hew, then drag up his little trucks
full of insight and erudition.

Elaine chokes then guffaws smoke—picturing her scholarly husband, stripped of his worsted suit and his wing-
tips, his bifocals and bowtie, and compelled to sweat it
out—and not simply by way of fetishizing the dignity of
physical work with a little hobby concreting. Why? Because
she feels no true love—only a dull and encompassing
resentment at being placed in this predicament. She may
type his manuscripts for him, and mull over the minutiae
of faculty politics, but she feels no great affinity for what
she must, perforce, consider a joint project—since when it
comes to Elaine's status in the world, her fate is *indivisible
from his . . . I'm a selfish person*, she concedes—and moreover: *I despise him . . .* precisely because he did nurse her,
detaching her damp hair from her tear-drenched cheeks,
and holding her shaking shoulders as she rattled her way
through yet another attack.

Abruptly, Elaine thrusts the exercise book to one side, stands, and looks back at the depression she's left in the red and yellow squares of the quilt: a *cloven-ass* shape, because of course . . . *woman is the sex devil*. She crosses to a small card table under the window, pulls out its drawer, gets out an ashtray, and then . . . nothing except absorption into her own cigarette smoke—its new-blue swirls and old-brown clouds.

The cat has padded so softly into the bedroom she's suddenly there—sitting upright on the dully shiny floorboards, and staring at the cigarette smoke as if it were . . . *a woodland stream* . . . in which the eye apprehends every element simultaneously moving, while all is at rest. Who is she, Elaine wonders aloud, taken anew by the tortoiseshell's poised inscrutability: the cat's mother? Because it's true: Karma isn't a mere personal pronoun—while neither is she some sort of acme of momism: Elaine has caught her holding her one remaining kitten, Maya, down by the neck, and savagely raking this smaller and yet prettier muzzle with extended claws.

They'd thought it humane to at least let her have one kitten remain from the litter of six—but on consideration, perhaps it would've been better if Maya had been given away with the others. Elaine feels a bitter culpability—after all, if she's the cat's mother, who am I? Surely, the cat's mother's mother . . . a game old pussy busting with lust. The poster Elaine's seen advertising the movie currently playing at the Cayuga Theater should've been pasted . . . *on me*, who's so blatantly been BORN TO BE BAD, TO BE KISSED, AND TO . . . MAKE TROUBLE.

John, Betty—Ted most of all: none of them take the
necking or the petting too seriously—it's only Elaine
who jerks about so: a puppet manipulated by . . . *human
desire.*

What will the coming Saturday night's party be like?
Quite likely the same as the Hucksackers' last weekend:
rugs rolled, furniture rearranged so couples can jive and
join in the confined space around the record player, their
feet slip-sliding on drunkenly discarded record sleeves. As
for all the drained and dirty glasses, the overflowing ash-
trays, and the canapé plates, cleared save for a few smears
of salad cream, pastry crusts, and soggy lettuce leaves—
this dishevelment is also de rigueur, even for those parties
that begin well buttoned-up.

At around midnight, running a jaundiced eye over the
Hucksackers' living room, Elaine had thought that the
true measure of success for Esmé would be not how long
and loudly anyone stayed, but how quietly and efficiently
she and her help managed to set all this straight—no
doubt while Rod Hucksacker, that thoroughly committed
moocher, slept his skinful off upstairs.

Because let's face it, all faculty parties started with this
sultry beguine rhythm, over which earnest talk about the
Army Hearings, or the Dean's hirelings, could be heard, but
soon enough, as everyone got fired up, they were gossiping
about who'd necked with who at the last shindig. Then,
fired up still more, the actual necking began—upright congress which always seemed to take place in the kitchen, and
if the room in question was too small, there'd be a queue of
hopefuls . . . *backed up in the hallway.*

Screaming bebop jazz, and modernistically distorted lives—cramped by bomb-terror, stretched by sex-hunger—and in the midst of it all, Elaine, evacuated long before fullterm into this wild scene, a highball in one hand, a cigarette in the other. They are incubators—these parties, and their very heat has quickened her, she thinks, towards final maturity, and towards him.

Because just as full bottles become empty ones, so new parties acquire their very content from those that have gone before. An eyeblink separates the Hucksackers' hootenanny from the Lemesuriers' rather more formal affair a year since. At least, it was straitlaced to begin with—but by the time Elaine was introduced to Ted Troppmann there'd been enough moral turpitude on display to gladden the witch-hunting heart of the Senator from Wisconsin.

Not that she hadn't been hearing all about him for a while. The Troppmanns had been making quite a splash since they'd arrived in Ithaca—he was a wunderkind who'd been hired to shake up the Cornell sociology department, while his chic and brainy wife had joined the College faculty. She was a scientist, apparently—and even before setting eyes on her, Elaine oozed with envy.

It's considered infra dig to teach at the downtown College by the savants up on East Hill, but Elaine was impressed: she couldn't have taught first grade if her goddamn lousy life depended on it. Besides, there are only a handful of women on the Cornell faculty, and they're downright intimidating. Rose Goldsen—who introduced Elaine to Ted—could only secure a position as some sort of research associate, and she's made it painfully clear to Elaine on a number of occasions that this was due to discrimination on grounds of sex rather than political allegiances—present or past—or because she's a Jewess.

Rose also told Elaine that Ted Troppmann was an intellectual ally—not that their scholarly interests are the same, but that they see eye to eye on many things. Elaine wonders whether it was this that led to the introduction—that Rose was offering her up to Ted in some capacity, a compensation, perhaps, for his loss of Mona Voss. Elaine doesn't imagine for a second that Rose thinks her particularly clever—how could she?—but the sociologist does laugh at her quips, a painful sight, a bit as if the Statue of Liberty's shoulders started . . . *shaking*.

So, Elaine knew about these fabulous creatures—blown in from the Midwest via Washington and New York—for a few months before she encountered them in the flesh. Apparently, their place out in Trumansburg is a first-class example of contemporary architecture: a wood, steel, aluminum, and glass palace, its enormous picture windows full of Cayuga Lake and the surrounding forested peaks, its angular rooms equipped with all manner of clever contrivances—lights that dimmed at the turn of a dial, open fires that could be kindled with the push of a button.

Elaine also knew they had two girls, and that Ted dropped them off at the little grade school Billy attended every morning—and once he'd been standing in front of her, with a wide grin on his rather red face, she'd recognized him as the guy who drove the beaten-up old jeep. Strange—and disarming—that a rich guy should favor such a modest wagon.

It gave her a shock to realize she'd been looking at him, unseeing, pretty well every morning since the fall semester had begun—and moreover, that this must also be the old friend of Rose's who John had had lunch with a few weeks previously, together with the head of Arts and Humanities, Harry Lemesurier. Not that John had said anything much about Ted, besides commenting positively on the other man's research work.

Which had been, apparently, to set up then oversee an important program for the War Department to do with analyzing the behavior of individuals in large-scale organizations then aggregating this data. From her husband's tone Elaine realized John found this estimable—which was seldom the way with him when it came to homeland heroes, who he usually knocked pretty hard. Digging a little deeper, she'd discovered the truth: it wasn't about sociology—but politics. In common with John, Ted had been more than a fellow traveller—but at the point where the paths forked, he'd taken the right one: *No left-deviationist, he . . . !*

Elaine kills her butt in an ashtray that once belonged to the Algonquin Hotel. Lily Rosenthal used to justify her thefts of hotel silverware and napery on the grounds that it was the Depression and everyone was hurting. Can her daughter do the same purely on the basis that she's . . . *depressed*? Cigarettes are cheap—but not cheap enough if you smoke a pack a day . . . *or more*. What fresh hell it would be if . . . she looks on avidly as, yawning, Karma arches her perfect pink tongue in her perfect pink mouth . . . cats smoked. They'd steal your Winstons—no doubt about that, then strut from room to room with a

smoky stole flung around their downy shoulders, purring
that they tasted good.

This encounter . . . this meeting . . . this *kosmic kollision*
of star-crossed lovers—Elaine's thought about it over and
over again for a year now, trying to recall every last little
detail: what they wore, what they said—how he looked,
and, more importantly, how he looked at her. Because she'd
been smitten more or less immediately—that much is a fact,
a fact about one of the individuals in *the large organization*
that's staffed with women—and no doubt plenty of girls, as
well—who're soft on Ted Troppmann.

No . . . not quite right, the truth is this: Elaine remarked
that she'd just returned from New York, where she'd been
helping her sister-in-law to move into a new apartment—
and he'd given her a curious look, then said: No, tell me,
why were you really in the city? Try as she might, she
can't summon any more precise memory of the next few
minutes—but somehow, they'd been alone together, while
Moon Mulligan sailed his dumb ship, also alone, and Elaine
hadn't immediately confessed to her on-off affair with Arty,
but she'd said enough to finesse this from Ted . . .

. . . there'd been a dalliance, quite recently, with a married woman. The entire situation had come to a ghastly
head, after which their respective spouses had found out.
Then he'd been on the verge of a full-scale breakdown.

The Ithaca Journal—which Elaine had read earlier that
morning, while eating a soft-boiled egg she'd beaten up in
a cup—editorialized in the same pompous way Freudenberg pronounced: *Emotional adjustment to everyday*

*happenings is a sign of emotional maturity. General happiness is the sign of adjustment* . . . and certainly, that's what Ted had tried to convince her of: the turmoil was over now—he'd regained the sunny uplands of marital bliss.

It had been so much phoneybaloney—the proof being that at the Lemesuriers' a year ago he'd pretty damn effectively seduced her—OK, it's not as if it'd been physical, but the emotional result was the same as if it had: a sudden and shocking intimacy, one in which, tight and in tears, she sobbed out why she'd really been there—specifically, in the lousy Italian joint near to Arty's office, 'cause the cheapskate couldn't be bothered to take her anywhere better. There, where the tears had also coursed down her cheeks once she'd said her piece and heard his reply. There, where a lousy haul of dried-out starfish and glass floats hung suspended in netting over a pokey ocean of red-and-white check tablecloths. Cast adrift, Elaine had stammered that maybe they might resume seeing one another—not on any especially regular basis, but now and then, as it pleased them both—because they were adults, weren't they?

In return, she'd received confirmation of what she's always feared . . . *that I'm a lousy lay*, because Arty had explained, *in the nicest possible way*, that this was quite out of the question. Sure, he'd been flattered—and of course, he still found her very attractive—but they were both married now, and had their children as well as John and Valerie to think of . . . In point of fact, while he didn't imagine it would make Elaine feel any better, he wanted her to know that their little moment together had had a most salutary effect on his marriage . . .

He wouldn't go so far as to say it'd saved it—but pretty close. Tears falling onto her rapidly congealing lasagna, Elaine nonetheless saw it all perfectly clearly—after all, she'd been Arty's secretary for a couple of years, and knew that he always delivered bad news to suppliers, customers, and employees with the same humble, shit-eating expression—but that once they'd gone, he'd puff his chest out with pride: just as it had suited him to do business with them before, now it suited him to . . . *not*.

Feeling herself an idiot quite as much as an ingenue, Elaine had refused this Judas her cheek and stumbled away in the direction of Grand Central, her only objective being to get away as fast as possible, and to return home to the security of the husband, home, and child she'd only minutes before been intent on betraying.

Her first impressions of Ted were that his were the deep, brown, trusting—and therefore trusty—eyes of a dog. There was thick hair on his wrists—and on his ankles above his socks, which Elaine had noticed when he'd hitched up the knees of his pants before hunkering down beside her. Faithful canine, maybe—but quite possibly a werewolf. As she'd sob-spoken, he'd nodded affirmatively, yepping under his breath—and Elaine felt they'd reached an accord immediately . . .

. . . He'd straightened up, gone to the makeshift bar and got them fresh drinks, returned to her side, and hunkered down again—his jug head tilted to one side, ready to receive whatever she *had to pour out* . . .

When it was time to go, and the Hancocks and the Troppmanns were standing with Selma Lemesurier on the porch, Ted had kissed Elaine very briefly, full on the mouth—and maybe it was merely her own impression, touched and retouched in the weeks and months that followed, but didn't he also, just for a brief moment, push his tongue between her teeth?

Now? Ow! Elaine drops the angry end of the cigarette she's lit without thinking and allowed to burn down . . . *without thinking*, into the ashtray. She's wearing a combination of inner- and outerwear: a floral-patterned housecoat, and beneath it a homemade skirt—the hem of which she now notices is . . . *who will knit up the ravelled sleeve of . . . care?* She ought to get the sewing machine out and mend it—but on the briefest consideration: What's the point? Her life's unravelling as well . . .

Stop it! she admonishes herself, aloud—and standing, strides from her and John's bedroom into Billy's, fully intending to make his bed, pick up his discarded pyjamas, and restore all these troubling, sick-making, scintillating *things* to some kind of order. She stands looking at his toy basket, his little row of books on the windowsill, and the strange little pulley system he's rigged up with string and thumbtacks, connecting his bedside table with his bookshelf, and his bookshelf with the little table where he does his beading and other handicrafts, draws, and writes with apparent—and quite possibly enviable—fluency.

Billy's made his cable cars from little strawberry boxes, and placed two or three little figurines in each—cowboys mixing promiscuously with Indians. The whole effect is *quite enchanting*—and, not for the first time, Elaine dares to consider the still more enchanting possibility that her son might be not just above averagely bright, but exceptional. Then *Hawkeye* turns on her heel and stalks out again.

In the room she and John grandly call spare—although one or the other of them often sleeps in the small cot, or works at the pine table next to it—Elaine pauses once more, staring at the painting by her friend Bobbie that hangs on the opposite wall. It's a gift she's sequestrated from any more public viewing—although she's not altogether sure why. It's not as if they have any finer pictures—pride of place downstairs is taken by a muddy piece of New York Postimpressionism: a wheeled market stall, up to its axles in the thick oil paint flowing along Houston, given to her . . .

. . . bien sûr, by Arthur Aaronson.

But this one of Bobbie's is an oddity—both canvas and wooden frame are coated in ochre paint, and every time Elaine looks at it with any attention, she perceives a visual metaphor for her own phobias: her reality and whatever frames it are the . . . *same thing*—there is no distinguishing inner and outer realms, they are . . . *the same thing*, which is why she fears them both, so suffers with both the pull of claustrophobia and the push of agoraphobia to such a symmetric extent that she really has found herself, dithering on her own doorstep, quite unable to either abide—or flee.

Then there's the troubling matter of representation—
what is the painting of? Superficially, a stylization
of stick-figure kids clambering on a frame of black
brushstrokes—but as soon as her back is turned, Elaine
worries one of them will fall. This is the essence of her
motherly dilemma: as long as Billy is in the room with
her—as long as she can smell his sweet-sour breath, inhale
his tangy boy sweat . . . *in deep*, feeling the rock-steady
tremble of his young life, she's reassured. Ironic, considering his is the very presence she finds it so hard to cope with.

Once out the door, though, his sharp image soon begins
to fade—once he's half a mile down the road, even though
she's sat in the classroom with him, Billy's a stylization.
Who knows, maybe if he was away from her for much
longer, he'd become a complete abstraction?

Impelled by *God knows what*, Elaine quits the spare
room and plunges back down the steep stairs. It's only
when she returns to the front room, and through its windows sees the dense cross-hatching of rain falling, that she
realizes the source of all her agitation. All morning she's
been struggling to be in the picture—not merely regarding
it from further and further away. But she's failed—because
she's a dolt and a dope and a dumb kind of Kallikak cow,
who wouldn't notice if a dead calf slithered out of her and
lay, steaming, in the long grass . . .

What other creature would be so adept at forgetting
her own noxious nature?—a smell of burnt hair and other
astringent things fills the air as more water brash gushes
into her mouth. The beadwork she tossed in the bowl is *half
gone* . . . the bowl is half gone, too. Billy's Mad magazine,

the Ithaca Journal, and the Moroccan leather pouf are also
subsiding into this: a cosmic kind of doodle—myriad iridescent little shapes and forms that, if she tries to focus on
them, merge in a kaleidoscope swirl—and if she tries to
carry on regardless . . .

Well! She can't ignore them, these squares, circles, tri-
angles, lozenges, trapezoids, and polygons—because they
are the stuff her world is made of, which explains why they
swarm then swim in through her gaping eyes, while at the
same time *they are those eyes*. Elaine sits down heavily on
the couch, jarring her spine. Her tummy is *bubbling* . . . and
up comes another half cup of bitter saliva. The Caffergone
is upstairs in the bathroom—but is it worth it? She'll have
to undress and go through all the sickening, smelly contor-
tions for its rectal administration, and by the time it starts
working she'll already be wallowing about, quite lost, in
the dank depths of the malaise.

Last Saturday night at the Hucksackers', Ted had been
warm with her—and this despite the awful scene at his
house only three days before that, when all three of them
had rounded on her. Sure, he'd probably been tight—she
certainly had been, but despite everything there it had
been: the same heat sparking between them as the first
time they'd met, and the same intimacy such that Elaine
could . . . *see right into him*, and Ted had laid his forearm
across her bare thighs.

The hem of her skirt had ridden up.

She'd felt as if she were the tiny lightbulb on the little circuit board Billy had made at school then brought
home to show his parents: Ted had touched the wire to

her contact and she had . . . *glowed*. Immediately upon meeting him, a year ago, Elaine had realized Ted was a strongly sexed man—and she'd been turned on by it, because she was already struggling to contain her morbid desire. Why? Because she has a migrainous personality, of course—tense, irritable, turning every neurotic feeling into a debilitating physical symptom that demands immediate treatment . . .

Not forgetting her flightiness—because she always wants to escape, and for any jailbreak you require an accomplice: she'd needed John to get out of lousy Johnstown—then again, to escape the messy situation in New York. As much as she'd wanted to make love with Ted there and then— she'd also longed to escape her marriage, the Cornell faculty party circuit, Ithaca itself.

At the Lemesuriers' a year ago—quite as much as at the Hucksackers' last Saturday, and at any number of the intervening parties and gatherings—she'd yearned to hold on tight to his solid presence and urge him to . . . *fly me to the moon—so we can play among the stars* . . .

Or better still would've been for him to've done the urging, saying, Come away with me, right now!—and suddenly they'd have been in his wagon, with the canvas top rat-a-tat-tatting in the wind of their own fugitive speed. On the Hucksackers' davenport, with the sweat trickling between her thighs, and Ted's arm feeling heavier by the moment, Elaine had looked away from his eager face and into the brightly lit kitchen, where, up against their hosts' futuristic Frigidaire, stood John and Elizabeth, as dull-looking as their names implied, their embrace wooden as joinery, their dry mouths dutifully clapboarded together—any spark that might exist between them falling, inert, to the tiled floor.

The jackhammering in Elaine's head has begun—and she knows the slightest tilt or inclination of her head will make it much worse. The day is a washout—that's for sure: she'll be lucky if she makes it to bed without vomiting. No, Ted would never say anything like that—because the truth is, Elaine acknowledges wearily, he doesn't really love me at all. He isn't capable of love's rapture—of giving himself freely in the act of . . . *taking a woman.*

Not that I'm much of a woman to take . . . because Elaine's half gone herself, sinking rapidly into that migraine world of darkness, afterimages, numbness, and nausea. She's struggling gamely to stay on the surface of things— but then, hasn't she always been?

# .2.

## November 1954

The last words of John's introduction to his study of the blind poet—ones Elaine had typed before her departure for New York, stayed with her the whole time. Perhaps not verbatim—but anyhow, as the cab turns into Hemlock Street they repeat once more, as food rejected by the stomach does, all chewed up into acidic little bits: *I have often regretted . . . the choice of a subject . . . which gave so little play to the gracious sentiments of generous appreciation . . .*

Ridiculous! The truth is he shares with his chosen subject a great pleasure in being peevish, ungrateful, and most especially ungenerous. Moreover, Elaine doesn't think much choice was ever involved—there's an elective affinity between the two Johns.

Now, looking up at the small and isolated suburban house from where she stands in the roadway, paying off the cabbie who's driven her from the station, Elaine wonders: Who am I coming home to—and why? Why not simply keep going somewhere—anywhere!—else? The thought of some mad meter reading for a two-hundred-mile ride up to the Canadian border . . . *and asylum*, makes her smile internally, *acidically . . . ulcerously*.

The two-buck fare from the station—including tip!—will be noted and filed in the hushed repository of her husband's highly efficient memory—and eventually it'll be . . . *held against me*. Because he's a parsimonious soul, is John—No! Not so—a grave misnomer: he's a goddamn miser, a puritan to his core, who, far from suffering their straitened circumstances as his wife does, positively . . . *relishes them*.

His judgmental presence has, she feels sure, swelled in her absence to fill the entire house. The front room is all his head—his lips are Dalí cushions. His rear end squidges against the back wall of the kitchen. Fuseli's artist is moved by the grandeur of similarly enlarged and fragmentary limbs . . . *to despair*. And even if she didn't know her husband as well as she does, Elaine suspects she'd feel the same were she to come upon his giant arms and legs lying athwart the dinky hallway and the tiny first-story landing.

Yet despite John's overbearing grossness, it's he who has the nerve *to find me vulgar . . .* ! Worse yet, he now feels free to express his scorn in company quite as much as when they're alone: the same sour look, as if he'd just this second bitten into the realization that *I'm too impossibly crude*. Not that it's any better at home—for he does it in front of their child . . . *our only*.

As Elaine mounts the stairs, then, opening the screen door, enters the glassed-in porch at the side of the house, she's compelled *yet again!* to this pained acknowledgement:

Billy is unusually close to his father, while John—unlike so
many other men—is perfectly competent when it comes to
his own and Billy's daily needs—so, really, there's . . . *no
room for me!* As for love, the angles of their triangle are
always altering, as each parent is revulsed by the spectacle
of the other enfolding their child in a sweetly endearing
embrace.

Opening the kitchen door Elaine smells the reheated
meatloaf they must've had for their supper—a dish she
prepared and refrigerated before she left—and again she's
overwhelmed by a desire to be alone and *lick my greasy
wounds* . . . On Saturday evening—if they do, after all,
attend the Lemesuriers' annual cocktail party—John
will do it again: pick-picking away at some mispronun-
ciation or grammatical error of his wife's as if . . . *I was
infra-his-dig.*

He cannot help himself—and doesn't seem to realize
this behavior makes neither of them look smart. On the
contrary, when he does this Elaine's certain the others can
see what she and John know to be always there . . . clinging
to their shaggy, unkempt coats—the wretched testaments
of our introversion . . . *and our deceit.*

They're not expecting her back until the following morning—so Elaine hesitates on her own threshold
between inside and out, claustrophobia and agoraphobia,
atomic Armageddon and the world peace earnestly hoped
for in the greasy disarticulation of the wishbones, little
fingers crooked, she pulls with her seven-year-old son, so
that even if everyone else's world is destroyed, hers will be
miraculously . . . *redeemed.*

She remembers getting back early from a shopping expedition with Bobbie at the beginning of the summer—before the Hancocks went to the cottage in Vermont for their vacation. That was an awful episode—will this be one, too?

Elaine had still been seeing Doctor Freudenberg every Wednesday afternoon—either driving there alone or, on the days when she couldn't face the bumpy boring through the small wooden townships, and the sinister whirring of the tires as the Buick bucketed across the open-form bridges, John would have to accompany her, having begged a colleague for yet another favor.

No surprise, then, that he's unpopular in the department—and thrashing about trying to get a promotion, or a Fulbright, or both. Elaine, bitter to a fault, conjoins her husband's lack of sexual vigor with his obnoxiousness, socially, and his failure to advance professionally—then cries out in the cramped confines of her own head: *Ça suffit!* That was then—this is now, when she's better—much better, so much so she's free to consider exactly how reliant he might've been on her illness . . . it suited him—saved him from having to face up to his own inadequacies.

There are Billy's outgrown clothes in upstairs drawers, together with old correspondence and saved string. There, upright in the dish dryer beside the sink are washed dishes, but they'll be dirty again soon enough. And there, on the mat beside the door, polished *with pathos*, are his school shoes.

All domestic objects have, for Elaine, this dread quality: they're hooks that, any time she sees or thinks of them, pierce her cursed flesh and drag her back, through months and years full of awful days and excruciating, inertial hours—times when she felt so bad, so worthless, and yet so very angry, she couldn't lay a hand on a plate without wanting to fling it at John's head.

While as for Billy's lace-up shoes: hunched over and shaking as she fumbled together their bows, Elaine was gripped by maniacal urges—wondering whether her best course, given the rotten state of the world, would be to pick her small son up by his heels and *dash his brains out against the wall . . .* After which she'd slump down on the floor, sobbing, and John would have to get their kid ready for kindergarten, then take him there.

Well, nowadays it may not exactly be *a circus of fun for everyone . . .* ! but for the most part that terrible, tense atmosphere has hissed out of the house—and this was coincident with Elaine stopping seeing Doctor Freudenberg. He'd doubtless say it was because of the work they'd done together, rather than its termination—Elaine isn't so sure, as she'd come to distrust his motivations, which at worst seem adventitious—she knew he'd wanted to get rid of her quite a while beforehand but had had no one to take up her hour until July . . .

. . . Well, is it any surprise she'd come to feel a sulky mistrust, not just with respect to this one egghead, coddled in his consulting room—but the entire apparatus of psychoanalysis, which she'd begun to see as just another American fad, one she's observed in the past five years heading West, as if its practitioners were gripped not just by the money-making zeal of carney men, hucksters, and four-flushers . . . *like my papa*, but by a weird version of

Manifest Destiny, compelling them to subdue the Indians of the id, and take possession of their unconscious hinterlands.

During the same period, she's noted the language of psychoanalysis creeping into ordinary speech and commonplace prose. It's no longer only the faculty crowd—among whom are plenty of quondam communists and renegade Jews—that speaks of attachments, complexes, and inhibitions . . . *everyone's doing it*. Soon enough, Elaine thinks, I'll go into Pete's to pick up some groceries, and he'll be behind the counter, sitting on the old barstool with the foam escaping from its crimson cushion, massaging his temples with one hand while he makes tragic gestures with the other, and he'll explain he can't go to the storeroom and get what I want because of his *oedipal issues* . . .

Now that she's stopped seeing Freudenberg, Elaine finds it weird that she was captivated for so long by this odd little man—whatever he did or didn't do for her, one thing's sure: he isn't one of those screwy, clever guys she can't help herself falling for. That was the nub of the problem—and when she tried to get him to say anything about his feelings for her, he'd retreat behind his wall of jargon, then begin chucking hand grenades: Elaine hadn't merely been what he termed a child seductress—but a castratory one as well, who, sidelined by that golden boy, her brother, resolved to cut his penis off and have it for her ownsome.

What could possibly be the connection between this mishigas and treating what ailed her? Her multiple phobias, her obsessional thoughts and feverish impulses? Elaine had trusted him to this extent: laying out for him all the facts of her for the most part dismal loves and attendant . . . *lies*. But

Freudenberg could make the most wanton act of adultery
seem as dully unappetizing as *Venus in support hose* . . .

. . . because along with the rest of them he was fundamentally dishonest about the mismatch between their real
beliefs and their espoused objectives. They knew it was all
pretty damn hopeless, really—that people are just animals
like any others, driven hither and thither by their lust, their
anger, and their insecurities—so doomed to be miserable if
they admitted it, and hopelessly neurotic if they didn't. So
what if shrinks were rapt as they decoded the secret language of their patients' symptoms—Elaine came to believe
they were the same as any other exegetes, and she knows
what such types are like: immersed in their symbolic world,
with little true affection or care for the *pissy and shitty*
real one.

None of which stopped them taking your ten bucks—or
chasing their bills just like any other tradesman. There's a
letter from Freudenberg upstairs in the file box Elaine uses
for correspondence that does just this, wheedling away for
a few dollars, money he thinks far more important than the
sum of . . . *all human happiness!*

*And yet* . . . to begin with it'd been different, with the
wind whistling happily through the Buick's broken quarter glass, she'd sung the Howdy Doody song all the way
to Syracuse: *Ev-ery day you'll meet a friend, but do you
know how to greet a friend* . . . ? Willing herself to be
open, cooperative—a girl who had many more than one
little curl in the middle of her forehead, and who was trying to be good rather than . . . *horrid*. Which was hard,
since the horridness is deep within her—may even be, she

fears, integral to her, such that she obviously could never be talked out of it, nor talk it out either.

If she wasn't so horrid, she'd run to embrace her child right away—Billy will have been in bed for only a half hour or so, and he's probably rereading Charlotte's Web under the covers with his flashlight. She should go up there and surprise him—he'll be overjoyed, if not to see her then at least to defer the moment when he has to go to sleep.

She should gather him in her arms—bury her shame-face in the warm and flannel-smelling hollow of his dear, dear neck. The way Elaine's mother never did *when I was little* . . . and frightened—because when she was little, she was often frightened . . . *of starving.* And this was when she was very small—long before the Crash. How could this have been? True, Lily Rosenthal starved herself to stay petite—but Elaine's papa and brother were lusty eaters, and there always seemed to be eating going on in the house: delicatessen cuts—hard and soft salamis, sour and sourer pickles, salt beef, knishes oozing kasha and cheese. Cans of salmon were opened and sucked up with fervor—jars of sweetly vinegary rollmop herring the same.

Lily fried latkes, sliced lox, molded meatloaves, hand-cranked out liverish worms, and made her own kreplach— as well as a chicken soup with carrot, celery, and bulgur wheat that seemed to Elaine, in its warm flux of liquid and solid elements, a complete and alternate world. All these dishes she now prepares as well—at least sometimes, because often she feels nauseated by all this pulp and slop, with its shtetl odors. Freudenberg's theory—*quel blague!*— is that the sickness arises out of this contradiction: the food was from the old country, where both Lily and Jack had been born, but they never so much as acknowledged this, dedicated as they were to effacing all they could of their cultural distinctiveness—scrubbing away at religion, community, language, and lore. All that was left were these heavy, fatty dishes, which were consumed behind closed doors, as if eating them were something to be ashamed of, like . . . *shitting*.

At last, Elaine takes a couple of tentative steps into the kitchen and sets her overnight bag down on the linoleum floor. She takes off her old squirrel coat with the bald patches, and finger by finger carefully removes her equally aged blue kid gloves, so as to not split the seams any further. The coat goes over the back of a bentwood chair—the gloves on top of the scrubbed-pine kitchen table, next to the egg timer Billy plays with while he eats, turning it upside down each time it's run its course, then watching just as intently, again, as all the tiny grains jostle their way to the . . . *exit*.

The facts, as Elaine sees them, are that she's never loved her parents—it's this, she thinks, that's the actual explanation for her all-devouring anxiety: the nameless and clammy-cold dread that settles over her betimes, like some shroud tailor-made for the living. At the age of only four or five she'd understood this much: if you don't love your parents, they're under no obligation at all to love you. It follows, if they decide to stop feeding you one day . . . Well, no one would judge them for it, because everyone could see that Elaine was an ungrateful, spiteful little girl, guaranteed to grow up to be gawky and ugly, with *a big clay blob of a nose* . . .

She couldn't keep company with Delmore Schwartz—
who she'd seen just the once, in the late spring of 1944,
when John was stationed on Guam, and she was cinq-á-
sept with Arty, twice a week, in the Sherry-Netherland.
She'd tracked the forlorn-looking poet downtown for
twenty blocks, trying to pluck up the courage to . . . *do
what, exactly?* before losing him to a noisily quacking
gaggle of NYU co-eds somewhere in the vicinity of Times
Square— What she'd wanted to say to him, she belatedly
realizes, is that the movie of her parents' first date was
inaccessible to her. If she looked for it in the plush darkness
of her inner eye, the images she found there became the
expanding whorls of the film's decomposition, as it caught
fire and turned to slick ash.

What could she say in the face of this annihilation—
the void out of which she, herself, had emerged? Nothing,
clearly—and certainly nothing like the poet's impassioned,
self-cancelling rant. He got it wrong, though: it was in all
their parents' dreams of non-Jewishness that her reckless-
ness and her impostures began.

*Don't belong to the league of the self-deceived* is what
the good doctor used to urge her, yet every time this hateful
homily worms its way back into her thoughts, she summons
the resolve to resign from it *immediately* . . . so goes from
the kitchen into the front room, where she finds someone
who's still paying his dues, sitting studiously in the yellow
light that burnishes him—an icon, indeed, preoccupied by
iconostasis to this degree: he's writing about it by the light
of a special lamp bought with the proceeds he's earned
from writing about . . . *it*.

Composing her face—although why should it be necessary for her to conceal from his that *nothing at all* has happened?—Elaine bends to bestow on his balding pate a kiss so perfunctory it isn't really a kiss at all, only an airy kind of allusion to what a kiss might be like, if, that is, Elaine ever *deigned to bestow one . . .*

Oh!

He starts, a little—and she instantly concludes: Aha! this is the marked card with which he's trying to finesse mine. Because no matter how deeply immersed he may be in his richly private realm of sympathy, figuration, and summation, John Hancock remains perfectly aware of that sublunary realm—the one in which he hears the cab drawing up, her paying the cabbie, her tread on the stone steps, the click of the screen door and the clack of the kitchen one—and wonders: Why is she back so soon?

I was going to stay . . . another . . . night . . . Elaine gasps, dropping down onto the couch, getting out her cigarettes, beginning the necessary fire-making and smoke-sucking . . . but Ginny didn't seem to really want me there— She stops short, rebukes the self-piteous puppet she believes herself to be: *Everybody you meet is a pal, but do you know how to treat a pal . . . ?*

When John finally returned from overseas and was discharged from the army, he returned to her, his person and everything he had about it smelling of *rot and rubber . . .* In the musty confines of a minuscule studio at the top of a decaying Brooklyn brownstone that she'd managed to rent with a combination of guile and connections, Elaine had for some time already been practicing putting on her expression of guileless affection.

Had John been deceived? No—not at all. Not for one goddamn stupid little picayune slippery second. He'd been a pretty damn difficult and disputatious fellow before he went away—lashing out with his sharp tongue in a way Elaine had initially taken for the frustration the very bright necessarily feel as they try to slash their way through the dense and shapeless ones. But afterwards, everything seemed sharper—as if he'd been *stropping it on his goddamn bayonet* . . .

He'd told her that first night of their reunion what the army censor had forestalled: he'd heard the news the A-bomb had been dropped on Hiroshima as he was on a transport flying from Guam back to Hawaii. Lolling on gunnysacks full of lumpy machine parts all jumbled together in the hold, he began laughing near-hysterically when the radio operator shouted the news back to him. His merriment had been both intensely selfish—it was over, of that he had no doubt, and he'd be heading home soon enough—and also egotistic: it'd been he and his unit on Guam who'd sourced, then shipped to Tinian, the extra-heavy bomb hoist needed to winch Little Boy into the Enola Gay.

So, in the great and ghastly chain of cause and effect that shackled together all sad sacks, he had played his part, entirely inadvertently, in making this—an event of global significance—happen.

For John Hancock, that sparkling sunrise high over the Pacific had—he told his wife—the intensity of the thermonuclear explosion itself: this was the moment when the exit doors in the world-theater had been wrenched open, and the daylight streamed in, and the movie all shackled humanity had been enjoying was seen to be over. Laughing, stiff, and sluggish, they all tumbled out into the brave new world—and for the eighteen months until he was rotated out, his hilarity continued, growing bitterer and more mocking by the day.

So he had been cynical—and she in an outright funk. With a zeal she never brought to English 3: Poetry, a study of selected British and American verse, Elaine had analyzed every line of his intermittent V-mails, trying to figure out if he'd read the truth concealed between the lines of her own: the job with Arty Aaronson had turned out to be far more interesting than she'd anticipated—she was no mere secretary, but an assistant with real responsibilities. Moreover, Arty and his wife, Valerie, had taken Elaine under their wing, inviting her for dinners at their swanky Upper East Side apartment, where she was introduced to their set.

Solid rather than starry types—other publishers and their wives, wholesale book dealers and theirs . . . together with the occasional younger person like Elaine, temporarily unmoored by the war, and a little *rudderless* . . .

Looking now at her husband's sententious lips—while avoiding his accusatory eyes, roving about behind their thick and imprisoning lenses—Elaine thinks how little analysis, by contrast, is necessary to understand the lines of the poet John's so preoccupied with—the one he's just been writing about . . . *again. Eve, but patiently resign what justly thou hast lost, nor set thy heart, thus over-fond, on that which is not thine. Thy going is not lonely, with thee goes thy husband, him to follow thou art bound, where he abides, think there thy native soil . . .*

Well, *he lies*, it's good to have you back—I reckon if you'd've left it 'til tomorrow, you'd probably be too whacked Saturday to want to bother with the Lemesuriers', um, gathering.

Have we got a sitter? Elaine queries, sliding effortlessly back into . . . *an administrative role*: Edith's gone away for the weekend, hasn't she?

The Tates' eldest lad is happy to oblige—I ran into Mrs. Tate in the Commons on Wednesday and asked her to ask him.

Oh, you think it wise?

By which Elaine means to say . . . *I have serious doubts*. At fourteen Larry Tate is an aspirant thug, with his heavy Neanderthal brow and heavier knuckles. He struts up and down Hemlock Street in a leather jacket, legs bowed as if a motorcycle were about to be *driven under them*. Of course Billy idolizes him, and pulls the collar of his own red cotton windbreaker up in tame emulation of a wild one.

It'll be OK—Mrs. Tate seemed grateful, I guess it'll keep him out of trouble for an evening . . . How was New York?

Oh, I'll tell you later—has Billy been in bed long?

No, not long—I shouted up five minutes ago, 'cause he was creeping around up there.

Elaine looks down at the typescript of John's book fanned out on the tray he sets across the chair's arms when he's working in the evening. It's covered in his handwritten emendations and amendments—she'll have to type him another draft, although *can it really be worth it . . . ?*

There's a Lincoln Log on the last stair, a window frame and a roof on subsequent ones. Weak light wells up and spreads across the landing—when she's away, John leaves a small candle burning here in a saucer full of water. Billy's bedroom door is ajar, and pushing it open Elaine sees his tousled head buried so deeply in the pillow it's pretty damn obvious he's only this moment thrust it there.

Hi, Honey . . . C'mon—I know you're awake . . .

With exaggerated blinking and yawning Billy pushes himself up onto his elbows: Oh, Mommy, you're back . . .

Two big strides and she's upon him—lost in his sweet-sour odor, compounded of milk and sweat. Do all mothers, Elaine wonders, feel this way: that their child's smell is a refined perfume decocted from their father's rather more repulsive one?

Billy worms from her embrace: Did you get it, Mommy?

Yeah, I got it, honey, don't worry.

It's only . . . I mean—when I heard you get back . . . I thought . . .

Elaine understands: she, too, finds it difficult to detach her current fears from the traumas she's experienced in the past. Ever since Billy saw the perfect little fire truck in an FAO Schwartz ad, he's been coveting it—and although she promised she'd get it for him, now she's returned early from New York . . . and . . . well . . . When Mommy returns prematurely *all hell can break loose . . .*

Which is what happened not long after they returned from Vermont, the Sunday before Labor Day. Elaine spent the next few days trying to sort the house out, as well as looking for a part-time job so that once school started, she could . . . *get out of it*. She and Bobbie either took turns having both boys, or Elaine got Edith, one of John's co-eds and their regular sitter, to keep an eye on them at Hemlock Street.

The skies had still been that hurting shade of blue—and the white heat haze lay undulant across the lake. Local lore was that the lakes and falls kept things cooler in Ithaca during the summer than elsewhere in the region, but Elaine thought this the kind of moonshine to be expected from people who . . . *drink it*. Still. There were regular trips to Flat Rock to slide across the slippery stones and lie, swathed in the cool curtains of water coursing over them— and when they had to stay at home, the boys had their water pistols and a hose for cooling water-play.

After a slow start during which they'd sized one another up, Bobbie has become Elaine's best friend in Ithaca. With her flat chest, blonde bangs, and gravelly voice, she's an irreverent presence—perfectly capable of hooking onto Elaine's barbed remarks about their in-group ones of her own. Although, where exactly Bobbie's piss-and-vinegar secretes from Elaine's unsure: she seems perfectly happy with her unambitious husband, Pat, who's still an assistant professor in the engineering department after many years. Happy, too, with her sons, Frank—who's Billy's exact age—and the baby, Daniel, who she lofts about the place as if he were a beloved sort of parcel: lifting him up by the bunched material at the back of his playsuit, or tucking him, bawling, casually beneath her scrawny arm.

Bobbie never seems that bothered about the boys, or flustered by her household responsibilities—in slacks and sweater, hair tied back in a big, black elasticated band, she chain-smokes and scrutinizes her latest canvas as it emerges from the obscurity of her own clouds. It was with Bobbie that Elaine first felt able to admit to the shape—if not the full substance—of her distress, and her apparently uncritical acceptance of this: *Sugar-bun, it's only a kinda grippe in the head* . . . is what made what happened that afternoon quite so devastating for Elaine . . .

. . . who, never having exactly warmed to Frank, agonizes, still, that it was this very adult antipathy that had really angered her. There are, Elaine believes, those kids other than your own who simply feel right—physically right, quite as much as if they were family. Then there are others who emphatically don't. Frank is a wholly inoffensive, tubby kid, with a fair, freckled complexion and fetching auburn hair—but there's something prematurely mature and funky about his small person—a very masculine whiff, quite unlike Billy's, who, at seven remains gracile and gentle.

The boys have been at home in each other's homes for close on three years now—but before the summer Elaine was already beginning to find Frank's nudity disconcerting. When he unashamedly stripped off his underpants, in preparation for water-play, she half expected to see he'd sprouted thick auburn pubic hair. Then she caught them playing *that game*.

Can I have some milk, Mom?

It's an innocent request Billy's mother answers with a quip: Milk as a straight beverage has long been regarded

with suspicion in France . . . This being something she'd
read aloud to him from the Times, and which they'd both
found screamingly funny. Now, in the dim illumination
from the half-open door, she sees his pleading expression
—no, he's no Frenchman, more's the pity. Elaine feels a
perfect rube, not having been anywhere further than Wisconsin in her thirty-three years—and hopes her child will
experience what other countries and their cultures are like
while he's still young . . .

. . . places where race relations aren't quite so terrible.

Pouring out his white milk, shining in the light from the
icebox, Elaine is tormented once more by her violent reaction
when, arriving back unexpectedly from town, she first saw
the two mud-plastered figures cavorting in the front yard.

They must have used the hose to create a wallow behind
the low wall separating the property from the roadway,
then stamped about in it until it turned gloopy, then
smeared this stuff all over their naked bodies.

Wow! she'd cried out. Look at you two!

Billy's teeth flared white in his deep-brown mud-mask:
Yeah, it's a new game, Mom—me an' Frank call it the nigger game.

She hadn't run at them—she'd pounced, grabbing at the
slick scruffs of these two . . . *animals*. Had she smacked
them both hard? Yes—she definitely had, but probably
more frightening was her screaming: Don't let me EVER
hear that word from either of you EVER again—it's a DIS-
GUSTING and DEMEANING thing to say!

The boys had been crying—from shock more than pain:
one moment they'd been in this primitive idyll: little black

Sambos playing patty-cake with mud-pancakes—the next there was this mad terror, mixed up for all parties with a dreadful sense of . . . *shame.*

Because Elaine hadn't only understood the boys' distress —she'd sympathized: as a child, she'd experienced exactly the same violent expulsion from a version of heaven, at least, to . . . *hell*—and for her, too, the race problem had been at the root of it. This episode was summoned up by Billy and Frank's behavior the way her awful experience of childbirth was by the odor of his crayons, which smell like . . . *ether.*

Edith helped the hysterical boys to hose themselves clean—Elaine had telephoned Bobbie right away, and told her to come and pick up her kid. A little calmer once her friend arrived, Elaine felt the need to justify herself—so while the still-dripping and dirt-streaked boys were comforted with milk and cookies in the kitchen, their mothers had an early cocktail on the back porch.

To begin with Elaine tried discussing the issue in general terms—the various boycotts, the school board decisions, and the sense that, at last, things might be changing. But somewhere into their second old-fashioned the truth began to . . . *will out*, and she told Bobbie all about Prudence . . .

. . . who'd never lived in with the Rosenthals—unlike Wioletta, the Polish girl who replaced her—but arrived at the Brookline Avenue house on the dot of seven every morning. From then on until six in the evening, she devoted herself entirely to the care of Elaine and Robert, her elder brother. Prudence washed the little Rosenthal children, dressed and fed them. She took them out to Wick Park and played hide-and-seek with them—and when they had to go to the bathroom, so long as they were at home, she accompanied them and made sure they cleaned themselves properly.

And she sang to them, her voice high and quavering: *Ezekiel saw a wheel a-rollin', Away in the middle of the air, A wheel within a wheel a-rollin', Way in the middle of the air* . . . Prudence sang to them when they walked hand in hand: *There is a balm in Gilead to make the wounded whole, There is a balm in Gilead, to heal the sin-sick soul* . . . and when they sat on her lap, and she deftly wielded the comb, and even more deftly removed the cooties caught in its steel teeth: *Green trees are bending, poor sinners stand trembling, The trumpet sounds in my soul, I ain't got long to stay here* . . .

Elaine wondered aloud whether the green trees bending were her abundant brown curls—while it was the cooties who stood, trembling, waiting for the comb to find them—but Prudence said this was foolishness, albeit kindly. From what Elaine can remember, she was an angular-looking sort of woman, who nonetheless had a big double chin—or some kind of dewlap slung beneath her first one, like a *fleshy chinstrap*. She smelled powerfully of Ivory soap and wax polish, and although she couldn't have been much older than Elaine's mother, she referred often to her grown sons, Ames and Aaron, who'd gone to Chicago for work.

Damn it, Jack Rosenthal exclaimed, a Zeus in his thunderhead of cigar smoke, I swear Prudence would school those kids—if she'd had any schooling herself.

Later, it occurred to Elaine that if she'd learned anything about what it was to love and be loved it was from

Prudence. If her mother or father bestowed any affection on her it was served with a sprinkling of criticism, always: *Aren't you just dear, although . . . Isn't she pretty, but . . .* their qualifications being just those features that bother her to this day: her big feet, her tremendous height, and her baleful, shapeless nose.

Her father's father had been a cantor and a widower, and as congregations were widely scattered and small in the Northeast of the time, he would leave little Jack with one Jewish family or another in Buffalo or Hartford, and be gone for weeks at a time.

It occurred to Elaine in her late teens, when she was in high school with Jewish kids who'd been raised in New York in Jewish communities, that her father's peculiar persona—he always seemed to be performing to an audience, even in the privacy of his own home—must've been the result of his childhood as a poorly paying guest in houses where they still spoke Yiddish, German, Russian, and Polish. He'd therefore been doubly displaced: a temporary foundling as well as an immigrant. Unsurprisingly, Jack Rosenthal found his community not in the seder or the synagogue—but in the street, and his language was his own patois of slang and business English. An aggressively atheistic man, he enforced the adage: everyone—including the Lord of the tabernacle—paid cash. No one could put it on his cuff.

It wasn't until Elaine saw him through the eyes of John and his prissy little Mutti on the day of their wedding that she found herself no longer able to suspend disbelief in Jack Rosenthal's performance at all, so was given away by just another vulgar, avaricious Jew, with no real culture save dirty jokes and corny cracks, and no real good cheer unless you counted what came out of a whiskey bottle. She and John had had to drive over to the county seat and bring the Justice of the Peace back with them—a flustered little fellow, who didn't seem at all familiar with the protocols . . .

. . . but soon enough was half-cut and cracking wise with Jack. Mutti's periwinkle-blue eyes glistered under the brim of her old bucket hat—and later on, as if to dissociate himself from it, John told Elaine there'd been a certain amount of shit-talk between her and the Justice about what terribly nice people the Jews were.

He'd revelled in this nasty little tale, and it was the first time Elaine realized that for all his vaunted philo-Semitism —he even liked to claim that he himself looked Jewish—the truth was he found it difficult—if not impossible—to see past the crudest types . . .

. . . she'd liked to climb up onto her papa's lap, just as she had onto Prudence's. Once seated on top of these elephantine legs in their gray flannel skin, she fidgeted and fiddled with his cold-bright keychain, and his yet more lustrous watch in its click-then-click-shut casing. He'd conjure candies out of his waistcoat pocket—Milk Duds and Juiclets, Black Crows and Red Hots, because he required above all something flavorsome forever to be swilling around in his mouth, together with cigar smoke and whiskey fumes . . .

. . . a mouth Elaine grabbed at with her chubby little hands—hanging on to his lower lip, then inky-pinkying through his clothes-brush-stiff mustache to tweak the waxen tip of his long and lumpy nose.

Everything about Elaine's papa was well maintained. The small metal objects and neatly folding tools with which he accessorized or otherwise carried about his many-pocketed person—fountain pen, billfold, cufflinks, tiepin, money clip, cigar cutter, cigar case, signet ring— were all of high quality and kept immaculately polished and shiny. This fastidiousness extended to the big bow-fronted chest of drawers that bulged with his beautifully clean and neatly folded clothes: black socks with clocks in one drawer, bilious yellow flannel BVDs in the next, and white cotton underpants together with white cotton handkerchiefs in a third, so there was no chance of some *unholy miscegenation* . . .

Lilian Rosenthal (née Cohen)—whose principal assurance in life was that her people were molded from finer clay—the ones who paid the piper, as it were—always managed to insert these words into any sentence concerning her husband: *coarse . . . vulgar . . . crude . . .* He never reacted directly—only persisted with the behaviors she found so distasteful, which included his compulsive punning, his off-color wisecracks, and his remarks about the Irish, the Poles, the Italians, the Negroes—indeed, about any people, not excluding his own. All other tribes were dirty—shitty, even—when Elaine's mother Lily's back was turned. And while the Jews were clean enough, they still smelled of dill pickles and gefilte fish. They were mean as well—oh, yes: unflinchingly ungenerous—while in line with their pettiness they crept about the place, craven, and effeminate.

When Elaine grew older, she realized . . . *well, what?* That towards the end of the day, when his cologne was beginning to fade, Jack Rosenthal smelled of gefilte fish and dill pickles as well—while he only saw in his daughter what he couldn't abide in himself? Her abundant, mousy-brown curls, her squinty myopic eyes, her long nose with the waxen-blob tip, and most of all her clumsiness, both physical and social: whatever it was, *shit or Shinola*, Elaine could be guaranteed to put her foot in it . . .

But no, that wasn't it—because along with his coarseness there was Jack Rosenthal's effortless facility when it came to being a man among men: horsing around, back-slapping, cigar-proffering, booze-pouring, and, of course, insidiously belittling. Whereas in the home, among his wife's watercolors of floral subjects, and her immaculately dusted Grand Rapids furniture, he'd cut a slightly ridiculous figure: especially since if his authority was brought into question, he'd turn bombastic—then get a little drunk, and eventually succumb to his insecurities, following his Lily about as if—fat chance!—she was going to take care of the poor little orphaned boy who'd been abandoned while his daddy went singing for their supper.

Papa didn't have anything to do with Prudence beyond authorizing her wages: The shvartze wants a pay raise? Elaine recalls his tone of happily incredulous . . . *contempt*. His children's nurse was always the shvartze to him, while when Elaine's mother said her name, it was as if the virtue named was being urged of the woman who bore it: Pru-dence, tread-carefully, watch-out and think-before-you-act . . . But to Elaine, Prudence's prudence was never in doubt—she was safe and enveloping breasts, firm and supportive thighs—and soft, smooth black skin, always smelling sweetly from its combination of coconut butter and coal tar soap.

One day, when Elaine was aged, she thinks, around five years old, she was sitting on Prudence's lap when her own dainty and demure mother returned home unexpectedly from a shopping expedition, and discovered her bestowing kisses on her nurse. Not just cursory ones, either—but full-blooded *smackers* . . . And, as she planted them on that dear face, she sing-songed her love: *Pru-dence . . . Pru-dence . . . I-love-you-oo . . .*

Lily hadn't run at them—she'd pounced.

Remounting the stairs, Billy's glass of milk in one hand while the other holds fast to the handrail, Elaine hears, emanating from some place of eternal mockery, Margaret Schlauch's throaty laughter. Elaine hasn't thought of the woman in years—yet here she is, plain as day, a jollily complacent sort of a Buddha, dressed all in dark tweeds, with a cream-colored blouse and bifocals that dangle down from a fine gold chain to jig about on her heaving and hefty bosom, as she tells all manner of jokes in all manner of languages . . . *I couldn't understand.*

She'd visited the summer ménage at Ken Durant's Jamaica place—and her reputation, which had preceded her, was as bulky as her luggage: two large suitcases and a collection of straw baskets, the obvious significance of which was she intended to stay for a while. Which she had a perfect right to do, given she, Ken, and Genevieve went

way back, and had been *waiting for goddamn Lefty* for
so long, the waiting had become the element within which
they existed.

Margaret also had a perfect right to be dismissive of
girls like Elaine—bourgeois alrightniks, who'd received
the benison of a free college education and done nothing
much with it besides entrap a man. Maybe so, Elaine had
conceded at the time, while also sulkily and silently main-
taining that *sex trumps everything*. Still, intimidated by
Margaret's brilliance, Elaine had stopped coming back
down after putting Billy to bed.

Was it the first night?—Impossible to say at this remove,
but not long after Margaret arrived, Elaine found herself
lying alone upstairs, and listening to the multilingual
hilarity echoing around the old colonial house. They were
talking politics, of course—and John was justifying his own
behavior, as he always did, by analogy with those other
deeply pragmatic accommodations whereby the intelligen-
tsia, realizing the premature character of the revolutionary
tendency, had sunk back down into the body politic, in
some cases becoming its most valuable organs—eyes still
seeing, ears yet listening, mouths ready to speak anew once
the winds of change were rising once more.

But that hadn't been Margaret's view at all—despite
her distinguished academic career, she was intent on leaving the States and its repressive regime. Not even sitting
at Ken's sequestered table, in his safe house, would she
vouchsafe more about her most primary allegiances—but
then this is what they'd all been like: getting a sly kid-
die kick out of belonging to clandestine organizations and

fooling each other quite as much as they did Uncle Sam—Elaine couldn't understand why someone as intelligent as Margaret couldn't see the whole credo was being fatally discredited, but instead she was going back to Europe, to a nation where progressive ideas still had a hope of success, while women were free to pursue independent lives, sexually quite as much as professionally.

Or at least that was the substance of what she'd said to Elaine the following morning, sitting at the kitchen table, breaking off from shelling peas into an enamel basin in order to take a gulp from a glass of buttermilk that left a white mustache . . . *thick as a clothes brush* on her top lip.

Elaine had never kissed Prudence again—it's worse than that: to this day, if she even considers what it would be like to press her lips on black skin, the smarting of her own from her mother's clout and the ringing of her five-year-old head return, together with these words: *Don't let me ever catch you kissing the shvartze again—they aren't clean . . . It disgusts me and now you disgust me, too . . .*

Would she—could she ever lose this grotesque and visceral prejudice? Objectively, Elaine understands it to be the worst possible nonsense—yet she still feels the full force of her mother's prohibition. On the days John takes the Buick and she has to do the grocery shopping on foot, Elaine picks her way gingerly down the path that edges the empty lot opposite. The tumbledown walls and mossy foundation of the old Williams place are lost in the deep crabgrass and ever-burgeoning shrubbery.

From out of there a lizard might run—or a rat: Billy says he's seen rats there, just one of the reasons he's forbidden to play on the other side of the road. His mother always wears slacks, or thick knee socks to make the trip.

One foot placed neatly in the space the other has just vacated, as she descends the hill Elaine imagines herself as one half of a fiercely dedicated couple—possibly Dorothy Wordsworth on her way to a local farm, where she'll get the eggs necessary to nourish her brother's creative vision . . . *or whatever it is that great poets eat.* The wide arena that the lake forms among attendant, brooding evergreens seems a suitable setting for this Romantic reverie—and while John's literary endeavours may not have the necessary sublimity . . . *what does he do, really, but write about what writers have written about other writers—and then have the gall to teach it to the poor sappy students* there's no gainsaying his commitment to *scribble . . . scribble . . . scribble . . .*

In the first year or so of their marriage, Elaine hadn't only believed John to be a brilliant fellow—she was emboldened by his worldliness, and especially his fierce anger with the color line, to address her own prejudices. When he was stationed outside Washington, and she stayed in Richmond, they were both revolted by the atmosphere of complete and surly segregation. Enough to pay their dues to the NAACP for maybe a year or so.

But every time when she reaches the bottom of the hill and crosses Floral Avenue, heading for the bridge over the inlet and the route to downtown, Elaine can't see people, only these vacant, gray-black visages. Faces hanging in

windows and doorways, or being carried aloft—like so
many placards—as their owners process slowly along the
sidewalk.

What does she read on them? John is a failure as a
critic if success consists in any kind of general assent to
his ideas—by contrast, the colored folk are masters and
mistresses of subtlety—far cleverer and more supple, she
thinks, than he when it comes to making their meanings
public: Yes'm and no suh are enunciated with absolute
neutrality—yet there's carefully concealed animus that
defies you to ask: What exactly do you mean by that?

She's frightened of them, though—it cannot be denied:
she may no longer have any intimacy with them at all, but
they remain, obstinately, in the margins. Margins that are
also kind of . . . *bleachers*, from which they whistle and
catcall as they spectate on her yellow-bellied behavior—
lurking, sly, waiting to *steal the moral bases . . .*

As Elaine had confessed then sought forgiveness from her
victim's mother, Bobbie had looked at her . . . *as if I were
sick in the head!* Which was fair enough—and when it
was her turn, rather than pronounce any absolution, she
instead spoke of her own racy youth in Chicago before
the war, where she'd encountered Negro luminaries, such
as the writer Richard Wright, and been to nightclubs and
restaurants that were defiantly unsegregated.

Then there was her métier as a painter—and this pretension Elaine had found hard to stomach—which, Bobbie claimed, meant she admired black bodies rather more
than she did white ones. Not, she stressed, because of their

athletic or statuesque qualities—for these weren't really what differentiated them, but were imposed on Negroes in order to emphasise their supposed animality. No, what she appreciated was precisely their color, which erupted onto the primed canvas, bringing with it the possibility of exciting compositions, tonalities, and chiaroscuros. Whereas white bodies? They were like unprimed canvases—nothing more.

Candidly, Elaine thought this was . . . *BS*. Whatever the ballyhoo with which their little set had greeted the Supreme Court ruling, and the ones in the state legislature as well—there still wasn't a single colored kid in their kids' school, while if a black man had had the temerity to enter the club car where Elaine had sat, moodily downing three cocktails, as the train chugged up the Hudson from New York—

Well! It was pretty unthinkable—the only blacks to be seen in the club car were white-jacketed stewards, the rest of them were somewhere else on the train, occupying the vehicular equivalent of Floral Avenue.

No—Bobbie's position when it comes to the race question is, Elaine thinks, pretty similar to her husband's: untested except by attendance at the occasional mixed party, or visit to a juke joint, and so dubious in a way that John's prejudicial remarks aren't. When Hetty had been with them at the Brooklyn apartment after Billy's birth, he hadn't scrupled to say of her, *who'd been his very own Prudence . . .* that when she had something she really wanted her employers to get or do for her, she'd *roll her eyes and play the dumb old nigger act . . .*

\* \* \*

Sleep now, Elaine says, as once more Billy buries his tousled blond head in his soft, white pillow. She remains sitting on the side of the bed and smoothing her son's hair, as she sings in what she hopes is a warm contralto: My pigeon house I open wide and I set my pigeons free, they fly so high they touch the sky and then light in the tallest tree . . .

He's fast asleep long before she reaches the coo-coo, coo-coo ending—which is just as well, as she can neither hold the tune, nor hold back her tears. A sickening sentimentality suffuses her as she remembers the huts and cages on the roofs of the tenements on the Southside, and in Brooklyn on those rare occasions she travelled into Manhattan as a girl.

Cages and huts the birds exploded from to swirl in mounting spirals, gaining height between manmade cliffs festooned with electric creepers and clothesline lianas, until at last reaching the refuge of the sky. As a girl, Elaine revered the pigeons: their broody burbling when at roost—their loose formation when in flight: each one allowed to find his own way, but all of them in it together. So that when they returned from their merry, merry flight, they did so together: a family as much as a flock, settling down cosily for the night on their perches.

Elaine sits, listening to Billy's deep and regular breathing —and its counterpoint: Karma's deep and regular purring, for the cat has crept in and sits, *predictably*, on the mat, as ever with a scrutable expression on its alien face: complete and content, the self-absorption of the female in *her most creative act . . .*

It's only when Elaine descends the stairs, and re-enters the atmosphere of cooling, staling meatloaf, that her most recent sins catch up with her, enveloping her tense shoulders. To be an adulteress is unquestionably a bad thing—although whether in or out of your furs, you're still *a Venus . . .* But to be a foiled adulteress, only too willing to err but denied the opportunity? To've proposed to her former lover this purely sexual arrangement—one entirely to his ease and advantage—then be flat-out rejected? Shame-upon-shame is now her double-ply garment, one providing *no support at all . . .*

On the contrary, as Elaine stands, soaping, scrubbing, then sluicing suds and greasy morsels from first one plate then the other, she's *crumbling . . .* a carnal kind of breakdown, as her bones liquefy, her muscles slacken, and her fat *sizzles . . .*

She hears John going upstairs. In the manner Elaine imagines unhappy couples behaving in the world over, they've figured out a way of avoiding each other in the evenings and the mornings, choreographing their movements so that while one uses the bathroom the other remains downstairs . . .

. . . and when they change places, the bathed one retreats to their bedroom, undresses, puts on his nightwear, and usually manages to be beneath the covers before the other one appears, already costumed.

No one says much during these interludes—but then there's no dialogue in ballet, is there? This evening, however, the timing must be off, and their pas-de-deux is a failure. When Elaine enters their bedroom John's still sitting on the side of the bed, his pyjama jacket lying beside him. Does he, she wonders, feel the same revulsion as me? She senses his gaze, roving slyly about beneath her nightie, its eyebeams stroking the pinkly-red marks left on her belly and thighs by her girdle and garters . . .

Does he gaze upon my sad, slack breasts with the same disgust that I feel when I come like this, unexpectedly, upon his swelling paunch and balding head?

Removing her glasses Elaine feels momentary relief: the world has returned to a blur. Then her tongue, at once dumb and painfully oversensitive, goes exploring—its tip stroking the molars to the right, to the left, up . . . and down. She feels the four, very distinct holes . . . *caverns, really*, and now, with their reacquaintance comes this future: an appointment with the dentist on Monday morning—a *failed Nazi*, with his ineffectual gas and punctilious manner . . .

The caverns are *fathomless* . . . out of them come flying the fleet pains of the future—ones incapable of being divorced from the drill's bit and its torturous whining grinding. Is it possible, she wonders, to die from anxiety alone?

Freudenberg used to say that dentistry was too sexual for me—requiring as it does the submission of my body to a man with a pointed instrument . . . This—and also that my anxiety was so extreme because my teeth—along with the rest of my body—belong to my parents, and by allowing them to become rotten, I was betraying them . . . What phoney baloney—only another thing he tossed out while he was *shaking me down* . . .

Besides, how could a small child be blamed for sucking on all those Milk Duds when she'd only just been weaned? Sitting on her Papa's lap, lost and contented, her little mouth full of syrup, her chin . . . *sticky.*

*Billy set off to school this morning looking awfully brave and serious in his little Pilgrim Fathers costume—and even though I ran it up myself from a couple of yards of blackout material, and with no pattern, I think he looks pretty swell. They're rehearsing the pageant at recess and I'll go along to see it, so I can't* . . .

Can't what? Elaine stops and thinks for a moment: Can't be bothered—or, more exactly, can't be bothered to write you more downright lies dressed up as evasions. Anyway, it's only three weeks since her parents visited— staying at the Statler, her father summing up the displays in Rothschild's with a professional eye, feeling a length of cloth with his *sticky fingers* . . . —so what more is there to be said, besides more of the stilted same?

She sits as moments stretch and twine with the smoke uncoiling from the tip of her cigarette . . . A strange sort of *fugue*, she thinks—having only this morning learned what this means, courtesy of Karen Horner on WQCR—in which the little blue curlicues unravel, as they pursue one another.

On the tabletop, beside the blotter and the letter she's been writing, is her spiral-bound exercise book *full of the truth.* Elaine swaps them over, leafs through her diary, finds the next blank page, and begins aggressive doodling: the letter *A* for Arty embellished with more and more wiry coils that tighten . . . and tighten. The ghastly little shit of a man, she thinks, as she obliterates his initial, he has no real feeling for me—and never can have. He took a piece when he was hungry—then sent the dish back when he was sated. Then he pinched the waitress's ass, saying, No, no second helpings for me . . .

Doodling gives way to listing: first Elaine writes the names of the couples she believes may be at the Lemesuriers' tomorrow evening. Why? Because by so doing she hopes to give them some substance—because when she's in this mood everyone starts seeming thinner . . . *translucent*, like cartoon characters on a TV screen *yapping away* . . .

John isn't translucent, though—he's opaque. And neither is he a little shit: he's a big, deceptive one, concealing his own childhood truth beneath a costume—one that's very definitely cut from a pattern: John Hancock, Elaine writes once, her hand clear and legible. Then a line down she writes it again: John Hancock . . .

It's no big deal for a play or a novel to be named after its principal character—but what about a signature? John's signature—his mark on the world—is named after the character he plays, not himself . . .

Elaine remembers him finally deciding on his alias, the morning he went down to the army office and signed up for the draft. It'd been a gay—if deadly serious—sort of game, for once one they played together: Hooper? Hewes? Pinn? Rutledge? Any one of these patriots' names might invite questioning about his origins, but Johann—as he'd been christened—required one that would not only erase his given ones but also be unimpeachable.

John Hancock did the business of forestalling any inquiries—after all, what was John Hancock beyond a fancy signature once the honor of actual consanguinity had been gently declined? Why, only this: a cliché—or a cipher that nevertheless conceals Johann Schitz.

Elaine had supported him—after all, she, too, was keen on *hiding in plain view*. And while no girl in her right mind would willingly become Mrs. Johann Schitz, neither had John's name change been at her insistence. Obviously, having a Kraut name wasn't going to look good once brave boys began dying, while as for Schitz's close proximity to shit—well, everyone avoids that, don't they? Everyone *steps over it . . .*

For someone who was already a professional interpreter of words, becoming John Hancock was primarily a matter of simple reinterpretation. None too gripped by their late-night bull sessions, Elaine understood this much: around the time he and she began dating, some of the members of John's little Marxist cenacle were turning their coats inside out—or perhaps they'd been wearing reversible ones all along.

The bulls could get rowdy, running between Columbia Circle and the queer little apartment in the Village he'd shared with another graduate instructor: some suspended disbelief in the theater of the treason trials, and went on toeing the Party line. For them, the anti-fascist war waiting in the wings had, following the Nazis' deal with the

Soviets, simply done a quick costume change, and become an anti-imperialist one instead . . .

Then it changed again, as German tanks dashed towards Leningrad and Moscow . . . But by that point, John, while retaining a materialist view of history—which, he was partial to reminding his *goo-goo-eyed* girlfriend, was made by *the great mass of individuals*, rather than great men alone—refused the deformations necessary to keep the march of time dialectical. More important than any of this was his overriding—hence overdetermining—requirement *to get laid* . . .

They married in Johnstown early in the summer of forty-two, then headed West in an old Ford John's fussbudget Mutti had handed down to him. Despite the world running amok, he'd managed to get an academic post at the UW–Madison.

Elaine doesn't have any rose-tinted recollections of their first few weeks of marriage—the days on the road were hot, dusty, dull, and kind of despairing when, after hours of boring through interminable fields of wheat, corn, and alfalfa, like some sort of gas-powered boll weevils, they stopped at a diner or a café in the shadow of a silo, and saw the Joads' stay-at-home cousins, shuffling along the warped boardwalk, giving these carpetbaggers the walleye.

In one forsaken settlement the proprietor had, in between hits from a bottle he kept below the counter, carefully laid a table for them in a room to one side, then ushered them in, explaining, You folks don't want to be looked at by the regulars while you eat—they're all retards . . . Picking at her ghastly salad, somewhere *well to the east of Eden* . . . Elaine wasn't exhilarated by her first experience of the agricultural heartlands—only enervated.

Proximately, this wasn't because of the burning end of a long hot summer—the sun flung daily across the white-hot sky to bury itself in the dust ahead—it was John. His vigor remained indisputable: he drove the car, did the budgeting, figured out their route, and, as of right, screwed her in one after another of the little shacks masquerading as motel cabins.

Lying alongside him on gritty sheets, with mosquitos dallying down to feed on her exposed flesh, she envisioned them equipped not with bloodsucking proboscises but with penises, and wondering at his peremptory behavior, concluded that all his courtly lovemaking *of yore* had merely been a means to achieve this end—at once sweaty and *rasping* . . . since she was dry *down there* . . .

There were others of his impostures that troubled his bride: he'd proudly numbered Jews among his Columbia crowd, and mostly because of this reckoned himself a philo-Semite, with privileged access to this ancient people's American sub-breed. One of his favorite tales concerned another westward road trip, in the company of a fellow Columbia man who was the son of a rabbi from Weehawken. To hear Johann-that-was tell it, as they'd made their way from one small-town kosher establishment to the next, following the trail of matzo balls, it was the rabbi's kid who'd been taken for a gentile, while all those pious Jews had assumed Elaine's future husband to be one of their own.

Of the two of them, who really passed? It's true, they had—and still do—a sibling kind of resemblance. Quite possibly this explained both their attraction to, and repulsion from, each other. Quite quickly, Elaine saw her own Janus face mirrored by John, and concluded she'd perversely managed to marry her own *inner antisemite* . . . One who, in turn, was harboring his own sworn enemy.

At a faculty party in Madison, not long after their arrival, where they'd skulked from group to group together, only being included in conversations under sufferance, Elaine had overheard someone bemoaning the way the English department was *filling up with New York Jews* . . . She'd said nothing, of course—although when the same bigoted ignoramus had remarked right to their bespectacled faces: My, you two look so alike, you could be brother and sister, Elaine snapped back: Actually, we are—we're adding *incest to injury* . . .

A line her husband liked so much, he went on repeating it for years after as an example of his wife's lightning wit. Which was gratifying—although still a slur, since Jews crack wise the way colored folk *blaze away at the congas* . . . Despite which, Elaine felt wistful about this past—a golden era, relatively speaking, when they'd at least maintained solidarity in public, even as privately they began drawing apart.

Now, snuffing her cigarette out in the ashtray, Elaine exhales and savors the acrid residue of last night's equally vaporous dream: men in midtown Manhattan—gray flannel masses of them, none with eyes or mouths, only smooth,

blue-veined skin covering their nevertheless leering faces—
and aggressive lesbians, cruising the block in station wag-
ons, one of whom picked Elaine up from the curb, drove
far and fast uptown, then, when they reached a windswept
bluff above the river, parked and pawed at her in the back
seat, in a way *which I didn't altogether mind* . . .

Now, this film—on her tongue, the roof of her mouth,
welling into and out of those goddamn cavities. And in her
belly a feeling both sharp and mushy, as if the sharp edges
of her broken daydreams are . . . *digging into me*—a corny
metaphor, one that makes her feel still worse. Who'll be at
the Lemesuriers' tomorrow evening? Only the usual crowd,
Elaine supposes—although where she's earned the right to
be so dismissive, *I've no idea* . . .

Given Elaine's periods of indisposition, it's taken the
Hancocks four long years to move from the periphery to
near the center of this—at times quite vicious—little circle.
They've attended faculty events of all sorts—picnics and
potluck suppers, lectures and fundraisers. Elaine's even
reluctantly attended some of the English department's
wives' luncheons, and made up to Selma Lemesurier, who
has the same fighting weight as Margaret Dumont *although
none of her sass or deadpan.*

Now that the affair with Arty has amscrayed, while
the one with Joe remains—if such a thing is possible—a
continuing unlikelihood, quite possibly she should, as the
Puritan poet schools Eve, *endure the livery of a nun.* Or at
least the white gloves of an obedient little faculty wife—
and live, *a barren sister,* for the rest of her miserable life. A

dumb bit of advice from a blind man, she knows, because while Elaine's never kidded herself that she can play the love interest, ever since she first began succumbing to her desires, she's known this much: her sole raison d'être is to love, to be loving . . . and to be loved.

But oh! Right now—this moment, there's this disgustingly squashy feeling in her belly, from the soft core of which emanate lightning-strikes of pain—there can no longer be any warding it off: the curse is upon her. *Falling off the roof* was Lily Rosenthal's queer expression for this—and she'd try, by bestowing this confidence, to draw Elaine into the conspiracy of her and her genteel kind—one dedicated to keeping the biological reality of life, as much as was humanly possible, top secret.

Could it be a Russian or a Yiddish expression? Elaine thinks, I'll quite likely come across someone from the relevant department tomorrow evening—and God knows, they're only too eager to share their hard-won scholarship— She shudders, as if arrested in mid-fall, because a fair- to middling-sized part of her wanted to stay up there, clinging to the eaves, a perilously pregnant Elaine. Since no matter how terrifying a prospect another child might be, its arrival would at least confirm her in the justness of her confinement—a Jewess, unfit for anything besides *Kinder und Küche*, if not regular attendance at *Kirche* . . .

Candidly, Elaine yearns to be had—rather than merely taken. Had being the operative word, since it's only as the object of a man's desire that she'll properly exist. Elsewise, she breasts muddy, turbulent fears—on her way to . . . *nowhere.* Yes, stated plainly her fantasies appal her with their clichés—but do they sound any better in Kinsey's dry socialese . . . ?

Rose suggested Elaine buy the hefty volume—but after a few forays into its forensic descriptions of the possibilities of penises and vaginas, clitorises, breasts, and anuses, Elaine gave up and secreted it down in the basement in John's old steamer trunk, a dusty-musty sarcophagus, plastered with labels for the Bremen Line, inscribed with customs officers' chalk marks. If she thought of it at all, it was as a *despair chest* . . . one to which she would no doubt add.

Yet it remains the case that at certain times, in certain lights, there he is: a dark shadow detaching from darker ones, then at once upon her, deftly unbuttoning and unhooking, smoothly removing her clothing and his own—and she . . . she . . . entirely receptive. Squashy—but in a good way.

There were men around who might fit the bill—Digby Henty is tall and dark enough, confident as well. A couple of weeks ago at the Wilsons' he'd asked Elaine to dance then guided her silkily between the other couples, simply by adjusting the pressure of each of the fingers poised on the small of her back. As they slid here, sidled there, spun and slid some more, she'd remembered the feeling of Joe's fingers on her mons, his thumb in her vagina—so what if Digby had a shapeless putty face and a donkey's bray for a laugh?

Then there's the boss himself. The rumor is, Harry Lemesurier—who exudes angered lust—beds his co-eds, and for this gives them better grades than he should.

According to John, he justifies his behavior to his cronies thus: What's the point of being a professor of French literature if you don't teach American little women how to become grandes horizontales . . .

It's a wonder any of them hasn't ratted him out long before now. Appalled by her own traitorousness, Elaine hypothesizes: He must manage the whole thing with some delicacy . . .

A hawk nose, snake eyes, and olive skin: Harry has thick gray-blond twists of hair sprouting from collar and cuffs, which Elaine finds . . . *perfectly ghastly*—still, he fits the bill, while there'd be no cause for remorse, since Selma Lemesurier—who's older than her husband, and wears her hair in a wintry sea of frozen waves—appears altogether complaisant, encouraging even. Last time they were at the Lemesuriers' she said to Elaine, I think it's a great help when a wife isn't too judgmental—don't you, dear?

Would she—could she—ever be like that?

Abruptly, Elaine screws the cap on to her pen and tosses it to one side: listing men—listing chores, neither action gets the one bedded or the other done. Besides, *who'd want me?* Not even John with his fishy lips and Jell-O belly really desires me anymore . . . Not even Arty . . .

Downstairs, Elaine peers into the icebox as Karma twines about her ankles. She turns her chilly regard on last night's meatloaf and a dish of cold potatoes waiting to be discarded —unless she mushes them up, adds flour, and makes Billy some pancakes. No . . . she thinks: she'll do something even simpler for his and the sitter's supper. Beans are in the cupboard—franks she'll get at Pete's. As for John and her, say what you will about the Lemesuriers, Selma keeps a beautiful table—there won't be only a few desultory plates spread with cold cuts or mounded with salad, like there are at so many other Ithaca parties.

Last time the Hancocks were invited, there was an entire poached salmon garnished with fresh parsley and cucumber slices, the centrepiece of an immaculately clothed and meticulously laid buffet table. Silver flashed from damask —and there were two heavy French casserole dishes, one with coq au vin, the other boeuf de bourguignon, steaming bowls of rice and potatoes dauphinoise. Elaine remembers accepting a portion of the fish, while being coldly regarded by its *dead and accusatory eyes* . . .

If she doesn't take the car, drive out to Loblaw's, and do a proper grocery shop, Elaine has time on her hands—but time for what? To scrub her menfolk's excreta from the toilet bowl? Or should she iron John's shirts? Of all the tasks required to keep the house going, ironing—or irony, as she calls it—is the one she detests the least.

Unlimbering the heavy old board, which is attached to the wall between the icebox and the sink, she always appreciates the cleverness of its cantilevered design, as counterweight sinks and legs . . . *open*. She couldn't give a shit whether John's shirts are well ironed—except for this: smooth or hummocked, these snowy expanses will, inevitably, *reflect on me* . . .

God forbid that John should go out into the world looking like Caspar Voss, the wrinkles on his shirtfront crinkling into letters proclaiming: MY WIFE IS A SLATTERN.

Arranging the front panel of the shirt with the buttonholes carefully on the ironing board, holding it in position with *poised* fingers, while those of the other hand deftly flick water drops across it, then applying the hot iron . . .

. . . If only, Elaine thinks, my entire life could be dealt with in this manner—all of its lies and hypocrisies evened out so there was no more smoothly saying things, when I'm all rumpled up inside. Irony, indeed.

# .3.

## Early evening, the following day

Papa loves mambo . . . ! The little portable record player is turned up too loud in the sitting room. Elaine pictures John and Billy unselfconsciously shimmying: letting themselves go with it . . . Mama loves mambo! But what if we were to separate? *No more mamboing then . . .*

From her descriptions of them together, Doctor Freudenberg had made one of his more elementary deductions: *Billy is a child who's unusually close to his father . . .* Meaning what, precisely? Only that John doesn't fear murdering him, then killing himself, on a daily basis . . . *the way I do.*

Thinking about such vile things, Elaine thinks, is what gives me this mean expression: the two deep grooves running from my forehead to either side of my hateful nose. She breaks from her mirror image's desperate eyes—ones full of her own just-pressed new blouse, quite as much as her *sour old puss* . . . In the Seventh Avenue store, it'd looked perfectly fine—just one fuchsia bloom in a silky and multicolored garden. But now it seems too frilly and flouncy, emphasizing the stringiness of Elaine's neck, its prominent tendons and empurpled veins . . .

Oh, Je-sus! she exclaims—a half-laugh, half-gasp that evolves into a liquid cough. She feels full of noxious fluids —a cocktail of menstrual blood and bronchial sputum— and has a dark and supremely personal little insight that makes her laugh still more, cough yet harder: *I've not only fallen off the roof—I've got goddamn lung cancer.*

Not that Elaine requires a fearmongering physician to tell her it's the cigarettes—she's been thinking it all by her lonesome these past three or four years, every fall when the first grippe of winter grows out of her usual and persistent coughing. As she decides, yet again, to stop—or at least to start stopping by not taking another full pack with her to the party tonight—Elaine knows her resolve is undermined by her perfidy, which means her private promises to herself are even more worthless than the ones *I make to others . . .*

Papa's looking for Mama! Who, quite obviously . . . is nowhere in sight, having fled into flattering fantasy: her smoldering cigarette held at a rakish angle in one hand, the lowball glass containing her pre-party drink cradled in the other. Reduced to the pen strokes and shading of an elegant drawing in the New Yorker, Elaine likes what she sees and begins to compose an anecdote to be deployed later that evening—why not something ironizing her prudish mother forever falling off the roof?

Which might seem either a little risqué, or terribly *worldly . . .* She enjoys the reception of this yet-to-be-coined witticism: the eyes on her widening, the shoulders

attached to them shaking—she hears waves of laughter
breaking over her, and sees the gloss of social success they
leave in their wake.

Can it be wrong, she wonders, to set such store by one's
own wit? There are others in their crowd who can hold an
audience while provoking hilarity—*but no one's as good at it
as me* . . . It's a crying shame, Elaine feels, that there isn't an
ad' in the Journal's Help Wanted section for a comedienne.
If she could pay her way with her antic abilities, perhaps she
wouldn't feel such violent jealousy when anyone else within
her earshot says anything even remotely amusing . . .

Feelin' that zing again, wow!—But then, does any man
truly admire—let alone desire—a woman who makes him
laugh? It's men who should make women *abandon themselves* . . . and for a woman to do it to a man is necessarily
to demean his powers and potential. Probably none of this,
Elaine concedes, would bother me if I were an independent
career woman—then again, if she were, she'd hardly be
likely to be included in the faculty crowd, which—apart
from the occasional singleton, usually passing through—is
exclusively composed of couples.

Composed. *Composed* . . . the prominent brown mole
on her chin dulled with foundation, her cheeks a touch
rouged, her lips likewise. Why bother with *Mrs. Magoo's
baggy old peepers*? No one's gonna see ya behind these *old
coke-bottle glasses* . . .

Downstairs, Elaine doesn't exactly make an entrance
to the sitting room, but props herself in the doorway, her
pocketbook dangling from her hand, clearly ready. John is
still bouncing Billy on his knee in time to . . . Papa loves

mambo, and quite likely doesn't want Mama to rumba or samba. Edith is curled up prettily on the couch with a book held in front of her face, to forestall any conversation, Elaine suspects, rather than from any real bookishness . . .

. . . though why the kid should be shy around John is a mystery—he's no lothario, and would rather mambo with his kid than *beat time with a woman, any day* . . .

You look great, Mom! Billy's soprano rises above the rhythm section— It's a merry mix-up, Elaine sings back at him: a wonderful whirl of colorful separates! Which is her way to make light of a skirt, blouse, and jacket that simply don't match, Papa loves—

John lifts the tone arm, twists the switch: delicate movements—sudden soundlessness . . . *perhaps he doesn't love mambo after all?*

Dad, Billy *solos*, why can't we have a proper hi-fi?

For a split second Elaine feels sorry for her husband, whose shortcomings as a provider are shot at him *from both sides* . . .

Coats and hats on, the Golden Boy in his adorable red pyjamas cuddled and kissed, the Beleaguered Patriarch recovers some of his authority, saying, We won't be back late, Edith.

That's OK, Professor Hancock, the pocket-sized blonde simpers, my pop'll come and get me whenever I call . . .

I wanted to save him the trouble, John replies—then, in the Buick, its headlights *drilling holes* in the *rotten* darkness, Elaine says: Don't you remember? You were pretty goddamn tight the last time you drove her home—either she said something to her old man or he smelled the liquor on your breath.

He can't've smelled it on me, I didn't go anywhere near the guy . . . John begins justifying himself—but then, sensing her scorn beside him, he trails off.

The Buick reaches the bottom of the hill and crosses the first of the open-form bridges that span the inlet of Cayuga Lake that separates West Hill from downtown. Tires and engine duet: the swish of wire brushes, the hollow hammering of tom-toms . . . They turn into State Street.

Mama does love mambo, Elaine concedes—but she loves literature a lot more—at least, she cherishes moments such as this one, when, warm in the November night, bourbon in her belly, and with a pleasant sense of anticipation regarding the party ahead, she thinks how very wonderful it would be if she could write one of the perfect short stories she so admires—like The Lottery: one in which the most mundane imaginable events—such as a middle-aged couple going out for the evening *like us*—would be told in such a flatly unemotional tone, they became macabre and hence superlatively . . . *troubling*.

The Lemesuriers abide, together with the majority of wealthier faculty members, up on Cayuga Heights. Poorer ones rent in College Town—but the Hancocks are exceptional, and the only other faculty they know in their neighborhood are the—at least, superficially—homespun and happy O'Briens. Over there, old farm equipment rusts in outhouses and there's abundant poison ivy in underbrush running along the old field margins. Here, the verges mound up opulently from the smooth tarmac roadways into still-smoother lawns, and the shaggy old-growth evergreens beat the bounds of the broad yards within which the houses repose, untroubled by arising from *their semi-recumbent posture.*

Cars are parked halfway down the long block from the Lemesuriers' place, which, Elaine thinks—as she did the last time they came—is *suitably eminent* . . . It's a misty-damp evening, far from chilly, and the sidewalks are slippery with fallen leaves. Feeling unsteady, she takes John's arm out of habit, as they mount stairs that uncoil into a path that snakes between Chinese lanterns hanging from the lower boughs of trees and ornamental shrubs. Ahead of them, the front door to the house opens and closes, *hungry for company.*

I heard from this new guy in Sociology, John says, who's done work with the military, that over at the base in Saratoga, the officers and their wives have parties where everyone leaves their car keys in a bowl at the beginning of the evening, and when it's time to go the husbands just grab a set of keys at random, and take the car together with—

The wife that goes with it?

Correct.

Elaine wonders what kind of car she goes with—certainly not the little old Buick coupe, something statelier, perhaps—although not a pre-war Packard, even if it does seem as if she's talking to her husband through a speaking trumpet while he reclines behind a glass partition.

Is that what you want, she asks him, that kind of unbridled promiscuity?

No! John laughs sharply—and in the gathering light from the porch Elaine sees he's either cut himself shaving *or has a hickey . . .*

Time was when she'd've unashamedly clothed her finger in a clean corner of her handkerchief, licked it, and done away with this dry crust of blood—because physical intimacy isn't only carnality . . . *I know that*, but an entire panoply of physical involvements, the principal aim of which is to make cavemen acceptable to cavewomen . . . *and vice versa.*

There's no way of subjecting this to the power of reason, Elaine thinks—either you can stomach it or you can't, and it has nothing to do with your morals either, even the *virtuous mind that ever walks attended by a strong siding champion* . . . may still be housed in a body you find flat-out repellent.

Elaine isn't so hot when it comes to architectural styles, but she supposes the Lemesuriers' place is of the ranch variety, what with its ornamental wagon wheels, low eaves, Dutch gables, and feature walls, but *no actual ranching to speak of . . .* unless you counted Harry himself . . . *rounding up co-eds*, and Selma's rather improbable ability, still, to heft her considerable bulk up onto a horse.

Her pride in this achievement shines from the heavy, cream-painted door, adorned with a large brass knocker in the shape of a horseshoe, and below it a Thanksgiving wreath of red berries and leaves twining *incognito . . .* The door swings open, and here's Selma Lemesurier poised to welcome her guests, with cleavage *you could lose a carving knife in . . .* and bare, wattled arms. The Hancocks hang back, as she pecks at the couple ahead of them—then it's their turn: How do you do . . . How do you do, dear . . . ? *How do, doo-doo, doo-wop-doo-bee-doo* . . . You can leave your coats in there . . . There being a walk-in closet presided over by a colored kid in a shortie white jacket, who's presumably been hired for the evening—Elaine knows they have a maid and a cook, but there are no other permanent staff, so far as she's aware.

Peeled from her old lambswool coat, she's *stripped bare . . . anything might happen*: because all parties have at least this moment of promise, Elaine believes—as young women do—when what they may turn into is moot: beautiful experiences, or ugly debacles. Which is why married couples wonder whether to stick together, or seek out something or person else. Elaine repossesses her husband's hand for long enough to feel his pulse—then they relinquish one another for highballs borne by a second colored kid.

*That pretentious pederast*—which is how John refers to Jimmy Castlemaine in private—is hard on the kid's heels, arresting him so as to exchange an empty glass for a full one—he turns to see his junior colleague *and his superfluous wife*, but nonetheless smiles indulgently: Oh, Sir John, he flutes, and his lady . . .

As they start chatting, Elaine considers this: whether Jimmy basks in exactly the same warm feeling of indisputable superiority to his interlocutor as John does.

Her husband says, You like a game of tennis, don't you, Jimmy?—and Elaine realizes he's committing one of his habitual solecisms: not just laughing at his own joke, but laughing . . . *in anticipation of it.*

Caught off guard in this way Elaine reels around in the vestibule of her mind, staring through this gaping door at the terrifying boundlessness of her own contempt. John continues: Better look out for that elbow, my friend, I hear there're some terrible cases of bursitis going around.

Sure, Jimmy mugs, but it isn't infectious, is it?

No, John concedes, but it's very likely contagious—one victim gave himself sinusitis when he picked his nose—

Dirty guy, Jimmy says, an' I heard his nose started out just peachy: a little retroussé thing—but now it stretches clear out of the committee room . . .

Both men snort with laughter—and Elaine joins them, but more to be companionable than out of any shared sense of humor. She knows what they're driving at, but she's fed up with these detours they think diverting: What I don't understand, she says, is why did the army allow Samuel Sears to be chosen as attorney in the case?

Jimmy—who she notes is wearing a plaid vest and matching bowtie—glances at John, then says: The whole farrago is finito, Elaine—no one's taking him seriously anymore, the old cluck. The army doesn't want its own doing any tittle-tattling—the top brass knows fine well the war wouldn't've been won without . . . He trails off, blue-button eyes dangling down, and Elaine wonders if he knows—or at least guesses . . .

Then he resumes: Now it'll just be business as usual—blaming and blame-fixing 'til the sainted press and its holy readers do the decent thing—

And forget all about it, John says, then moves so's to cut his wife out of their conversation: Not to be infra dig, he says to Jimmy, but there's this business of mimeographing all the notes for next semester's courses . . .

Elaine wanders away. She's been to the Lemesuriers' house a couple of times before—the Labor Day party last year was held in its extensive grounds, but the faculty wives' coffee morning had been inside, and she recalls the layout as she paces, peering in at open doorways to the right and the left.

The décor is pretty damn chintzy—yellow-and-red drapes, carpets, and cushion covers. A lot of flouncing about and ruching up. The rooms are wide—but the ceilings low, and overall, what with the great profusion of pedestal tables, standard lamps, club chairs, bookcases, and jardinieres, the feeling is . . . *oppressive.*

She finds herself in some kind of conservatory—at any rate, a large room with floor-length windows and earth-toned tiling. Two more colored kids are readying the buffet, and Elaine's tummy rumbles, which never fails to revulse her . . . *maidenly soul.* One's fanning out the cutlery on the damask cloth—the other's doing napkin origami. Elaine thinks: If I could be that deft and diligent a hostess—I'd be so well loved . . . I'd lose my inferiority complex . . .

*The way you hold your knife* . . . The way we danced 'til three . . . The crooning is so softly insidious she hears not statements, but secret instructions—but to do what? There's no doubt that these large parties provide excellent cover under which to hunt down love, she concludes, as a platter of meticulously arrayed cold cuts is placed on the buffet: 'cause I'm hungry as hell, *and I'm not getting any meat at home* . . .

*. . . anyway*, who would want cheap hamburger meat when there's quality ribeye steak available? If not Arty, some other sophisticate who knows how to make love to a woman properly—how to savor her charms, rather than *slobber over them . . .*

Turning from the buffet she sees the party is filling up with guests, who, as she observes them, coalesce into gossipy little colloquies. In each one, Elaine thinks, given the number of people who dislike and avoid me, there must be a quisling, who, while they don't have any firsthand knowledge, has nonetheless heard *whssh-whssh-whssh-Well-you-know . . .*

Could she really conduct an affair right here in this goldfish bowl? Not likely. Her crimes—subterfuge, stolen kisses—are opportunistic ones:

*What did you get up to in the city?*

*Nothing, much—Ginny wasn't so keen on me once I was there. I packed some boxes for her but then she didn't scruple to tell me I wasn't too efficient at it . . .*

*How long did you stay with her at the new place . . . ?*

Adding up hours with a vacant cow face: *Not long . . .*

But long enough: a false-bottomed suitcase within which to conceal the Italian joint where she'd lunched with Arty: a dark little booth, starfish . . . glass floats—icons of Stella Maris, bounteous sea-mother, ocean-tidier, and *straightener of straits . . .*

Do have a drink and something to eat, will you, please, Elaine?

Selma Lemesurier has manifested—a friendly enough, if substantial, ghost. With her arrival, the colored kids jump

to it—one sallying out from behind the bar to ask Elaine,
What you'd like to drink, ma'am? And before she's put
away half the old-fashioned, she wants another . . . *it's the
same as cigarettes*. She swigs the rest of the cocktail, strides
to the makeshift bar, asks the keep for the same again, and
spills some on the collar of her blouse, such is her thirst.

The truth is . . . well, what? That for parties where
they think their hosts may be a little stingy, the Hancocks
have been known to bring their own pinch-bottle of Haig?
No . . . dabbing at herself with a snowy napkin, Elaine sops
up this dirty little secret as well.

Selma's still clucking about, so Elaine joins the
short queue for the hot dish—which is a soufflé, served
with . . . *coleslaw?* and chunks of French baguette, part-
baked with wedges of garlic and butter. No great surprise,
considering the Lemesuriers' French connections—ones
they drop into just about any conversation. Propped up
by an inglenook, Elaine feels awkward. With plate in one
hand, glass in the other, she's unwilling to sit lest she be . . .
trapped—but she is—by Harry Lemesurier, who comes
towards her with an older couple in tow.

Vladimir, he says, and: Vera . . . this is Elaine Hancock, the wife of one of our most brilliant young assistant
professors . . . Elaine—his diction slows to enunciate *for
the stupenagel*: these are the Na-bo-kovs . . . Then he disappears, leaving Elaine blinking in the face of this *balding
old coot* . . . who has a neat, aquiline nose and hooded
eyes which . . . *pierce into me* through the thick lenses of
his horn-rimmed eyeglasses. The wife's gaze is yet more
coldly appraising: *no coquetting for this honeybunch*,

with her cotton-candy hair, and pursed, mauve-painted lips.

Her husband says, I'm not in the habit of judging a woman solely in terms of her spouse's profession—do you work yourself, Mrs. Hancock?

Flushing, Elaine deposits the small congealed ruin of her soufflé on a convenient table before replying: No, I confess . . . I mean, apart from a little copywriting for a department store here in Ithaca . . . That, and typing up my husband's work for publication—he can't do it himself, and his handwriting is appalling.

Not so alien to our situation, says *the ice queen*. Elaine's finding the strange couple's accents hard to place—there's Russian there, certainly, but twisted together with one or more other European tongues. There's no shame in such work, Mrs. Nabokov continues. I take a great deal of responsibility for those practical tasks associated with my husband's work that some might think extraneous, but which he and I know are as necessary as his imaginative labors. I typewrite his manuscripts as you do your husband's—and I don't doubt that you, as I do, also take a hand in editing them. I correspond with his publishers— where necessary translating submissions . . .

Elaine isn't listening—she's heard it too many times before: the woman who claims to be engaged in a mutual endeavor, so as to elevate herself into the male world of power and consequence. It's the inversion, she thinks, of the way intellectuals like John made an equation between writing and sex need: their need for one to be admired and the other satisfied.

Also, there's something bothering her about this fellow . . . Suddenly, she recalls what it is and unthinkingly
snaps her fingers—instantly regretting it, for it's as loud
as a pistol shot in this still, subdued atmosphere, while the
elderly couple are visibly startled . . . I'm so sorry, my kid
does it all the time, and I've got the habit . . . anyway—I've
heard of you, of course, Professor Nabokov—sometimes it
seems we've a surfeit of critics at Cornell, but scarcely any
actual authors . . .

They ignore this—instead, Mrs. Nabokov says: Do you
have several children? And Elaine sees several little pseudo-
Schitzes of descending sizes, looking blond and unctuous,
before answering, No, just the one son.

We have that much in common, then.

Not to be so easily dismissed, Elaine blunders on: Are
you working on a new novel at the moment?

Oh, a little divertissement, er, Elaine—nothing very
sen-sational . . .

Forgive me, if you will . . . she feels her face growing
puce . . . I've wanted to write ever since I was in high
school, but every attempt I make— Well, the results are
fairly wretched, so that . . . They're still looking at her
expectantly, with an air of rather chilly objectivity, as if *I
were a bug they were studying* . . . although words stir in
me, and I start with great enthusiasm, convinced I have a
tale to tell, pretty soon I run into trouble . . . while every
line I write seems so very banal . . .

There's a harsh noise that for some seconds Elaine cannot identify—then she realizes it's Mrs. Nabokov, laughing: Forgive me, my dear, she says, wiping a tear from a

cornflower-blue eye, but the idea of Nabokov giving anyone advice concerning such matters is wholly ridiculous—he writes, you see, as a spider spins its web or an ant builds its nest . . . It is, I think, entirely instinctual.

Well . . . yes . . . maybe so, her husband joins in, but you know I read this very interesting—quite possibly germane—article in the newspaper only the other day. Apparently at a zoo in the environs of Chicago, a keeper gave one of the apes in his charge some sticks of charcoal, and showed the creature how to use them to create sketches and so forth . . . Well—and d'you know what this furry Fragonard chose to depict with his very first attempt?

I can't guess, Elaine replies, sounding, she hopes, suitably intrigued.

Why . . . the Russian's own charcoal-stroke eyebrows levitate . . . the bars of his own cage, of course!

For what seems a long and penitential while, Elaine wonders whether this man, a real writer, has somehow surmised her terrible claustrophobia—how trapped she feels in her body, her marriage, her entire lousy life.

Do you mean . . . she chooses what for her are incendiary words, carefully . . . that I should paint the bars of my own cage, symbolically speaking?

But before he can reply, John appears—hair mussed up, face a little red—and announces: Professor—Mrs. Nabokov, an unexpected pleasure, but I'm going to have to forego it as well as deprive you of my wife's company . . .

Turning to Elaine he takes her arm: There's someone here I'd especially like you to meet . . .

\*　\*　\*

It isn't until they've said their goodbyes, retraced Elaine's route, and entered a large living room, dominated by a full-length portrait of Selma Lemesurier, in oils, together with her ample embonpoint, that Elaine checks John: Why the rush . . . ? I was enjoying talking to them . . .

then takes a fresh drink from a conveniently passing tray . . . True, she was looking at me as if I was an old burlap bag, but he seemed kinda screwy and interesting.

Her husband says, Bishop brought him here from Wellesley not long after the war—they're virtual recluses. He's apparently a good if unorthodox critic—but not much interested in the students per se . . . Can't say I know anything much about his own writing. Look, I wanted to make sure we caught Steeves before he leaves—he's on the selection panel for the Fulbright, and . . . well . . . y'know if I got it, it'd pretty much guarantee my promotion as well . . .

Closing in on a big, self-important man, who, together with a bulky rotary bookcase and a tiny, timorous-looking woman, is occupying the corner of the room, Elaine ponders this question: If her husband is made a full professor, will he become any less pompous and arrogant?

And what about John's Fulbright, which, even as he stalks it seems to forever retreat into the distance—just as his application for promotion is passed from one ad hoc committee to the next, but never seems to reach the Dean. If she pictures their little family in Europe, they're either huddled up with bedrolls and bundles—like immigrants who've gone the wrong way—or else posed in front of assorted towers—London's, the Eiffel, Pisa, et cetera —tourists, who remain very obstinately American: Pop in a pale-blue seersucker suit with a fistful of travellers' checks, kiddo in a cowboy costume, and Mom an ageing bobby-soxer, complete with a poodle skirt that shows off . . . *my meagre can.*

Oh, hello, my dear, says the big grant-giver, you must be John's wife—he's been telling us all about you. This is my wife, Dolores.

Elaine shakes hands with the Steeveses, but wonders if she should curtsy. Soon enough she realizes her presence is entirely a token one: the men are busy impressing one another, leaving her to commune with ditsy Dolores—not that she seems like a woman whose pretensions need pricking, she's sheathed in a sleeveless satin dress that exposes stringy arms, while her bony fingers fidget at its neckline.

I don't know about you, she says—her voice a surprisingly warm contralto—but I find it harder to have a jolly time as I get older . . .

Elaine's taken aback—Mrs. Steeves is surely closer to sixty . . . *than I am to forty.* Something of this must show on her face, because the other woman continues: Oh, I'm sorry—I can be such an idiot at times . . . I didn't mean to imply I wasn't enjoying your company, it's just that we've been having such a hectic time—we were in Buffalo the day before yesterday, then Syracuse, now here. And everywhere there are receptions laid on for Gideon—sometimes it feels as if he's being feted . . .

He is being feted, Elaine thinks, looking sideways at her normally saturnine and superior husband, wearing his cheerful suppliant's mask: and shamelessly grovelled to. While to the influential man's quite likely influential

wife she says, I've only just resumed going out in the evening after a long period of illness—and quite frankly,
Mrs. Steeves, I don't know beans anymore when it comes
to having a jolly time. Saving your presence, I'd rather be
at home listening to Around Town than be, ah, around
town . . .

This remark galvanizes the little woman: Do you listen
regularly? she coos, stopping fidgeting and instead smoothing the bodice of her sadly slinky dress . . . I do believe that
man to be a beacon of light in a darkening world . . .

And so it'd gone wearisomely on, Elaine reflects a couple
of hours later, in the hushed seclusion of the Lemesuriers'
bathroom. Really, the evening could well have ended with
Mrs. Steeves's corny remark, followed by *good night, and
good luck* . . .

She can hear the soft thudding of a bass fiddle downstairs, as she smears between thumb and forefinger the
greasy residue left there by the collar of the last man to
propel her about the improvised dance floor. Now—at
least for a few minutes—she has the luxury of being alone,
of slumping any old how, and registering only this: her
heart, at first thumping in time to the music, then . . . at
last . . . being outpaced.

This bearded lady's been left behind—the carnival has
moved on.

Outside, rain sweeps across the broad lawn, sending
leaves skittering ahead into the maelstrom of the trees.
Entering the room, Elaine had gone straight to the unshaded
window, peered out, then pulled down the blind. Taking

off her glasses, massaging the bridge of her nose—looking around once more, she saw she'd brought the storm inside.

Or the astigmatism—which is what optometrists call it: a strange word that's nonetheless familiar to her—*since I've been hearing it all my life* . . . Hearing it—and seeing the distortion it describes: a world not simply grown bigger or smaller, but . . . *twisted out of shape.* Not for the first time, Elaine considers whether or not it's bad eyes alone that brought her and John together: *We're both creatures kept behind glass—maybe that's why we occasionally make such exhibitions of ourselves?*

Increasingly rowdy partygoers have been using it all evening, so notwithstanding the colored help the small john downstairs is a mess. Elaine came in search of a more secluded place to void herself uninterrupted, and rest her hammering head. It's part of an en suite, albeit with a lock on the door leading to the adjoining bedroom—and it's almost as big as a bedroom, too. There's a tawny carpet, the deep pile of which rises up and over the two steps bathers must mount before lowering themselves into a deep and glossy tub, and twirling the brassy faucets.

The opulent surroundings somehow make Elaine's ablutions seem more . . . *respectable.* Slumped on top of the commode, her navy-blue skirt hiked up, and her panty-girdle down around her ankles, she contemplates first the bloodstained Kotex that lies discarded on the carpet—then her bare calves, barer thighs, and the thick brown pelt in between them. *We're animals,* she thinks—*there's nothing truer than this, so why should I feel shame if every month I wind up behaving like a bitch in heat . . . ?*

But she does—biologically, it seems rational enough to want a man when you're fertile, but to continue doing so once you've fallen off the roof, and you're lying there, legs apart . . . well!

She pees, passes wind—and notes *the barnyard odors of my own making* . . . mixed with the smoke from the cigarette she's just lit. Leaning her heavy head against the vernal wallpaper above the toilet roll holder, it strikes her quite how *drunk I am* . . . She must pull herself together, go find John, and get him to take her home—but will he be sober enough to drive? Buttering up the Fulbright man hadn't gone well, not that it was Elaine's fault—she'd got on fine with his wife, it's John who'd screwed things up.

How funny . . . Steeves had quipped, his fat little mouth puckered up in anticipation of his own witticism . . . that so many partisans continue to read the Partisan Review.

John, instead of dutifully laughing, had—after some further exchanges, during which he composed his devastating retort—replied: Well, either that frail paper barque has at long last completed its passage across the great political divide, or its readers—having arrived there first—are waving little Stars and Stripes . . .

The fat little mouth puckered up still more—its possessor really wasn't at all amused. Bye-bye Fulbright, Elaine had thought, and quite possibly bye-bye promotion as well, given how in cahoots the man is with Harry Lemesurier.

After that, the Hancocks extracted themselves with alacrity—then threw themselves into the revels. After all, what did they have to lose? They'd drunk far more than they'd promised themselves they would—and Elaine gave one of the colored kids a couple of dollars to go down the hill and get her a fresh pack of cigarettes from a local bar.

By midnight, the older and more sedate attendees had all left, and the Lemesuriers went to bed as well. Standing on the wide staircase that swept up to the second floor, Selma called out in the lull between numbers: Do please stay as long as you like and enjoy yourselves, everyone—but have a care, please, for the carpets . . . and the staff.

In that order, Elaine had thought caustically. And besides: the carpets in the room where the guests were dancing had been rolled up a couple of hours earlier, at the same time as an impressively large hi-fi system had been wheeled in. Soon enough, it'd been turned up to its maximum volume, and couples were either jumping and jiving— albeit in a restrained, Cornellesque fashion—or, poised in each other's arms, scooting about the polished floor.

Pat O'Brien had asked Elaine to dance . . . *then trod on my clumsy feet*. Caspar Voss smelled of the mints he sucked to disguise his liquor breath from his equally wayward wife—while Gordon Burtt plodded in between the other, fleeter dancers as if he were *a tweedy donkey . . .* tethered to . . . *an irrigation system*.

Of the men she'd danced with—and there were, at least, a gratifying number who'd asked her to—the one who'd made her feel least like a heavy piece of equipment, difficult to operate, was Jimmy Castlemaine. He'd led her so smoothly that for the three minutes his left arm encircled her waist, and their right hands clasped, she felt *lighter than air* . . . So what if he's a fairy—and so what if all the other men Elaine danced with are married, all of them must have at least a scintilla of desire for her, or else they wouldn't've asked her to . . . And if all these scintillas were added up . . .

Bobbie O'Brien has been asked to dance even more than Elaine—not that *anyone's counting* . . . Being blonde helps—as does a fuller figure, and hair cropped boy-short. Men find that sort of androgyny sexy—at any rate . . . *sexier than my unruly curls* and rangy, mannish figure.

Elaine sighs out smoke—and the roses on the wallpaper . . . *catch fire*.

It was me, she decides, who gave it a push, so made the party go with a real swing: *Have you no sense of decency, sir? At long last, have you no sense of decency?* This brand new Nunc Dimittis had come to her unbidden—then been flung at anyone in the immediate area, until they, too, picked it up and tossed it further afield, so it became a collective catchphrase, one met with greater and greater hilarity as everyone got tighter and tighter, then began disappearing off into the kitchen to neck with each other's spouses.

*Decency . . . decency . . . decency . . .* was their watchword, even as their behavior verged on its opposite. Was it funny? Up to a point—and at that point, finding herself alone, Elaine's bubble of hilarity had . . . *popped*, leaving a revolting residue on the Lemesuriers' dimity drapes and their overstuffed armchairs and couches.

What the hell was she doing? She has the curse—now's not the time to angle for admirers. She'd fallen off the roof—and down here on the ground everything was dirty and *smeared with snail trails* . . . the coming and going of children—they had at least one son at Harvard, didn't they?—together with all their mess.

Standing, wiping herself with two quick-torn sheets of her hosts' luxury toilet paper, Elaine flutters them into the commode, followed by her flipped butt. To thrust down the lever is to trigger local—but total—devastation, albeit destruction from which—she banters with herself the way she might with a complicit sister—*civilization soon arises anew* . . .

She retrieves a fresh Kotex from her handbag and begins the necessary folding, pulling, and fastening required to impose a feminine silhouette on her *scrawny* . . . *squashy* . . . body.

No . . . Arty didn't want this—John, either . . . There's a liner in the wastebasket in the chintz-hidden cavity beneath the sink, so Elaine leaves the used Kotex there, swaddled in toilet paper. No one will conceivably know it was her—and if they do, Harry Lemesurier's influence hardly extends to a dragnet . . .

. . . and a squad car at the bottom of the steps outside 1100 Hemlock Street: *Mrs. Hancock, we have reason to believe it was you who disposed of* . . . *the* . . .

He can't say it—while the other patrolman, a mere boy, hides his blushes in the shadows of the porch . . .

C'mon, sport, Elaine addresses her reflection, as it leaps from the mirror above the sink to the one beside the door.

Then she's standing on the penultimate stair, looking at a hallway empty but for a redhead of about her own age who sits, head down, knees together and feet splayed, on a chair beside the front door. As Elaine watches, this *wigwam* of womanhood collapses a little more—canting sideways so she can cradle her head in her crossed arms, which in turn rest on a—

Whoa! Elaine reaches the scene just in time to prevent several empty and half-empty glasses, an ashtray, and a standard lamp from sliding onto the carpet. She sets the table upright and rearranges the woman. John comes banging through the swinging door leading to the kitchen, sees his wife, and slurs, You gotta come an' meet the Troppmanns.

Troppmanns?

I tol' you about them—he's the new guy in Sociology, come from Northwestern . . . Clever guy—and a sound man . . . Then, as an afterthought: His wife's joined the College faculty as well—she's in veterinary science . . . or somethin' . . . Anyway, you should meet them . . .

And then what? Elaine thinks, as she dutifully trots along behind him: the traditional ticker-tape parade from Bowling Green to City Hall? I know who these homecoming heroes are already . . . Jesus! I should go home—and if necessary . . . alone.

As the Hancocks appear, Rose Goldsen is talking to a tall, handsome couple. There are the sloppy grins of fast, fake friends, and a sort of haven in the hubbub—albeit one palisaded by their own hilarity. Rose cackles he-he-he-he, and the man back-cackles he-he-he-he, and the woman joins in a-ha-ha-ha-ha-ha, which means John has to h' h' h' h' h'.

Breaking ranks, the man turns to the makeshift bar, asks for a refill, so that he's turning back when Elaine says,

Hi, I'm Elaine . . . What are her first impressions? He's a clean man, big, and with a swarthy skin—his face reddened by liquor and an evening shave.

We-ell, Elaine, he drawls, did you have a good time in the big city?

Unnerved, she takes a small step back and averts her face before answering, Oh OK, I guess . . .

The other member of their new quartet is a severe-looking yet pretty woman—a dark brunette with angled rather than arched eyebrows, precise lips, a sharp chin, and long, white fingers . . . *like asparagus* that she offers Elaine.

John says, This is Elizabeth Troppmann, Ted's wife.

She says: I've no decency whatsoever.

Which Elaine takes as her due, laughing—it's this that triggers general conversation about the Army Board, and the University's oppressive behavior—not only regarding faculty members' politics, but their religion and race as well. Elaine can tell John is trying to find out where Ted stands, but the other man has a feline quality—such that he curls out of the way while his interrogator blunders after him.

Elaine resigns herself to wifely chitchat: the enumeration of offspring—her deficiency in this regard, and, slyly, by hint and concealed direction, the remuneration of any employment as well, since no job goes unaccompanied by a paycheck. But Elizabeth Troppmann must be from money, because these contentious matters—which have remained, unresolved in, for example, Elaine's relationship with Bobbie O'Brien, for years now—have been dismissed within a few moments, and instead they're talking about Betty's recent flight from Ithaca down to Newark, and how she could see her birthplace near Forest Hills with crystal clarity as, on the cold, clear morning, the Mohawk began its descent over Long Island.

Elaine gives nothing away—even as she joins Elizabeth, her arms-for-wings rigidly extended, and they glide over Jews with money and without . . . *Alrightniks*
*and losers . . .*

. . . then, somehow, Ted Troppmann is alone with her on a Chesterfield, while Elizabeth and John remain standing—in the next room, other couples will be entwining as the crooner urges on them her own couplets, Hold me, hold me, Thrill me, thrill me . . . And as if heeding this, he's leaning into her, his voice a warm burr: Now, tell me . . . what you went to New York to do, really, that turned out so badly?

Aghast, Elaine stares at this tall, dark stranger—then bursts into tears, because something quite unaccountable has happened: an emotional drought lasting for years has suddenly ended, as the tears glittering behind Elaine's glasses then coursing down her cheeks prove. The marathon dancers and the colored kids working long overtime have disappeared—together with all the gawkers, the gossipers, and the campus ginks: she and Ted are islanded alone in a dark night he wards off with his warmth, his . . . *radiance.*

He knows, she thinks tipsily: he knows but he can't possibly know—and I don't know how he could . . . possibly . . . know . . . he must see through my alibi . . .

For the briefest time, he takes her gently in his arms, kisses her hair, and releases her—then, as she weeps a little longer, he makes his confession . . .

I've had bitter, shattering affairs, he says, one of his hands stroking the other.

This is the precise point at which Elaine realizes who he is—because contrary to what John's just said, Ted isn't that new a guy—he's been around long enough to've had an affair with Mona Voss back in the summer, and because of this to be referred to among the vicious-circle types as the Sociologist, or that Chicago fellow.

. . . and the point is . . . he plows on . . . we had terrible times, Betty and I . . . I felt so remorseful—it was eating me up, and she . . . entirely understandably . . . His eyes keep flicking to the door through which his wife and her husband must've disappeared—and Elaine cuddles up closer to Ted's guilty warmth, understanding: He's like me, he's erred enough that she no longer trusts him to be alone with someone of the opposite sex—and he's like me because our adulterous thoughts are as bad as physical betrayals, since we've done it already, so forevermore may do it again.

All of which may be true—but taken in sum, it still doesn't explain why she tells Ted about the affairs she'd had while John was overseas—tells him, as well, that while she told John she was going to New York to help her sister-in-law move into a new apartment, the truth is this was just a pretext—and what she'd wanted to do was rekindle one of those affairs. She even tells him who Arty is—and how his rejection made her feel she'd just been something to have a piece of because he'd been ravenous, and now . . . Well, now she's all bitched up inside . . .

When John and Elizabeth return it's clear to everyone that the witching hour is at hand. Saying goodbye to anyone

they encounter along the way, all four retrieve their coats
from the makeshift cloakroom, then say their farewells out
in the street, exchanging phone numbers and promising to
be in touch. The whole evolved world of the Lemesuriers'
party is immediately pushed deep into the past—or at least,
that's how it seems to Elaine as they clamber into the *damp
jail* of the Buick.

From some temporary part of her own memory—as it
were, a makeshift repository, established simply for its
duration—this strange little recollection is retrieved: Selma
Lemesurier alighting on Elaine again, saying: Do come and
say goodbye to the Nabokovs, my dear—they did so enjoy
talking to you . . .

At the door, they'd found his high-domed head coddled
in an astrakhan hat, while one of the colored kids was
helping Vera Nabokov into a squirrel coat almost as shabby
as Elaine's own lambswool one.

Feeling stupid and awkward she told them how nice it
was to meet them. Vera seemed about as impressed as she
would've been by a *goddamn gumboil* . . . but her husband
made an effort: You asked before . . . he reminded her . . . if
you should, metaphorically speaking, be painting the bars of
your cage—on that matter, only you can be answerable, as
only you know if there are bars, let alone how to paint them.

But one thing I can say is this: if sex is the servant maid
of the contemporary novelist's art—and I very much suspect it is, whether what is meant is a biological category or
a mode of intercourse—then love remains the lady of the
gaunt and isolate tower within which he composes . . .

\*    \*    \*

What can he have meant by this, Elaine muses as, with a worrying lurch, John gets the Buick underway. The eccentric émigré and his . . . Well, what was it with them?

She'd stood on the Lemesuriers' porch, watching the Nabokovs, arm in arm, walk away between the now-extinguished Chinese lanterns—and although Elaine would've said, if asked, that Vera Nabokov was a virago type, what she'd heard, floating back to her in the wind, silvering the darkness, had been the couple's complicity: not mere merriment, but *unrestrained laughter* . . .

Of which there's none in the Buick—only the wind snickering through the broken quarterlight, John's annoying little effortful grunts as he turns the wheel, the mournful groan of the heater, and the mutinous silence of a couple who've had a far better time in public than they ever do in private, so await the opportunity—in bitter word or wounding action—to tell one another so.

The car caroms down from Cayuga Heights, crosses over the gorge, and passes through dank, shuttered downtown, where the stop signs strung up across the intersections swing in the wind. At the last, John gives the engine some gas, and the impetus propels the car over the inlet, then, switch-backing up, at last, to their own . . . *gaunt and isolate castle.*

All the way, Elaine keeps shifting about in her seat so the cold draft plays on her face. All the way, she considers first the disastrous meeting with Arty—and then its annulment by Ted Troppmann: when it was her turn to say goodbye, she'd embraced him and kissed him full on the lips, then, leaning in, whispered in his soap-scented ear: Thank you.

A thank-you she keeps repeating to herself—because it's true: a few simple, heartfelt words from this Sociology guy had been enough to put all those years of pain over Arty in their correct perspective: *my yearning puss* . . . harboring a dream that, the instant she'd seen his, it'd been clear . . . *he didn't.*

At home, Elaine understands she's drunk—and proceeds accordingly and unsteadily to go through her parental paces, receiving a report on Billy's behavior from the sitter, in return for a couple of bucks stuffed in her jeans pocket, then escorting the girl out into the night. Her father's waiting for her in a tan sedan, hic! What's the deal? He sits staring straight ahead and says good night sideways through a cartoon cheater's lips. Elaine, turning away from the auto, attempts a skip that almost becomes a headlong fall . . .

So . . . what's the deal there? These older and over-protective parents have, John says, upped sticks from Palm Beach to keep an eye on their only daughter. *Well* . . . slumped in the least comfortable of the three mismatched chairs in the front room . . . Elaine rubs her shin: so what if they think we're *a pair of rummies*—she's gone, *so everything's jake.*

She can hear John creaking about upstairs: taking Billy a glass of milk, settling him—then using the bathroom in the prescribed way.

It's only later, when she's curled up inside the warm, cotton-lined burrow of bedclothes, that Elaine realizes: He simply can't've known . . . and what's worse: I must've told him about Arty first—before he said anything at all . . .

What can it mean? Her head swims as Arty's face flows into *this new guy's* . . . She rolls onto her back—back onto her side. John snores—a bass note, deeper than his own speaking voice. Elaine's back in a fetal position, gently rocking herself, and able to anchor herself with this: It feels . . . feels . . . like a union of some kind—as if *we're involved*.

A queerly shaped thought that stays with her all night—holding fast to her no matter how sweaty and disordered she becomes. As for the successive generations of dreams, that appear, birthed from the indubitable reality of their predecessors—well, these are visions of herself as an empurpled and bawling newborn, an Elaine just birthed from the indubitable reality of her predecessor, who is herself an empurpled and bawling newborn, an Elaine just . . .

Birthed into a bare and windswept winter morning—her first impression the whack of a slack powerline against its post—followed swiftly by a heavy, sick-making feeling . . . to be expected when coming ashore after so many months at amniotic sea . . . *salty as Saltines . . . crisp . . . brittle . . . desiccated . . .* And in the grip—she soon enough, whimpering, concedes—of an absolutely *first-rate hangover . . .*

A state of being that her husband simply won't acknowledge—nowadays, he cares more about his blind poet's constitutional theories than he does about . . . *the state his wife is in*. She can hear them downstairs: Billy fifing—John drumming, so makes this familiar, faintly

desperate calculation: Can she remain abed long enough
for them to march off? And if she does, how badly will this
count against her? Would it be a flat-out lie to say she'd
feared the onset of a migraine—or even a worse collapse
of some unspecified kind?

John doesn't often talk about his time in the army—and
when he does, he certainly doesn't come up with the tales
she's heard more and more as the war's receded, from men
whose very masculinity is founded on this: a few weeks
or months sacking down in a stinky Quonset hut on the
far side of the Pacific or the near one of Europe—and its
apparently inevitable consequence: a great love for each
other, and for the obedience that once governed their life
together.

Her husband, Elaine knows, takes the greatest pride not
from facing enemy bombardment, shoulder to shoulder,
without cowardice—for he'd never actually come under
fire—but from withstanding the cussed spit and spat curses
of the sergeants charged with breaking him during his offi-
cer training. A hazing that'd taken place in a comman-
deered hotel on Miami Beach . . . highball glasses choked
with fruit . . . the near-fecal smell of pineapple mixed with
the still-shittier one of stale liquor—

Elaine hics . . . splutters . . . rolls over onto her back.
The one thing John will talk unashamedly about in public,
when it comes to wartime experience, is how he *boozed
with the best* . . . To hear him tell it, on Guam, flyboys
would take cases of beer up to twenty thousand feet to chill
them—and there was always someone who knew someone
who was deploying from Honolulu with a bottle or three

of Old Guckenheimer, and who—with a little persuasion—
would be prepared to pour it down the dry gullets of the
Logistics Corps, for a reasonable consideration.

The moral of all these tales was the same: nothing to do
with happy, back-slapping inebriation—rather, braggado-
cio: it didn't matter how much you'd drunk, or how wild the
horsing around had been, so long as you were up on time
for reveille, shaved, pressed, dressed, and fully prepared for
another courageous day . . . *pen-pushing*. So, while he may,
even now, try to allay her fears and phobias—appease her
carping and nagging, too—he won't tolerate a slattern for a
wife, unwilling to do what's required to *keep the domestic
machine running smoothly* . . .

Elaine ducks down into the neck of her nightie and
inhales deeply, and with childish repletion, her own bodily
odor: likely she should rise now, in timely fashion, and get
a pill from the bathroom cabinet—after all, she'll do it
*sooner or later* . . .

What is it—what is this fear that grips her?

Shrouded in damp folds of brushed cotton, thrust deep
between her clenched thighs, her hand is clamped on her
vulva—and she thinks first of an A-bomb's mushroom
cloud, then of Ted Troppmann. First of that eerily horrible protuberance—flickering within, boiling below—then
of its annulment by his strong, clean body. Oh! *base and
baser* . . . her mouth and throat are lined with last night's
congealed liquor and leathery from cigarette smoke—yet
still, she'd welcome his tongue in: she is struck dumb, slack-
mouthed, by the very prospect.

Freudenberg once said that people who worry the US and USSR leaders will prove incapable of controlling the bomb are really terrified they'll be unable to control themselves. By his own exacting standards, Elaine still thinks this a particularly self-serving example of shrinkish claptrap. In fact, *a crock of shit*—one only a childless man could come up with.

Mornings like this one, she thinks, I'm simply aware of a jittery state I've been in for . . . *almost a decade*— A sickly luminescence plays about the clothes discarded on the Shaker chair in the corner, and the little framed sampler hung on the wall above: *A, B, C, D, E, F* . . . Since all her thoughts end in disaster, disaster must already be what envelops her—must be *the element I'm in.*

Only a childless man—or a hateful one—has this luxury: freedom from this daymare, one in which the sirens begin howling, closely followed by you . . . *and your children.* When Billy was little, she thought she'd drown him in the bath, but she hasn't even this awful recourse anymore—he's too strong for her, sinewy as well. She shudders, imagining his tense, drenched body . . . *battling with mine.* No. Inconceivable—the only other option would be the sedatives in the bathroom cabinet, and in common with so much in the Hancock household, there almost certainly *aren't enough of them* . . . Which entails a crazed calculation: Maybe I should take my share of them now . . . *and get it over with.*

Because it's the only way she can think of to end this awful tension that, stretched between moments, pulls them closer and closer together—until something snaps.

What is this feeling, if not the vertigo that overtakes her every month, for the two or three days she creeps about on the steep eaves waiting to *fall off the roof*—or not? Nausea . . . so insidious—yet so superfluous, because she can choose whether to fall off the roof or not. All she has to do is leave the Dutch cap in its icky, flesh-colored box.

In between the lists of names in her journal, and the laments she can't ever stand to reread, are neat tables, decorated with her doodling, that attempt to correlate the dates of her monthlies and her migraines. Are the two somehow linked? After all, they both . . . *throw me for a loop.* Does one provoke the other—and if so, which? Sometimes her period precedes an attack—other times it succeeds one. Elaine counts the number of days separating the onsets of each, racking her brains for any other significant factors, as if by this act alone she could pull off a medical first like . . . *Linus Pauling.*

This Troppmann fellow—he'd be a better cure for *whatever ails me* . . . He seemed beautiful to me last night—but did any of it really happen?

She imagines him taking her in his arms, his breath sweet as goddamn *cotton candy* . . . She pictures him, taking her in his arms—then senses one hand caressing her back, moving lower and lower still, until arrested by her trembling one. What was it she'd said last night to Caspar Voss, who enjoys breaking taboos as much as she does? Yes . . . she'd said they should build a JEW rather than a DEW Line: an early-warning system comprised of excessively sensitive New York Jewish intellectuals spread out in a wide arc across the Canadian Arctic.

After all, suppose they failed to alert the big cities to the incoming Soviet missiles, at least out there in the wilderness they'd survive the blasts themselves, so be in an excellent position to begin hair-tearing, wailing, garment-rending, and generally lamenting—which *is what we do best* . . .

Caspar had thrown back his shiny little pinhead and cackled so unrestrainedly, Elaine saw his tonsils flutter. She thought at the time—and does so again, now—that while their friends may be smart—and some very smart—none of them . . . *is as witty as me.*

Knees rising, arms swinging, as their little troop marched down the steps to the grocery store, Elaine would sing: With a step that is steady and stro-ong, the Camp Fire Girls march a-lo-ong . . . and Billy would harmonize . . . *kind of.*

They had scads of little games they played together—songs they spontaneously reworded, sketches from radio shows they relived by playing all the parts—and of course, they spoke baby talk fluently to one another, often ventriloquizing for Karma, and Billy's threadbare old teddy, Donald, too. Well . . . they did this when Elaine was well enough—well enough, she concedes, often being *too much* . . .

Which is probably why she admonishes her son, in lieu of herself, *enough is enough*—because she can't help herself when she's high any more than she can when she's got the blues. Besides, good Freudenbergian that she remains, she understands this behavior is wholly compensatory: that the mania with which she mimics and improvises and scats is an attempt to cement an intimacy with her son that always feels fundamentally insecure.

*If only he knew* . . . being the cudgel with which she ever belabors herself; it's bad enough— No, it's *too much* that he's already exposed to her often-venomous anger, and her poisonous asides—that he already must sense the yawning abyss inside his mother, one she longs to pitch headlong into. She knows his night terrors include the fear he may lose her—the problem is *I want to be lost* . . .

The distinctive creak of the little Buick's passenger door notifies Elaine that: I've won. Yet what kind of victory is this, given the nature of its prize? A shameful one, surely— not having to put up with her menfolk while she still has this pounding head and turbulent belly. Anyway: that's it—the celebration is momentary and it, too, is followed by a hangover: If *Little Miss Roundheels* lies here a second longer, she thinks, she'll either start to masturbate, or cry . . . Sleep is out of the question without a Nembutal— yet that's what she longs for the most: sleep, *sleep that knits up the ravell'd sleeve of care* . . .

. . . Although not the one that lies rolled up in her knitting basket downstairs. Oh, Christ! She can't even knit with any application—

The next second, she's standing shaking on the dully shining floorboards, squidging from one sweaty sole to the other. From then on, it'd been automatic: the little white tablets shaken from their canisters—aspirin for the physical pains, Miltown for the mental ones—then the chilly hand-clasp of the faucet, followed by the gulp of pewter-tasting water. Elaine completes her toilet with a damp washcloth.

Dressed in slacks and a sweater she descends . . . *she descends, dressed in slacks and a sweater—in sweater and slacks dressed, she descends*: each thought corresponds to a word or words, right? Mix 'em up and you get a wordy sorta salad, like the *mess in my head* . . .

Downstairs she sets to, a chastened Campfire Girl, her objective being to complete her chores in double-quick time. Colored beads—awarded for domestic skills quite as much as for woodcraft—clickety-click on her slack bodice.

First, she does the dishes—taking perverse pleasure in the awfulness of congealed egg yolk, smeared bacon grease, and the *everywhere* of coffee grounds. She relishes, too, her own coughing and retching—and from time to time turns to the garbage can, opens and neatly spits into it.

The very thought of lighting a cigarette makes her retch: Put that piebald teat between her peeling lips! Set fire to it! Draw in those toxic vapors! Ach! She's revolted by the sight of cigarette-shaped objects as well: so, pencils, the handles of wooden spoons . . . *the damn rolling pin!*

For the two hours it takes her to *faire mon ménage* . . . she remains tightly focussed on the matter at hand. The giddy panorama of last night's party hangs, migrainously, in the periphery of her vision, and, if she glimpses it, it's as a connoisseur of her own embarrassment: relishing every shameful and shaming remark, embrace, hand-clasp, and . . . *glimpse.*

It isn't until she's done with the sweeping, sponging, brushing, and burnishing that Ted Troppmann reappears. Elaine stands, legs braced apart on the kitchen linoleum, the hot iron held aloft above one of John's outspread shirts—and here he is, a phantom *draped in it* . . . Shaking off this vision, she endures another: the shirt is no Halloween sprite, but John's flattened torso—the creases are their marital failings, and her task is to *smooth them all out* . . . But she can't manage it, no matter how hard she presses down the iron, or firmly she passes it over the wrinkled expanse. The afternoon light is bright enough to leach the color from *everything*, so she lowers the blinds and draws the curtains, and thereby transforms herself into *Mrs. Tiggy-winkle* . . . bustling about in her ill-lit cottage. John's face, seamed with sarcasm, rises from the collar of his shirt—and his spikey wife annuls all his resentments with a few deft strokes of the iron.

Yes: their besetting sin—as well as the glue that binds them together—is irony, and its most active compound, sarcasm. John's sour as a lemon, bitter as the blackest coffee. But Elaine is at one with him—for she's always *hissing*, and primed to make *the insupportable remark* . . . Unless, that is, she's a temporary resident of Miltown, that pacific community where she can safely take up her knitting needles, her crochet hook, or pump the treadle of her sewing machine so as to bind this fraying little family together.

Yet, when she's done with *irony*, it isn't any such wholesome activity that occurs to her—rather, she lunges from room to room, transfixed by all that she's missed—a smear here, a scattering of minute crumbs over there. Why had she bothered to dust it, *when we'll all be dust soon enough* . . .

Each time she crosses the tiny hallway she eyes the pale face of the telephone, hunched up on its little plinth. It's the real household god—and a vengeful one, since at any moment she expects it to explode into derisive peals, ones that, upon her lifting the handset, will give way to the hissing of one or another of the women she calls her friends . . .

. . . *Bitches, really*, whose own insupportable remarks are borne on *hostess trolleys jockeying for preferment* . . .

No, Elaine's better off pitching camp alone in this wooden house—doing handicrafts, bow-shooting, and planting Indian corn—it keeps her calm enough. Until mid-morning, when there's still been no explosion in the hallway, and she deserves, she feels, that orphaned ciga-rette—the one that fell from the pack into her handbag sometime during last night's party, and spent several hours there being rumpled and crumpled by its clinches with com-pact, keys, lipstick.

Smoothed out, lit, its smoke, accompanied by the first astringent gulp of hot coffee, surges into the four caves in her mouth—because that's what they are: *caves . . . not cavities* . . . Vast and rotting caves full of exposed nerves, ones she understands with utter certainty she shouldn't touch with the tip of her tongue—so she does.

For a heartbeat it stops. *So much for honest labor* . . .

Pain shifts agonizingly into this shape: the gingerish aureole of the dentist's head as, ducking in front of his operating light, he bends over her. But not Phillips snug in his suite on State—this is the tooth-puller who tormented teenage Elaine: Weiss . . . *the ugly little sandy-haired Jew*, who did his awful thing in a third-story room, in an equally seedy building on Lefferts Boulevard—a prize example of the Olde English phoniness Kew Gardens specializes in, with its mock beams, mock plasterwork, and successive stories jutting out further and further and further . . .

. . . Such that, together with the fear overwhelming her as he fitted the rubber mask to her face, came this other compelling anxiety: the whole ghastly stack of wigmakers, prosthetic manufacturers, podiatrists, and other borderline quacks was about to pitch façade-forward into the street below, flinging Elaine end-over-end out the window, so *my panties were showing* . . .

*Oh . . . damn it, damn-and-damn it— No! On consideration, fuck it: fuck-and-fuck it* . . . Phillips may be less of a fraud than Weiss—while the practice of dentistry may've moved on, nonetheless, Elaine feels pinioned between the pain now and the pain-of-the-future, the horrible drill *grinding away* . . . In point of fact: the very near future, since she's due at Phillips's office at nine forty-five on Monday morning—

Then the phone rings.

Elaine . . . ?

For two or three more leaden beats, she seriously considers severing the connection—but then, cradling the mouthpiece as if it were a *second chin* . . . she says, Uh, hello . . .

And Bobbie squawks right back at her: You didn't say goodbye last night—I guess you were too tight, we were, too . . . Saw you saying goodbye to that guy Ted Tropp-mann very warmly, though . . . Did you know he had a mad thing with Mona Voss . . . ?

# .4.

## December 1954

Downtown it's raining harder than when they left Hemlock Street . . . *or where the Logos came to die*, as John jokes in his labored, unfunny way. The puddles in the roadway . . . *are getting drenched*—if, that is, such a thing is possible. The downpour has cut the line for the movie in two, and each of its slick halves has taken shelter in the shallow alcoves to either side of the glassed-in box office.

They circle the block, prevaricating—is it really worth it? They say nothing to one another, yet Elaine suspects John feels exactly as she does: better to sit, damp and fumigated, in the crowded little theater than at home—where they'll either hide behind book jackets and magazine covers or, comradely as two fellows painting different portions of a bridge, work on their allotted portions of his manuscript: he revising—she typing it up.

There's a kind of warmth between them still on these humdrum evenings—or, at least, so Elaine wishes to believe. They may've shown romance and passion the door, but it's

precisely because of this that *we've abided* . . . Founding
the marriage on more enduring things—shared endeavors,
and the love they each have for their *only* . . .

A love like the milkily pearlescent bubble that she
remembers swelling in the adorable corner of his cupid's
mouth as he fell away, drunk on milk, from her nipple . . .
swelling . . . swelling . . . and swelling . . . Until—until . . .
until . . .

Well, what?

Third time around, John, who's driving, cries out: Look!
There're Betty and Ted!

As if this alone has decided the matter, he parks the
Buick in front of Hair-a-Phayre and they get out.

While he locks the car, she ruminates: Elaine likes puns,
precisely because they make a mockery of meanings—but
she knows that for her husband they're one of the lowest
forms of wit, and her enjoyment of them places her in the
same vulgar company as her father, who keeps a card file
of *gags for all occasions* . . .

His daughter keeps a list of businesses with punny
names in her journal—no doubt she's coarsening Billy by
sharing them with him so *we gurgle like storm drains* . . .

Oh, boy! John blurts as they cut in line beside the
Troppmanns—and then: Hel-lo, winter!

Yuh—I guess . . . Ted's preoccupied—*have they been
fighting?* . . . I looked for the chains in the garage this
morning, but they may've got lost in the move . . .

He falls silent—both John and Betty compete to fill the
gap. He says, Well, it's pretty damn rare to get much snow

or freezing hereabouts before the end of the year. She: Have either of you heard anything about this movie? It doesn't seem like our kinda thing . . .

Elaine knows only too well the small town where this idle remark coasts to a halt: it's all around them—gabardine-wearers and gum-chewers yakety-yakking away: but can Elizabeth Troppmann really be an anesthetized woman of the worst sort? Occasionally, they show European movies—more exotic ones, too—at one of the auditoria on campus, but you can wait a long time before anything other than a thriller or screwball comedy is shown at the State Theater downtown.

When they do, these offerings aren't, for the most part, remotely sophisticated—merely risqué, like the one about the middle-aged woman seducing the schoolboy set at the French seaside. They'd gone to see it because she'd enjoyed the Colette novel which it'd been adapted from. But it was a dumb little picture so far as Elaine was concerned—less budding wheat than . . . *a bust.* The idea of an older, worldly woman, inducting a teenage boy into that holy of holies: the temple of love, had seemed, at least on the page, thrilling.

On the screen, the kid had bat ears, looked a mere child—and Elaine found the whole conceit suddenly rather sickening and overripe.

Some hot little punks are buying ice cream and popcorn for their bobby-soxer girlfriends—but their sophisticated quartet disdain such fripperies and head for a row close to the back. Elaine's amused by this coincidence: both men insist on aisle seats for their long legs—and it's the first time she's noticed that they're the same height, although Ted Troppmann has a heavier, more muscular build.

When the lights go down, and the last yakker has been stifled by the growing soundlessness, the beam suddenly pokes over their heads at the screen, and fingers things into being—a Babylonian hydroelectric dam, God knows where, that will generate more electric power than . . . than . . . Well, some other equally gargantuan lump of concrete.

Elaine cannot prevent herself from seeing, in among the myriad workers swarming over the dam, a little Prof. John Hancock, as he was last summer at the Vermont cottage: stripped to the waist and sweaty, manhandling fieldstones into place then smoothly cementing them.

When she brought him a bottle of beer, John's dazed smile had been a strange sort of revelation—he oozed male pride and satisfaction, far more than he ever had *after making love to me* . . . She had stared, pointedly, at his white, wobbly belly.

The movie is sublime, Elaine thinks: for once, the screen lives up to its silvery reputation, and she's announced, then ushered through it into this glittering and self-reflective realm—one in which the gay characters whirl one another through receptions followed by parties succeeded by midnight suppers, perfectly aware they're in the Belle Époque, as they regard their own reflections in boutique windows, and the heavy, gilt-framed mirrors hanging in the opulent salons they giddily frequent . . .

. . . and frequent again.

Regarded one way it's the fluffiest piece of Frenchy froufrou she's ever seen—yet the tale is told with such conviction Elaine, too, is whisked away, first by her husband, the icily composed Count—then by her lover, the dashing diplomat. Then by her husband again. She dances delightfully—she demurs most prettily, and when, finally, in his elegant carriage, she allows herself to be *taken entirely* . . . her powerful lover lifts her up in both arms, so her pretty head falls back, and her soft throat, white as doeskin, is exposed.

It's a moment of exquisite tension—and while the dizzy rondo continues, Elaine remains within it . . . and extends it, seeing the Diplomat's leonine head descend, while his elegant fingers make quick work of myriad hooks and eyelets, until she's at last revealed. It must be the total conviction that allows her to luxuriate in an equally ridiculous reverie: she's as alluring as the actress playing the enigmatic Countess. A woman torn between husband and lover, true enough—but who's also wrenching them both apart.

Elaine must stop thinking about Ted Troppmann—at least in that way. While the Countess must forget her sleek and seductive lover. So it is that when the camera's dizzying motion finally returns them to the beginning that contains every ending, the salons, the smoking rooms, the carriages, and the couchettes dissolve into the dusty-red velour upholstery of their theater seats. The Count's valedictory remark is . . . salutary: *Unhappiness is our own invention . . .*

Regarding Ted critically as the house lights come up—his jutting ears and receding chin—Elaine thinks, But he's already made me unhappy—he just has . . .

. . . while if I were as beautiful as Mona Voss, well . . . he'd still be as a moth to any flame that burned as brightly . . .

The atmosphere in the foyer is, Elaine thinks, postcoital —the moviegoers pulling on their coats and scarves with movements paradoxically furtive and forthright: Yes, we admit we've done this . . . they seem to be saying . . . now we'll redeem ourselves by picking up where we left off: going out into the stormy November night and *getting on with it* . . .

One couple after another opens their little rigid parachute then jumps into the slipstream of the street. The Troppmanns and the Hancocks linger longer—so long, a fat kid, his scarlet nylon usher's jacket unbuttoned, begins sweeping up scattered kernels of popcorn with a long-handled brush and pan.

They aren't rubes, so the two couples studiedly avoid discussing the movie they've just seen—instead, the cash-prize question is: Should they all go to the faculty club for a nightcap? It's getting late—and it's in the wrong direction from both their homes. Ted is already a member—and this, at last, may decide the matter for the Hancocks, who've been weighing up the pros and cons of joining for a long time now: Can it be worth paying dues when they're flat broke? Indeed, they've ridiculed those couples they know who talk about going to the club as if they were English lords and ladies—when the truth is they'll be sitting in front of a feature wall all evening, getting tickled by maidenhair ferns—albeit sipping slightly cheaper drinks than they would at any other joint, while watching the white-jacketed waiters squeak about on rubber soles.

Elaine isn't thinking anymore about this evening—she's lost in all the evenings at the club to come: Ted grinning, Ted laughing, Ted looking adoringly . . . *at me*. And if the Troppmanns are members . . . well, she knows John well enough to feel the gritty truth in his airiest evasions: Is it really worth it? he asks. I mean, we've considered it in the past, but . . .

Last week, Ted and Betty were at Hemlock Street for the small surprise party Elaine organized for John's birthday: I can handle the liquor—she told the prospective guests when she phoned them—and we definitely require only your presence, no presents . . . But it'll need to be a potluck supper kind of a do, if I'm going to keep the secret from him . . .

They'd brought a big stainless steel tray swathed in tin-foil, which, once unwrapped, revealed an obscenely lush collation of cold cuts . . . *so much red and white flesh*. And there'd been a gift for John as well: a fishing hat decorated with elaborate hand-tied flies that appeared—at least to Elaine's mocking gaze—to be a little cheesy, and far too costly.

Anyway . . . it's one thing to have this wealthy couple over on the weekend, when the little saltbox house is full of others roistering—but the dull, workaday reality is quite a different affair. So they all stand, mulling over the possibilities, until John takes the initiative: Come back to our place for a coffee, won't you? After all, it's on your way home.

The Troppmanns had already known the way when they
came last Saturday— Somewhere in fluid swirls of music
and movement it'd been Ted who'd stiffened, saying, Wow,
I've only this second realized—you guys must be little
Billy's folks . . .

Wow, indeed—although why Elaine hadn't seen fit to
mention it when they first met at the Lemesuriers, she
doesn't know. Or at least, is reluctant to acknowledge
—the truth being, from the very beginning she hadn't
wanted him to think of her shackled by the chastity belt
of momism—or, for that matter, draped in the homespun
garment of poverty. The little elementary school at the end
of Hemlock Street mostly fills its roll with kids from the
rather humbler families in the immediate locale: the sons
and daughters of workers at Ithaca Gun, or the typewriter
factory over at Corton, but it isn't exclusively blue-collar
—Billy has a little friend, Cal, whose parents are both
lawyers.

Bobbie has already breathlessly vouchsafed to Elaine
that the Troppmanns live out at Trumansburg in a beautiful, modern, and absolutely chic house overlooking the
lake. Speaking in hushed tones—as if she thought the
phone was being tapped by the Feds—she gave her opin-
ion concerning these exotics: that for all their dough,
they were bound conscientiously to their careers—within
which necessity were these virtues: their daily commute
took them right past the school, so the drop-off was convenient, while it suited their liberal sensibilities that no
matter the lifestyle they very reasonably provided for their

daughters, they remained aware of how the ordinary folk live.

Wow redoubled, though—because it isn't only that Stella and her sister, Karen, are attending West Hill. It's that poor Billy . . . Ted had laughingly told his mother . . . has become the unwitting object of my elder daughter's affections.

Ones not, Ted had continued, to be trifled with—although the following morning when Elaine asked the pocket-sized Don Juan about his conquest, he'd been delightfully dismissive: Yeah, she nags me 'til I hold hands—then she says that means we're gonna get married . . . But we aren't—'cause she's a stupenagel . . . She doesn't even know what Vatican sources are . . .

A reference to the radio newscasts he listens attentively to—ones which for days have been carrying bulletins regarding the Pope's declining health, which make frequent reference to these mysterious . . . *sources*.

Maybe if she'd had the right sources—not just Rose Goldsen's belated introduction—Elaine would've realized Ted Troppmann had been driving past her house for months. She isn't altogether sure what use she could've made of this intelligence—but in some mysterious way she believes it might've forestalled what he'd said to her much later on in the evening.

Now, splashing along the sidewalk, Elaine sees Ted and Betty clambering into a shabby-looking jeep, its cover loose enough to let in the rain. It's a queer kind of wagon for him to be driving: they must have something showier in the garage at home.

It's cool, though—Ted's jeep. Cool and kinda manly, so Elaine adds this to the image of Ted she's assembling—one, she tacitly concedes, is mostly *idealization* . . . and has little or nothing to do with the large, very live, and rather wet man who, soon enough, is standing before her at the door, trying—like a bashful dog—not to shake the raindrops from his coat. Beside him is his wife, neat and unruffled.

John has got his way—and is driving his co-ed home, salvaging his reputation for puritan sobriety with every careful signal and deliberate turn. Elaine ushers the Troppmanns in and takes their coats—noting that hers is not only a real but also very dear fur. Shooing them along the hall she asks, Would you like some coffee?

Would they? Heck—Ted looks almost pained at the suggestion: No, he says, we could use a drink—a short, *snuffly* laugh—like any sane individuals.

A category . . . Elaine concedes as she pads back along the hallway . . . that doesn't consistently include me. She fetches down a flimsy rattan tray from the cobwebby top of a kitchen cupboard, stretches to retrieve a half bottle of Haig from the back of the pantry, then gathers together four highball glasses, some ginger ale, a dish of ice cubes, and a soda siphon.

What the hell, she wonders—and not for the first time—am I gonna do when we run out of liquor?

As she's mixing the drinks to order, Elaine hears the Buick cough then die in the roadway. Then John's in the room, rubbing his hands together in the unctuous, Uriah-Heepish way that sets his wife's only recently filled teeth on dreadful edge.

Cigarettes lit, drinks inhaled, conversation turns at last to the movie they've all just seen, and becomes at once trivial, and *portentous* . . . I really couldn't see the point of it, Ted says—I mean, what's this Count fellow up to? First, he's giving his wife the go-ahead to have an affair—then he turns nasty . . .

For a disconcerting moment his mask slips, and Elaine sees a boy like her brother once was, in striped knickers and a sport shirt, all teeth and ears. This is the monster she's been trying to escape all her life—a coarse fellow, without a scintilla of sophistication, who balls women not from any real desire for them as they truly are, but only in order to add dirty pictures to his secret album.

She feels like replying: What game is he playing? No game, my sociological friend, only a man's most personal possession—which isn't a diamond stickpin or a Jaguar convertible, but his honor. It's the same for the dashing diplomat: he desires the Countess close to distraction, but once weighed in the balance his honor must tip the scales . . .

*Why*, Elaine shrieks in the confines of her own hurting head, *do you imagine the whole business ends in a duel for the men, and inevitable loneliness for a woman who's simply had the temerity to behave in affairs of the heart the way that they do?*

Yet all that emerges from her mouth is smoke and a polite inquiry: Does anyone have the chucks? I mean, I can rustle up a sandwich—or something else for . . . a snack . . .

But nobody wants anything—instead, they begin, with grinding predictability, to discuss television and its advisability for children. Rose Goldsen, Ted's colleague, has surveyed and written on the subject extensively—and he cites her research to explain that, while they couldn't resist getting a set, they're careful to monitor both the amount their girls watch and the kind of programs.

Elaine hears her own banalities even as she utters them—stereophonic embarrassment: She and John would like it if Billy grew up to be, firstly, a proficient and enthusiastic reader.

Ted, ignoring this, continues: Besides, isn't the whole scare over TV the same as the comic book one—mass hysteria, really . . . Folks always imagine new forms of entertainment are going to create juvenile delinquents . . . it's an anxiety as old as society itself. But if I put my professional spectacles on, what I see is study after study showing that the most significant factors—when it comes to delinquency—are good ol' poverty, together with a lack of paternal discipline . . . Both usually operating in tandem, since when the man of the house departs, the household income goes with him . . .

If I weren't infatuated with the guy, Elaine thinks, I guess I'd find him a bit of a bromo . . . And she lets the conversation rattle on without her along these well-worn tracks—while she thinks about the ones in back of the lakeshore, beneath the bluffs. The long cavalcades of high-sided freight cars are so infrequent, and go so slow —waltzing through the underbrush—that even she feels brave enough to place a penny on the shiny rail, and speedily retreat . . .

. . . returning once the train has passed to find it hammered flat by forces that, she hopes Billy will now understand, are indubitably real, as well as to be feared.

Tuning back in to the others, Elaine wonders: How long can we go on? Because the truth is we have very little in common: They watch TV—we like proper movies. They read newspapers and magazines—we tackle serious works of literature, and not only because it's John's area of study or my major. We do it for pleasure.

Elaine rehearses saying something like, Oh, is that the time . . . But John then chooses his moment: I've finally got my promotion—old Lemesurier told me a couple of days ago: my appointment as full professor will be officially announced before the start of next semester . . .

Elaine's wise to this obvious attempt at reeling Ted and Elizabeth in with an intimacy. John only vouchsafed his wife this important information yesterday—and swore her to secrecy about it. The other couple are suitably flattered—and it gives the flagging conversation a shot in the arm. All at once, they're all talking excitedly about the politics of preferment at Cornell—who are the players, who the fixers, and—most important, this—to what extent there's a quota still operating, albeit covertly . . .

One likely utilized by those malcontents for whom the vague, vatic nature of pronouncements from on high is a strategic gift, enabling them to spread both malicious rumors *and outright lies* . . .

\*    \*    \*

Later, in bed, Elaine uncurls from fetal comfort—*not even my mother was able to render her own womb inhospitable, although if she could've, she would've*: Why, she hisses, did you tell the Troppmanns about the promotion? You told me not to tell a living soul 'til you had written confirmation . . .

But he's asleep—lying, as he often does, contentedly on his back, his hands loosely clasped on his *weakling's* chest, as if he were about *to sermonize to some sectaries*, while his prominent little belly bobs beneath the blankets, and his breath comes in the little gasps and groans like *abortive snores* . . . his wife finds supremely irritating.

Throwing herself back onto her side, Elaine raises her legs, and inserts prayerful hands between her warm thighs. Bubbles form in her tummy, and chase one another . . . squeaking—which awakens her still more, as does the cat's tongue when, a few moments later, she rasps at Elaine's now-outflung fingers . . .

. . . which Elaine transforms into a sling with which to winch the cat aloft, then deposit it in between the *graven images* in the bed. Some animal warmth, Elaine thinks, is better than none of the human variety at all.

Yes, she's kept it zipped about John's promotion—with one shameful exception: Bobbie O'Brien, who she swore to secrecy on this matter, as she has, futilely, on others in the past. Yes . . . because it's Elaine who's the real stupenagel, far more so than poor heartsore Stella Troppmann, let alone the impeccably turned out and darkly sexy Mona Voss.

Why did she defy her husband and confide in her friend? For the same reason she stands at the open icebox door, spooning down mayonnaise: she's hungry—therefore provocative, and not only with men: she has dreams with lesbian themes, although now that she considers it, it could be that her subconscious began to produce them on demand—Freudenberg's, that is . . .

. . . Anyway, the hunger is real enough—and it includes a hunger for the least little morsel of news concerning Ted: How do they live, the Troppmanns? Who do they see? And, most importantly, is there anyone he confides in? She'd offered Bobbie this choice nugget about John's promotion as a kind of payback for her telling Elaine about Ted's affair with Mona Voss. Why shouldn't she speak of it? What with all her lobbying on his behalf—dancing with clods, charming old fools—and her work on his book, she has every right to regard this preferment as something they'll share. Still, Elaine has no illusions concerning Bobbie O'Brien: as soon as a debt's settled, *she'll advance the proceeds.*

At John's surprise party she'd been everywhere: upstairs, downstairs, in *my lady's goddamn parlor* . . . Her sleek, white-blond head, combined with her fondness for brightly colored clothes, and yet brighter accessories— dinky blood-orange bags, wide puce-pink belts—made her seem like some exotic little bird: a humming one, flapping about men's fluttering lips, then taking all the pollen she's sucked up and depositing it in some other woman's receptive ear.

Still, at least she came—at least they all came: the boring Burtts and the annoying Vosses, the dull Hucksackers—and the yet duller Goldbergs. All the usual crowd, including those wild cards who, thank God, make play a little bit interesting: Jimmy Castlemaine and his gentleman friend— and Claire Beamish, who lost her baby last year, and who, together with her fat and formerly jolly husband, Marv, has been on a toot ever since.

And when, well past midnight, Elaine began to flag, Ted Troppmann had appeared in first-aider guise, and offered her one of his happy pills.

Hours before, in the late afternoon, Elaine had dispatched John to deliver Billy to the Troppmanns', where he'd been sent—with great reluctance on his part—to have an overnight with Stella and Karen. A date Elaine had arranged earlier in the week when she'd phoned to invite Ted and Betty, as well as enlist their support for her plan: they would keep John for a drink at their place while the other guests arrived at Hemlock Street.

Was this kind of spontaneous gathering something her husband would actively enjoy? Emphatically not. Even as she'd done the drudgery required to make it all happen, Elaine took malicious glee in the knowledge that he'd have to bear it. A lesson she hoped he might learn, remember, then apply to other areas of his life in which he'd been none too careful concerning what he wished for.

Hadn't it been John who, right in the middle of her nervous troubles, beseeched Elaine to be more outgoing? Hadn't he further implied it was, in fact, essential for his career as much as for their marriage? So, now he'd be compelled to face all these people—to be outgoing indoors, in his own home. And to smile and laugh, and concede that yes, he is a jolly good fellow, since so say all of them.

There's a sadistic side to Elaine—*I cannot tell a lie* . . . one that revels in revealing the baffled boyishness he displays in their intimate relationship *for all to see* . . . at the exact point when his ambitions are about to be fulfilled. The malformed idea being that as a consequence, maybe—just maybe—he'll be able, for once, to empathize with his wife—rather than merely pity her. Empathize with her, because in the very instant of his own overexposure, he'll apprehend her far greater vulnerability—not as a woman, and hence a representative of what he considers . . . *the menacing sex*, but as an individual *like him* . . .

Diligently, all week, Elaine rounded up the necessary party supplies—digging into their pitiful savings, as well as shaving a few bucks off the household budget so she could buy potato chips, nuts, and of course . . . booze: whiskey, vodka, and the required mixers.

Calling all their friends, she'd explained her need for both secrecy and some help as well: it was next to impossible for her to shop for and prepare a buffet without the birthday boy getting wise. So, a potluck kind of a party with everyone participating—what could be more celebratory, or communal?

As the week wore on and this fakery began to rub off on her, Elaine almost convinced herself that she was, at long last, happy in her allotted role as the good little wife: ever ready to cook up a storm—and happier yet to clean up after it. Almost . . . but not quite: because inasmuch as she wants to punish John, she also wishes to ensnare Ted.

Some men, she knows, take a positive delight in home-wrecking—women, too. Maybe an image of connubial bliss ready to be violated is what he needs to put some lead in his goddamn pencil. Does he even think of her in that way at all? That kiss! Since it'd happened, did he think of it at all? Did he recall each tentative tongue-touch and taste? Did he think not just about what had happened but about what it meant? Did it mean anything to him whatsoever? Elaine obsesses, or is he in the regular habit of kissing other fellows' wives . . . ?

Looked at through the distorting lens of her infatuation, the party is an elaborate contrivance designed to give an answer to this vital question: Does he care? Is he even capable of caring? That men should try and reach for the women they desire rather than vice versa . . . Well, this is a truth *graven on my maidenly soul* . . .

Besides, why shouldn't she—who's suffered so much, lost so much—have both: continue living closely with John—and of course, Billy—yet still have Ted around as a floating kind of love object? Other women managed to have casual flirtations without them becoming crazy and ruining their lives . . . *Why can't I?*

The answer is pretty obvious: these mystifying other women don't need pills or psychoanalysis—these other women don't fear Bellevue's brown brick jaws opening to feed on the mentally ill. Au contraire: they're the sort who rustle up a perfect casserole for an impromptu supper using a can of pineapple and some leftover chicken pieces—with maybe a carrot and an onion tossed in for good luck, together with corn starch or flour . . . *to thicken the gravy.*

These other women—these hay-riding, hallooing, and lassoing women—these frontier gals, who have their druthers and their . . . *lovers.* Well, it stands to reason that they're not the kind who allow their raw feelings to be *lacerated beyond reality* . . .

On Thursday morning, Billy was at last persuaded—after several tearful fittings—to wear the pilgrim costume his mother had run up for him, rather than his preferred outfit of felt Stetson, plastic holsters, and a pair of plastic six-shooters loaded with caps. One his mother explained to him was deeply anachronistic.

He'd still been sniffing back tears when she tucked his shirt into his voluminous black breeches, while brushing off—as best she could—her blue chalk marks. Look, she'd conceded, I know it isn't the best fit, but if you're set on planting corn, raising hogs, and having something substantial to feed those helpful Indians, you need a little give in the waist and the crotch, sir . . .

At times, Elaine's certain Billy enjoys her near-limitless capacity for ironizing *more than I do* . . . Then there are those other occasions, when, even as the quip departs her lips she'll see his sunny features become overcast with what she suspects is his fundamental uncertainty about the world and his place in it.

When she's gone too far—and he's truly hurt—her child will pick up Karma—who's more biddable than the kitten—and womb her in his shirt or pullover, while also retreating into a den made from carefully arranged sofa cushions.

Sloppy invitees, who couldn't be bothered to follow simple instructions, loused the whole business up anyway: everyone else had dutifully parked their cars around the corner, or further up the block, but the Burtts were getting out of theirs right in front of the house as John returned from Trumansburg.

By the time they were all coming in together by the kitchen door, John was prepared for any eventuality—so beamed as he was toasted, grinned his way through the ragged chorus of Happy Birthday, then proved beyond anybody's doubt what a jolly good fellow he was by either bussing or glad-handing everyone present. The only one who could see through this act to his sulky frown—as if, like one of Billy's comic book heroes, she had X-ray vision—was Elaine.

Then, efficient bottle-feeder that she was—who'd learned to check that the formula was well mixed by squeezing a few droplets onto her elbow . . . *and licking them off*—she'd set to, and within an hour had two drinks inside every woman and three in all the men. Liquor inhaled, cigarette smoke exhaled together with ceaseless chatter—these were what inflated the party, and gave it shape: a strange tatterdemalion balloon, sewn from suits, skirts, blouses, and shirts, that swelled, wobbled, rebounded from the walls, then swung *rapidly aloft* . . .

Soon enough, someone had turned the little record player up as high as it would go, and the dancing began. Backing herself into a corner, Elaine watched this, the very choreography of desire itself—and gave herself a thorough talking-to about drinking too much, smoking too much, and—of course—flirting too much . . .

Within a half hour more she was backed up against the folding ironing board in the kitchen, cigarette in hand, pretty damn tight, and necking with Ted Troppmann . . . *hard—my leg in between his . . . hard.*

When the serpent slithered away, she felt so dazed she slumped onto his chest, while the ironing board fell against her back, making the sound of *one derisive hand clapping* . . . Into this charged atmosphere—*dark and dirty wisps of cloud teased from the massy base of the thunderhead by the winds gathering over the lake*—Ted said, It's lucky I didn't meet you six months or so ago—If I had, I'd've surely fallen in love with you . . .

Elaine saw light flicker in the heavens, so the sky was illumined in precisely the way a painter would want it to be if he were to show all is for the best in the most amorous of worlds. And Ted's lighthearted remark concerning the matters weighing heaviest on her heart had zipped Elaine more tightly into her dazed condition . . . so that for what remained of the surprise party, she'd sensed the other women's eyes on her, assessing the cut of this most revealing garment.

\*    \*    \*

Now she feels the saliva trickling from the corner of her mouth—and recalls how she *got pretty goddamn gabby* . . . dancing in the front room with whichever man showed the last inclination to accompany her—then, in the intervals between these increasingly woozy gyrations, the words had spilled from her—wisecracks, intimacies, pointed observations: everything their circle summed up under the heading BANTER.

Each time her mouth was empty—more words filled it up, together with more liquor and cigarette smoke, everywhere she went there was another group of her guests, waiting to be entertained—since, *like the well-dressed bums they are*, they'd taken up residence in every room in the house.

Aw, come down offa those character heights, John had said the first time Elaine poked her head into their bedroom and found him, full-length on their bed, wearing the absurd fishing hat the Troppmanns had given him, with its hand-tied flies hooked into the canvas material. Elizabeth Troppmann, as correct as if she were standing, erect, at a lectern, was laid out beside him. Elaine hadn't got his point—true, she liked to snipe, but what character heights? Surely they're reserved for the wives of wealthier and more senior faculty. Anyway, the next time she stuck her head in, they were still there—and had been joined by several others, including Jimmy Castlemaine and his gentleman friend.

She'd only been intending to tell everyone the buffet was open for business, but shortly before this second visitation, someone must've had the temerity to quote a few lines of contemporary poetry—or at least allude to them having been written. Because John was by then in full flood: a steady stream of put-downs, send-ups, and side-swipes, aimed at the luminaries of a scene he affects to despise . . .

. . . although she knows there's nothing affected about it: he loathes anything and anybody that takes away from the sum of attention he believes should be devoted to his namesake, the blind poet—and by extension to his own critical endeavors . . . his own *secret gilding expositions*.

Elaine thinks it must be the very intensity of the joy he once took in the poetic impulse that makes his disaffection quite so bitter: this is a civil war, in which contemporary writers of all stripes stand as proxies for his own, formerly naïve and gushing self.

So it was he wrote off the old guard as not only has-beens—but senescent: Papa befuddled unto the grave—while Faulkner, befogged, sinks with every step deeper into his experimental swampland, from the depths of which resounds the raucous croaking of Mallarmé's American imitators . . .

. . . the Cranes overboard, the shipwrecked Stevenses, the marooned Williamses and capsized Cummingses of this turbulent wordsea, all of whom—so far as Professor Hancock was concerned—know rather less about prosody than his auto mechanic. And if they're meant to be poets, but are only poetasters—what's to be said of the prosaists? Pushy little Mailer, pulled along by the sanctimonious Trilling, or the lubricious Vidal, or Capote, the cavilling little queen . . .

Elaine had heard it all before—was grateful on this occasion, at least, that John refrained from including Elaine's old squeeze, Ted Roethke, in his dolorous roll call.

It may've been Betty Troppmann's presence—her inscrutable pale-gray eyes fixed upon him, her hip resting companionably against his—that made him, for once, capable of
*reeling them all in*, but leaning in the doorway, Elaine had
thought back and back to times that, if not any happier,
were at least *more complicit . . .*

Parental meals when you could hear a pin drop, confrontations with salesclerks and tradesmen, and faculty
gatherings where everyone seemed paralyzed, so anxious
were they for preferment. In any number and kind of social
situations the Hancocks had been *a team . . .* Elaine had
the native wit—John the erudition that inevitably accretes
when you're a third-generation Ivy League professor.

Yet, now that their nemesis is himself being hounded
out, she realizes her most crucial role as her husband's confidante had not been to say anything—but rather: nothing.
John's career could well have ended like those of his former comrades in the little communist cenacle he belonged
to while doing his postgrad work at Columbia. Good
teachers—good men and women—who'd fallen foul of the
Rapp-Coudert Committee.

But John had been, in this most important of matters, surprisingly adroit: moving on—and so muddying
the waters—a camouflage from which he emerged having
reverted to Brahmanical type. These were deceptions Elaine
ably assisted in—although more from her innate lack of
conviction than from any instinct for their preservation:
*What has the working man ever done for me . . . really?*

But it occurs to her, now that she's met a fellow traveller who, far from advancing his parsimony as factitious evidence of solidarity, is successful, and has money as well as brains, that it's all been a useless sort of cover-up. The cartoon she cut out from the New Yorker, intending to give it to Ted at the party, is still in the drawer of the gateleg table under the window . . .

. . . it shows a jeep like his, jacked up in an auto shop, with the mechanics lowering down onto it an entire new body—that of a sleek two-seater roadster.

Beyond the basic sight gag, Elaine isn't altogether sure what to read into this transformation—yet it speaks to her. Is it, perhaps, that she wants Ted to quit with his Mississippi mule-skinner act and become the fabulous creature she knows he has it in him to be: a dashing fellow—and a vigorous lover.

Anyway . . . she'd intended to give it to him—and why shouldn't she? It's hardly the sort of billet-doux Madame D would send her diplomatic amour. But since the kitchen kissing, Elaine suspected he'd find it too calculated a gesture—one that would repel him.

The Troppmanns had been the last guests to leave—and, flamboyantly blotto by then, Elaine tried to go with them. Now, in the dark barn of their marital bedroom, listening to John's heavy breathing duet with the winds gently pummelling their little frame house, she winces, remembering the exhibition she made of herself: lurching down the outside stairs and into the street in pursuit of them—then clambering up and into the jeep's jump seat.

Why shouldn't she go with them to Trumansburg? They were both not only fast but passionate friends—and Billy was already at their house waiting for his mother. Standing on the steps, his tall frame and pale face making of him a sickly sort of beacon, her husband had been as far away as the moon.

Ted made some crack about carfare—she thinks.

Then Elaine had been back in the roadway, and watching the jeep's taillights as it turned at the far end of the block. John slouched back inside and straight upstairs, calling over his shoulder she should come to bed, too—the cleaning up would wait for them.

But *dutiful little drudge that I am*, she'd stayed up two hours longer. In the morning, the only remaining evidence there'd been a party at all were the plates, platters, Tupperware containers, and aluminum trays their guests had brought with them, bearing food—which, all clean, were stacked on the countertop.

Elaine's hangover was so savage, it kept her confined to her bed with *pain-tipped spears*. There, she fantasized not about Ted, but about a gadget she'd seen advertised in the Journal: a disc recorder looking like a miniature record player, on which the hard-pressed mom could leave instructions for the help concerning child-rearing and domestic matters . . . But what fucking help?

All jangled up—jumpy although lying flat out—Elaine had ruminated, fitfully: When I'm alone, I'm merely in my habitual situation—and like a person tied by ropes, I've gotten the knack of breathing lightly . . . Yet it didn't matter how lightly she breathed—there remained this awful constriction: was it her old friend, anxiety neurosis, or was she becoming a full-blown rummy? A blowsy lush like

Mrs. Tate, who sits, fat and frowsy, on her stoop, swigging openly from a gallon jug of port wine . . .

As for Ted Troppmann and her grand passion for him—was there anything real about this at all? Surely, he was only a substitute for Freudenberg: who, having effectively rejected Elaine, had *propelled me into Ted's arms* . . .

The following day . . . *yesterday*, she'd driven John to his office, then circled back by Olin Hall, where the Anthropology & Sociology Department is located. Glancing up at its ugly-modern brick-and-concrete façade, she'd wondered if Ted was in there—and if so, what he was doing. Then she'd driven straight home . . .

. . . where, after an hour or so of neglecting her chores while she doodled in her diary, she'd retrieved the cartoon from the drawer, put it in a plain envelope, and written this: Professor E. Troppmann. Then she got back in the car and returned stealthily to the campus—if by stealth is meant taking the streets a block over from the ones you usually do, and at each junction stopping and casting wildly about . . .

Half convinced some kind of anti-Cupid is gonna transfix you with a hypo' full of tranquilizer. Aiming the Buick's bulbous hood up the steep section of Seneca Street, then bumping in second over its capacious potholes, Elaine felt the awful gravity of her own situation: What in God's name was she doing? If she ran into Ted what the hell would she say? She felt as exposed as a wooden horse full of Greek warriors *trundling towards the gates of Troy.*

Objectively, there was nothing to fear—they were friends, right, so what could be more natural, given you were passing, than dropping by a friend's office to show him a cartoon you thought he'd find amusing?

Except she hadn't been passing—she'd driven clear across town, only to find herself trembling, busting for the can, and standing looking wildly around in the cold, institutional hallway. Scanning the directory for his name, she established Ted's crib was on the third floor—and avoiding the obvious trap of the elevator, and the exposed stairwell, found a smaller flight at the back of the building that she scaled effortfully—lifting one dropsical leg after the other, her breath coming in wet wheezes. Was this the winter's first attack of the grippe? *Or fear* . . .

. . . not only of this ridiculous predicament—what would she say if he suddenly and boyishly appeared, swinging one-handed around the bannisters?—but her hangover, which, she worried, was a dread harbinger of worse to come, as it surpassed its predecessors by lasting *three whole days* . . .

Running into Ted would be bad enough—but what if it were one of his colleagues, who then asked this woman—too old to be a student, too scatty-looking to be a member of the academic staff—what she was doing, wandering about in the building in the middle of a weekday morning?

Hearing a door slam while she was still mounting the stairs, Elaine lost her composure altogether—and fled. Back in the Buick, she piloted it off the campus, knuckles white on the black wheel—then pulled over and slumped down in the seat, shaking for a long time before she regained sufficient composure to drive home beneath low-hanging clouds she wished hung yet . . . *lower*, so as to hide her shame.

Because it's obvious, isn't it, what the cartoon means? She wants Ted to cover her, to absorb her into his ruddy, confident body—or, more troublingly, she wants to cover him, and feel his rigid bodywork grow soft and pliant.

Now, lying in her fetal position, her prayerful hands still clamped between her judgmental thighs, Elaine sighs—it was a lucky escape, one the Troppmanns' behavior this evening surely confirmed. The crass remarks about the movie—Ted's clumsy pivot from discussing it to grand-standing on his own subject area, where—given his pro-fessional standing—he thinks every one of his remarks *a zinger* . . .

Not that she'd expected the two couples to end up in some kind of orgy, *but . . . no . . . well . . . if . . . and* . . . It's a diffuse but very real insight Elaine has, like *the particular odor of a household*: I don't have to do this—I don't have to throw my life away, or ruin those of my husband and child, because of some *half-formed girlish fantasy . . .*

Dull silver shadows bloom, wither, or fragment on the dark-white walls of the bedroom, while the troubled little house seems, to Elaine, to be rocked in the wind's incon-stant embrace. On edge, her own breathing seems effort-ful, she sits at a deathbed vigil for herself, waiting for that eternal moment when it ceases. One that bears an analogy, surely, with awakening . . . Someone you love awaken-ing beside you . . . and you registering their transformed breathing first as their awareness, then as their arousal—as they reach out for you in the darkness, their very touch a perfect marriage of *ardor and assurance* . . .

rather than lust and nervosity—for which she mostly blames herself: If only I weren't so homely, so lacking in sex appeal. If only I were myself a better and more confident lover, then his hands wouldn't be swarming over my back, or his fingers fidgeting with the hem of my nightie, preparatory to yanking it up—as if it were the lid of a cookie jar, and he some *greedy little boy—!*

Rearing up, rolling over onto all fours—then springing off the bed, standing upright, at once enraged and hysterical, she cries, What the hell?! You fucking pervert . . . !

John snaps on his bedside lamp. Blinking owlishly, he gulps then regurgitates this pathetic pellet: Elaine . . . without his glasses his eyes are small and sneaky . . . Elaine, what is it?

Yes, what is it, given that ofttimes the weak little drudge will submit to these demeaning advances? Why? Because she's desperate for the reassurance even of his flabby arms, the warmth of his wobbly belly. Desperate for this—as she's desperate for his own desperation: a desire she knows, in her heart of hearts, is born of repressed hatred:

What're you trying to do? she belches—then, with shuddery spasms of mounting nausea: You disgust me! You disgust me! You disgust me!

They both know what comes after the ritual chant—the ecstatic shrieking. Is this why he's on his feet now as well? Is this why he's pinioning her arms, frantically shushing her: Sssshhh! and Sssshhh! again: Enough! You'll wake Billy.

Wake Billy?! Her tone is so sharp it ought to cut him—cut his *fucking throat* . . . Yeah, great idea—why don't we wake Billy, get him in here so he can see—see what a fucking charade his parents' marriage is . . . then . . . then—we can make him choose between his beloved papa and his de-de-despised mother . . .

She's sobbing now, which is why, presumably, he thinks it's safe to take her—entirely chastely—in his arms: take her as he's had to so many times before—take her, so as to rock her as you would a baby or a very small child . . . *My pigeons' house . . . I o-open wide . . . and I set my pigeons free* . . . its sobs slowly subsiding into a soft susurrus.

*Stupid man. Stupid damn fucking man.*

The mechanics of this interaction should be obvious to him as she remains completely rigid in his embrace. It's the same with the foldaway ironing board in the kitchen: if you hug its tapered torso . . . *up come its legs!*

John doubles up, the breath whistling out of him—he lets her go, and when he straightens up, it's into a rage the like of which she's seen only a couple of times in the thirteen years of their marriage: You bitch! he mewls—and then, more authoritatively: You slut! You can't keep your goddamn eyes off that man—your hands, either. I disgust you? That's rich, when you disgust me far more—

Not enough for you to keep your filthy hands off me! she howls.

Now it's cartoon time: fists and feet emerging at all angles from a dust cloud—or at least, once it's all over they both wish there'd been one to obscure what they did to each other, because Elaine's lying full-length against the baseboard, while John's rubbing the stinging palm with which he's clouted her.

For an odd moment Elaine thinks of Ted—specifically, his nervous habit of rubbing his fingers with his thumb—after which there's a curious pause: a kind of commercial break during which, by all that's right and proper and wholesomely American, they should be preparing to apologize and wash this very dirty linen of theirs *whiter-than-white* . . .

Instead, Elaine remains supine, sobbing over and over: It's over . . . it's over . . . it's over . . . thick blood surging back and forth between her ringing ears: It's over . . . it's over . . . it's over . . . *Why the third-personal impersonal pronoun—Will I*, she wonders, *remain such a fussy grammarian 'til I die?*—referring to their marriage quite as much as the fight. And if her marriage is over, Elaine's life is as well . . .

. . . 'cause what future can there possibly be for a thirty-four-year-old divorcée with sagging, stringy-veined breasts, pitted thighs, and a complexion like . . . *old oatmeal.* What future can there possibly be for a woman conspicuously lacking those graces that would enable men to happily sustain and protect her? Let alone for one who's also failed to acquire those aptitudes essential if she's to make her own way through this dark and hostile world . . .

Thrashing about in this slough of anguish, she howls at the *fucking sadist!* who's tormented her for years—first with his sexless, pitying concern,—now with his disgusting desires . . .

What does he want of her? Another child, with all the bloody agony and bloodier misery it'll entail? Or that she should force herself to the bathroom each time he's inclined—in the middle of the night, if required—and first force it up, then fiddle about . . . *until the cap fits*. And not some wispy creation from a Fifth Avenue boutique with a delicate veil trim, but *a nauseating rubber one* . . .

Yes . . . she'd rather have his blows—even expert ones—than inept caresses! Which is why she's on her feet again, with her fingers . . . *in his face*, as she half sobs, half shrieks, You bastard! You goddamn fucking bastard! Until he hits her again—and this time, harder: so her head is clamorous with this revelation: *He isn't going to stop . . . as long as I carry on, he isn't going to stop . . .*

A few minutes later they're in the front room, as far apart as possible, each cradling a full glass of bourbon—a favored potion for neither of them, but all that's left in the house. Elaine's shoulders shake, and as she drags on her cigarette, then exhales, coughing, she takes sidelong glances at her husband, whose mien is satisfactorily abject.

Since the hitting stopped, they've been behaving towards each other with the studied politeness of diplomats representing nations that have only just ceased hostilities: now she asks him to pass the ashtray—which he does with such economy of movement it's clear *he regrets being so free with his hands* . . .

Through her own toxic fumes, Elaine glimpses this grim aftermath of their row: as if subjected to many kilotons of radioactive rage, everything in the room has been half burnt. Billy's old beaten-up teddy bear, his beading, his cowboy pistols—a magazine rack, a table lamp, John's

reading one, her mother's still life of flowers, her own sewing basket: all of it crisply calcined on one side—untouched
on the other.

The Hancocks sit, silently sipping in these smoking
ruins.

Once or twice, John begins stuttering an apology—then
stops, sensing it's either too early for that . . . or too late.

After this pained interlude, during which he finishes
his drink, he sighs, stands, and heads back to the kitchen.
She hears him rinse the glass and place it upside down on
the draining board—she listens as his footsteps ascend the
stairs, then move about the upper story, as he fetches sheets
and covers from the linen closet, then retreats to the spare
room.

Lying once more in the murk of her marital bed, Elaine
thinks: It's a miracle we didn't wake Billy . . . And then: It's
a miracle I'm still alive . . . Why? Because she'd wanted to
attack John again—which she acknowledges, with a sick
shudder, means: *I wanted him to hit me again* . . .

Hands sheathed once more between her bare thighs,
Elaine has turned against the wind—its embrace isn't
inconstant, *it's perfidious* . . . The wind would like to
smash the little house to smithereens—is that why she's
praying like this? Praying for deliverance from the great
and terrible outdoors, quite as much as from her domestic
plantation, and its cowardly tyrant of an overseer.

She recoils from this: the mile upon mile of wooded
hills, surmounted by bare crags, which undulate their way,
hundreds of miles north, to the Canadian border. And in

every thicket and clearing of those forests, wild animals lurk, waiting to claw and bite and tear and chew their way . . . *into my vagina.*

In an undertone, she sing-sobs, There's nowhere for me to go . . . There's nowhere for me to go . . . There's no refuge or haven for me . . . Nowhere to go . . . N-nowhere . . . and carries on until she's asleep, and dreams of herself as a giantess, slumped down on the bare earth and weeping inconsolably for the bounty she's destroyed—not by slashing or burning, only by crying, such that her tears cascade down the gullies in her face, their salt penetrates the soil, and barrenness spreads out from her further, and further.

In the morning, the atmosphere is no better. Up early, she and John edge round one another, as if they aren't people *but precipices* . . . As for Billy, he has, Elaine thinks, the baffled air of someone who's slowly realizing something terrible has happened to them *while they weren't paying attention* . . .

Because, while the battle may be over, his parents are intent on winning the peace with their *entirely self-interested* solicitations. Only this last summer, after years of propagandizing, John at last succeeded in persuading his son that sports are interesting—and not just the playing of them, the watching and the amassing of statistics concerning them as well. Now, when they breakfast together, they discuss the minutiae of batting averages and yards per carry, as if they were connoisseurs mulling over *fine wines* . . .

Billy's mother is equally two-faced when it comes to her intimacies: Would he like an extra peanut butter and jelly sandwich in his lunchbox? How about having Frank over to play after school? And as she hectors him, she realizes: she and John may be precipices to one another, but for their son they've combined into a single—and almost certainly unavoidable—*pitfall*.

What was it Freudenberg had said about Billy whenever Elaine had raised the possibility of ending her marriage? That for a boy who was as close to his father as he, the psychological effects might well be disastrous. A meaningless equivocation Elaine's long since corrected to: *will be disastrous* . . .

Then they're gone—just like that: Billy, swept off to school in the Buick with John driving. There's no pep talk today about the benefit of a brisk walk as an antidote to all that sitting still . . .

. . . instead, she imagines John driving more expeditiously than usual—then hustling Billy out of the car, and accelerating away, keen to get as far, and as quick as possible, from his shrewish wife. God knows there are other women in their circle who'd be more to his taste—someone like Betty Troppmann, who, in addition to her two girls, has a doctorate and a career of her own. True, it's nowhere near as illustrious as her husband's—or John's, for that matter, now that he's got his promotion—but nevertheless, some people must actually call her Dr. Troppmann.

Struck by this, Elaine doodles for a few moments in the margins of her mind: *Dr. E. Hancock D. Litt . . . Dr. Elaine Hancock . . .*

But really, to speak of these academics and their spouses as a circle is idiocy—if it is one, it certainly isn't charmed.

The truth is—she flagellates herself—that she has no great affection for any of these people, so deserves to be rebuffed: Put me in any waiting room, she concedes, and I'll strike up a conversation with anyone who's seated there—why should it be any different with the waiting room that's our life here in Ithaca? No, these are only adventitious conversations, that in some instances have led to equally adventitious *couplings* . . .

Mary Burtt is a physician—and Elaine's well aware she's also recently qualified as a psychoanalyst. That wise little owl Freudenberg has had nothing to say on this matter—but Mary's told Elaine that now that her youngest is in school all day, she's considering setting up a practice here in Ithaca.

Maybe a woman will be better able to understand Elaine's predicament—sympathize with it as well. But where are the dollars needed to fund this further treatment to come from? The only way, nowadays, she can get John to shell out a few extra bucks is by sturdily typing up his manuscript—that, and speedy dispatch when it comes to the copywriting she does for the department store downtown.

The Rothschilds' marketing manager, Fishburn, pays her piece rate to churn out sales technique guides for the various departments. At least this is work she picked up herself, by showing moxie and marching into the poor guy's office. But Christ! How dispiriting it is to be instructing salesclerks on how to *gouge more effectively* . . . I am, Elaine thinks, my father's daughter—and like him my real literary talent lies in penning discount signs and banners ballyhooing MASSIVE REDUCTIONS.

I'm a shyster . . . she mutters under her breath, as she retrieves items of crockery and cutlery from the sudsy water, then arranges them in *intuitively artful* piles to dry . . . and a huckster . . . I'm a snake-oil salesman like the old man— and like him also in this respect: I'm only two cents short of being an out-and-out con artist . . .

She swoons over the sink: last night's violence—naked, feral—still prowls about the house, smelling in equal parts of metallic, dried blood and stale liquor. Gasping, she wrenches open the kitchen door—but there's no finer mold out there to shape her, only anemic sunlight and the feeble motions of grass and shrubbery animated by the chill breeze . . . *There's nowhere to go . . . There's nowhere to go . . .* Sure, the night may conceal myriad rapacious mouths, but this bright gray day is agape: a nowhere hungrily awaiting her.

She lingers on the doorstep, appalled.

Another dumb item in the Journal repeats on her, smelling eggy . . . tasting acidic—this time, one about kids' bath times and their concealed dangers—and not just the normal fuss and muss: frisky youngsters may *chew on razor blades* as readily as they slip on soap. And if their dad tries to forestall this danger by buying the latest-model electric razor, then the aspiring suicides will simply drop it in the water, such is their longing to expire in a pungent broth of singed skin and burnt hair.

Does the woman who wrote this BS, or the editor who syndicated it, realize quite the extent to which they're feeding Elaine's ravenous anxieties? The soap isn't only dissolving in the bathtub—it's spread slippery mush all over the little house's wooden floors. Now, standing at the kitchen sink, she feels her feet sliding about: *Bambi on ice . . .*

If she tries to tidy the front room, her feet will shoot out from under her and she'll fall *flat on my can . . .* So, instead, she skates about upstairs—which always feels a little more secure to her—making Billy's bed, then stripping the sheets from hers and John's. A momentary hallucination: her scholarly husband lying full-length on the bare mattress, naked, with an erection in one fist and a gun in the other.

Elaine shudders. Even so, she goes to strip the bed in the spare room as well—whatever rift there may be between them, this is one way of preventing it from widening: welcoming him back into her bed, and, *if necessary . . .*

But she can't complete the grotesque thought—any more than she can master her trembling limbs and shaking hands until she's sat back down at the little table in their bedroom, with a cup of black coffee, a cigarette, and John's manuscript—a sheaf of yellow pages, narrow ruled, and torn from legal pads. These are covered with his neat, angular, yet scarcely legible handwriting.

Why does she do it? Why does she assist him any further in this business, for which she has no real feeling or sympathy? Elaine would say she was passionate about literature—and she is to this extent: she takes refuge in a book the way others do in . . . *a bottle.* By contrast, John's critical writing seems the very opposite of such escapism: his words are the systematic denial of any possibility others can provide refuge.

Words she can, however, transcribe efficiently, at between thirty and forty per minute. She may lack any true poetic gift herself, but Elaine finds her métier in this—which gives her at least some leverage when it comes to the rat-a-tat-tat of their percussive marriage.

First, she fetches her Olivetti and a fresh ribbon from the roll-front cabinet in the study, and puts its box to one side for Billy, already hearing his delight at receiving this very ordinary gift: *My, but this little box is just darling* . . . which is a catchphrase taken from one of his favorite radio shows.

Slotting the cartridges onto their spindles—feeding the ribbon through the rollers, then tightening the knurled knobs: these near-reflex actions are reassuring. Elaine becomes calmer. She feeds a sheet of paper into the machine then types a few test sentences to make sure the ribbon's OK: *The quick brown fox jumps over the lazy dog . . . The quick brown fox jumps over the lazy dog . . .*

Her fingers, spread wide on the keyboard, bring this surrealistic scene to life—albeit for a utilitarian purpose: what's required for this tester are letters on adjacent keys, to check that typing can be done at speed, without any of the spasmodically upraised arms interlocking. The quick brown fox jumps over the lazy dog works well enough—but for maximum efficiency it's best to alternate with a second test sentence: *Now is the time for all good men to come to the aid of the Party . . . The quick brown fox jumps over the lazy dog . . . Now is the time for all good men to come to the aid of the Party . . .*

Better still, mix things up further: *Now is the time for quick brown men to come to the aid of the Party . . . The lazy fucking bastards*— She tears out the paper abruptly, balls it up, and tosses it to one side. It bounces—then rolls beneath the newly made bed. Now she recalls one of last night's troubled dreams—there were others, but this is all that remains from their confused wreckage: Elaine plunging, head down over the edge of the bed—in the same position she makes Billy adopt when she's administering nose drops.

From this vantage, the feline eyes in the back of her weird head were able to penetrate the dusty darkness: under the bed were two neat and desiccated cat turds lying beside a pool of cold urine. What does it mean? That our marriage is shit, of course—which is what happens if you marry a goddamn Schitz: acts of excretion rather than ones of love. Did this: the soft warmth of Karma's flanks against Elaine's bare ankles precede or succeed the memory? Was it the cause—or some occult effect? She glances down into the cat's green eyes—she's so goddamn knowing, but about what, exactly? Is it, perhaps, the self-satisfied expression of *the pregnant female . . .* And if Karma is enceinte, will Elaine be . . . *jealous*? An absurd notion—or is it: the cat is beautiful, free—and on one or two shameful occasions, Elaine has taken her anger out on her the way she does on . . . *my own son*—and yes, somehow, it seems worse behavior with the pet than with the child.

Karma wants to be picked up—she wants to snuggle down into Elaine's lap while rubbing her head against the underside of Elaine's breasts . . . *Fat chance!* Because Elaine

wants to be picked up as well—Elaine wants the comfort
of a lap, too.

*Ça suffit!* She lights another cigarette from the burning
tip of the last—but is it the last? Is it meaningful to divide
them up in this way—after all, the line of smoke, like the
line of poetry, is unbroken . . . Enjambment—isn't that
what it's called? Some Elements of Versification, taught to
Elaine by Ted Roethke at Penn State, return to her as she
turns her attention to John's manuscript and begins typing,
*Parenthetically, if Milton really meant to suggest sexual
relations between Eve and Satan, it is odd that no least
suggestion of the serpentine attaches to Adam after the
Fall* . . . No least? Surely, no less? She stares hard at the line
she's just typed, its letters stretching, twisting, breaking
apart, and reforming into: *The quick brown Satan jumps
over the lazy Eve* . . . she sees herself, sultry in nothing save
a striped towel, and spread invitingly across a bed under
the quizzical eyes of this composite: part Dick Powell, part
Ted Troppmann—

Another abrupt rip of paper from typewriter. Another
balling of the sheet—and another underhand pitch, which,
*base-stealer* that she is, Karma's already running for before
it hits the floor. Elaine earnestly believes she could cope
with her husband's high-minded intellectualism if it weren't
that he so often employs his bully pulpit to . . . *bully
me.* True, he may be learned—but she believes there's a
self-serving quality to John's sentences that imbues them
with meretriciousness as much as wisdom. This, and the
heavy-handed humor of a writer who imagines the strategic
deployment of erudition alone will qualify . . . *as wit.*

For his book seems to be less about what the poet meant by what he wrote than about John's clever dismissals of other critics' interpretations. Nitpicking that makes it difficult for her to maintain much faith in the scholarly enterprise—beyond the raw fact of the money he's received for it. Especially so when transcribing footnotes of this form: Page 150, line 16, for V, 602, read IV, 602; p. 158, 1. 22, for V, 186, etc. read VI, 186, etc. p. 166, 1. 28, for V, 832, read V, 837 . . .

As she types, each keystroke seems to tamp down further the bricks that comprise his heavy wall of ratiocination—one that immures . . . *me!* According to Professor Hancock, critic C's remarks about critic B's remarks about critic A (A being, so to speak, the primary secondary source regarding the blind poet's works) are unwarranted. It follows, ceteris paribus, that this essential dubiety, in being transmitted back up from C to B to A, necessarily casts such epochal events as the Reformation in a quite different light; and if the Reformation, then the rise of capitalism predicated upon it as well.

So it is that he connects his picayune determinations back to the *greatest story ever told*, namely, the inexorable rise and eventual victory of the proletariat.

Each time she reaches the end of a line and the carriage bell pings, Elaine pictures the squat black telephone crouching in the vestibule downstairs—crouching, and *silently brooding* . . .

Ted might well phone—or Elizabeth. They've all got quickly into the habit of chatting with each other in this way, as either a finale to the previous evening's entertainments, or as a prelude to ones soon to come. But in this instance, it seems extraordinary to Elaine that they shouldn't, by some clairvoyance, already know what transpired after they left the previous evening, and be eager to commiserate.

Surely Ted senses her desperation—so feels equally . . . *desperate*, as he longs to take her in his arms, the way he did on Saturday night.

Ten pages later Elaine finds herself in the kitchen. The glasses from which they drank their last sedative draft are still upended on the draining board. She twists the faucet and switches the radio on—a Bach piano piece flows out in a run of notes of such liquid clarity they twine with the water, weaving discrete moments into eternity, then unravelling it.

She knows the name of the piece: Sheep May Safely Graze—and recalls her friend Rae playing it at a little clapboard church where concerts were held, close to Ken Durant's place—Ken, who was another screwy, smart guy, although by no means a wise ruler, watching over his woolly-minded creations with love and wisdom—but rather, *a cold, selfish type*, intent on his own projects—and pleasures.

Perhaps she should've let John have her last night. Maybe that's what the feces and urine underneath the bed in Elaine's dream were symbolic of: he needed, urgently, to mark her with his scent, because at long last there's *another male sniffing about me . . .*

In which case, even his lust and his violence were to be welcomed as signs of jealousy—because anything's better than indifference, besides, *I gave as good as I got* . . . kicking and scratching, half welcoming the awful moment when she understood from the set of his body that with sufficient goading, he could well do away altogether with the *miserable little dolly that's me* . . .

While also knowing, throughout the entire vile contretemps, that the following morning everything would go on exactly the same: the man of the house at work, the child at school, and the man's wife cleaning that house, then picking up the child, and preparing the supper for all three of them to eat once the man returns . . .

Rather than being already scores—if not hundreds—of miles west of here, and jumping another freight car on her way to *join the fucking Joads* . . .

Elaine thinks: we'll have a hearty pot roast for supper —I'll get some stewing steak from the butcher, and I'll make biscuits to go with it . . . and John and Billy'll eat it right up, then they'll love me so . . . and all will be copacetic . . .

In the zip-up compartment of her purse—where she keeps receipts, and phone numbers she's scrawled on scraps of paper—Elaine finds an undreamed-of five-dollar bill, and thinks: *a wise ruler must be watching over me* . . . So, sets off on foot, almost merrily, to graze downtown.

After getting what she needs for their supper, she stops by the liquor store and buys a bottle of vodka and one of vermouth, too. Then heads to Woolworths, where she sits at the lunch counter, eating a chicken sandwich.

For a moment, she tries to imagine herself the sort of moody-looking vamp who's so very sultry, even a solid citizen who's just parked his car outside and popped in to get some *puppy biscuit* . . . can't help hitting on her.

For all the other moments, she sits in what still seems like *the wreckage of my life*: odd recollections of other jangled-up times, walking fast, or otherwise hurrying away from rows, or worse, with John, or others.

Then she drags her mulish self home. Climbing the steep slope from the bottom of West Hill, then plodding along beside the little stream edging the old Williams property, Elaine keeps her eyes downcast—as there's nothing much to fear in her sensible brown shoes, her dull dun stockings, or the slow swing of her calf-length pleated skirt.

It could be the rhythm of her footfalls—or the typing that morning, but as she reaches Hemlock Street, Elaine is smitten by this: *Is it not perhaps true that we are all dying now* . . .

*In this courtyard, crying* . . .

*Faces against this brick wall* . . . and exclaims aloud: What a goddamn lousy lyric!

No music to it and precious little meaning, either, because how could she—a high school senior in Queens, of all places—have known what it was like when you're about to be executed during the Spanish Civil War, when to this day she can *scarcely face a mirror* . . . ?

Reaching home, Elaine puts her groceries away, taking special care with the quart of vodka—which she cradles in her arms and coos to for a few moments, a sick sort of parody of loving, to be sure—both funny, and not funny at all, *because it's true* . . .

Then she goes and slumps down heavily on the stairs beside the telephone table, thinking back bitterly to the yet gawkier girl she once was: *Nature's chief masterpiece is writing well* . . . which, set beside the photo of the mousy blonde with her hair fashionably marcelled, read more like an injunction than a description. But then who looks to a high school yearbook for accuracy when it comes to the present—let alone the future?

Yes, her mutinous hair had at least been professionally waved—while her white ankle socks had been rolled. She had a fine leather pocketbook and satchel—and a fountain pen that was the absolute must-have, all courtesy of *Daddy Warbucks* . . . Elaine remembers meetings of the Richmond Hill school magazine's editorial board—she'd already had a sharp tongue, and was funny with it, she believes. And yet she hadn't shone, despite being surrounded by tyro writers of no greater ability or talent.

Her poem about the firing squad was the only one published—and no one had complimented her, or so much as demonstrated that they'd read it. Her parents interleaved the magazine with Time and the Saturday Evening Post in the bamboo rack—but unlike these other publications *it stayed there* . . .

The telephone still loiters in the dark cave of the vestibule —gaping at Elaine with its cyclopean dial. She wonders if it might be possible, short of paying for the service—which was unthinkable—to discover if someone has called while you've been out. Would French chalk dusted over the handset show some disturbance? Or what about a hair, glued with saliva between handset and cradle. Hot face in cold hands, Elaine berates herself for such crazy speculations: so what if these Nancy Drew methods worked, she still wouldn't be able to tell who it was who'd called—only that they had. It might just've been Bobbie, eager as ever to tittle-tattle . . . *a real, giving spirit, eh . . .*

Creakily rising, Elaine turns about and goes heavily up the narrow, oaken staircase . . . *rising heavily, Elaine about-turns and creakily goes up the oaken, narrow staircase.* If she begins this short journey as her father's daughter—tall, rangy, and a man of the world—she finishes it having transformed into her dainty mother, who's no more capable of enjoying a smutty joke than she is *the goddamn sex act . . .* There can never have been any *golden moments* for her—which makes it bizarre, her daughter thinks, that I feel her in me at all.

Her brother, Robert—he has a body: and he takes after the old goat quite as much as his sister does. More so nowadays, since he has the necessary means to afford the same flashy accessories as their father. The handmade silk shirts and leather shoes—the gold wristwatches, and the silver money clips inlaid with mother-of-pearl.

But he—like some old roué who hits on a girl a quarter his own age, as his brown hair dye drips down onto his collar—can't seriously believe he passes? A ridiculous notion, not least because Bob Robinson is far too dark-skinned to be of Scots stock. You can, Elaine thinks as she unhooks then unzips, disguise German blood any number of ways—but not a Jew who closely resembles *a cigar-store Indian . . .*

Notwithstanding the fact that nobody's fooled, he's polished his façade, has Bob Robinson—and they must also succumb to his other, not inconsiderable charms: the endless patter, the natty outfits, and a zest for life in all its most obvious, material manifestations that, for all she's revulsed by it, Elaine still envies. She sits, hunkered down inside herself, hearing the hissing of fire hydrants on vanished summer days, and mulling over a paradox that, along with their shared past, distorts everything between them: he could never pass—yet with a show of trying to, he's now one of the senior copywriters at a Madison Avenue ad' agency that, before his arrival, never knowingly *let a Jew in the building* . . .

Whereas his sister—who believes she does so *well enough* that there's no perceptible benefit.

When she was seeing Freudenberg, he took no interest in this—aggressively so—while exhibiting an unseemly one in the sex games she and Bob had played as children—at one point suggesting she'd gone some way towards seducing her brother. That, or he had molested her—or both. Insinuations that after agonizing about for some time she tried putting down to sheer malice on his part—not least because he cited this as an explanation for Elaine's own promiscuous behavior.

Lying, with her thick curls scratching the paper napkin he better've replaced after his previous patient, Elaine fixated on the small window, high up in the corner of the room. She looked at it for the full fifty minutes—except, sometimes, it looked at her. It was that, or a reproduction of Picasso's Blue Nude—a wilfully insensitive choice of wall covering on the shrink's part, if it had been his. In summer, leaves fluttered against the window's single clear pane. In autumn, wet, they slapped at it—and come winter, the trees' bared twigs scratched at its hard lens.

Over time Elaine allowed herself to be convinced of this much: that in earliest childhood she'd experienced this same *insatiable itch* . . . But it was a belief that didn't survive the analysis itself: now she could see that the things they'd done to each other were only what kids do—she'd've realized far sooner if Billy weren't . . . *an only*—and a male one, to boot.

She stands, tears two sheets from the roll, folds them and wipes herself. She sniffs, if not exactly savoring her own intimate odors, at any rate *accepting of them, too* . . . She peers down at her thick and curly pubic hair, and tries to imagine what it might be like to be . . . *an outie rather than an innie.*

Is it true what shrinks proclaim as holy writ, that men are forever in a state of anxiety lest they lose their penises? And not only in some freakish accident—but quite possibly by having them bitten off at the hilt by the full set of gleaming white teeth that are hidden inside *all women's vaginas . . . Arrant balls!*

She stands back, bumping her belly at the rim of the kitchen sink . . . *my workstation*, looking through another small window at agitated greenery, her tongue skipping from stopper to stopper: they say you can't really *remember pain—but I can!* A thick coating of pain, spreading out from the sickly green paint of the dentist's office downtown, flowing along the sidewalks and streets, gurgling throatily in the gutters—and all who touch it recoil . . . *howling*, for it burns—burns like corrosion and fire at the same time, such that flesh bubbles . . . *then fries*.

As for humiliation, it abides with Elaine in her every last fiber—as does her own ceaseless poking and probing into why this should be so, investigations which, inasmuch as they bare her, *humiliate me . . .*

She's unwrapped the meat, placed it on a chopping board, and assembled the vegetables in a bowl beside it—all without any thought at all. Maybe that's what happiness is like: as if the pleasure taken in skills so well learned they're automatic—*like knitting*—were somehow transposed to the whole of life. As if you're so skilled at living you just *don't have to think about it . . .*

It being in the first instance: this second Thanksgiving supper, convened in order to celebrate their little family's deliverance from . . . *domestic violence.*

There's certainty—if not much security—in the big stoneware bowl, pale green on the outside—paler still on the inside, and finely networked with cracks. Certainty, too, in this wooden chopping board, already scored by this well-sharpened knife. Then there's the subdued roar of the coal-fired furnace in the basement, which, knowing her reluctance to do so, John will have raked out then banked up before he left.

Because he, by contrast, takes a positive pleasure in scraping and clanging—as he does with others of the chores: whether mending broken stuff around the house—or doing yard work. No, Elaine's husband doesn't get hangovers—and if he does feel a little foggy-headed in the morning, then he gets up, has a cold shower, and mends the broken rail on the back fence—or checks to see the tire chains are ready for winter. He does this because he is responsible and competent, which is why she . . .

Can't stand him: the very set of his body is *pure reproach* . . . So, why should she cook for him—why should she put more meat in that fish-white belly? Half gagging, Elaine angrily cuts up the steak, repelled by the thought of this carnality: meat prepared so it can be chewed, swallowed, and transformed into . . . *more meat.*

The carrots, parsnips, onions, and potatoes peeled and chopped, the stock simmering, she retrieves the heavy iron casserole from below the sink, where, behind a red gingham curtain, the pots and pans are jumbled together on a couple of shelves. When she retrieves one pot, it slips or slides from the others—there's something congealed in there.

Really, Elaine thinks, I must, must, MUST clear the shelves, clean them, sort through that clutter, and weed out the ones with bent lids or broken handles. Just as I must, must, MUST go through Billy's old clothes and toys and pick out the stuff to go in the five-dollar chest . . .

So often, though, it's this thinking that takes the place of doing . . .

And why wouldn't it?

All the ingredients are in the casserole: the meat and vegetables *lolling* somehow *obscenely* in the murky stock. This much Elaine does know: to be a Jew, now, ten years after, is a solecism raised to the power of . . . *millions.* Moreover, this is what she mostly feels when she scrutinizes herself from a chilly triple-decker pulpit—that she's not simply unwelcome, but altogether a *cosmic embarrassment* . . . The very stars can see her skin's too sallow— while the nebulae know her nose is too big.

Is it too early for a drink? If it weren't for the coolness between them, Elaine would call Bobbie up and get her over—both for a party postmortem and an attempt to *raise it from the dead* . . . It wouldn't be the first time they'd alibied each other's daytime drinking—both mothers have cause to be grateful their kids' school is within *staggering distance* . . .

No, she admonishes herself, as she hauls out the garbage pail and pours all that peel in the trash can. No.

Another pot percolated—another cup, thick and black as paint, poured—Elaine settles herself back upstairs in front of her typewriter. It would be much, much easier, she thinks, to believe in what her husband calls, portentously, his intellectual project if it weren't that he's already received the money for the book, and it's long since been swallowed up by the household budget. There'll be a raise with his promotion—but that, too, will disappear soon enough.

Imagine not just writing the clever, deadpan story that's acknowledged, by critics and readers alike, to be brilliant—but being the sort of writer who's personally revered: mobbed at public readings, and in receipt of so much fan mail they have to *hire a goddamn secretary . . .*

Her fingers rest on the typewriter keys—and Elaine remembers Saul Bellow, who came to Cornell at the beginning of the semester to give a reading at Statler Hall. For no reason either of them could discern—contemporary fiction certainly isn't one of his specialties—Harry Lemesurier had asked John to do the introductory remarks. John griped about it, of course, but in the event spoke so well, and so well of Bellow's work in particular, that at the reception afterwards the novelist thanked him profusely.

Standing awkwardly amidst the hubbub, Elaine sipped steadily at her drink, while taking sidelong glances at this vigorous, self-confident, and above all successful man. She'd dutifully read the book in tandem with her husband —delighting in its portrayal of a vigorous, self-confident, and ultimately successful Chicagoan, whose native wit and kishkes allow him to triumph over just about every adversity. In a way, she couldn't believe this character's creator was right beside her—it was as if a movie actor had stepped through the screen and pushed down the next seat.

Bellow had, he told them, given such a great reading partly because of Professor Hancock's inspiring words, so it'd be his pleasure to invite them to join him for dinner at the faculty club.

Thinking about the incident later, it'd struck Elaine there must've been only a fixed amount of self-confidence to go round in their little colloquy, and that Bellow—the protagonist of his own highly regarded novel—must've got it all: because John had screwed up his eyes and ducked his

head in the way Elaine knows is the evidence of his enduring shyness, then politely refused the offer . . . *on behalf of
both of us!*

What!? Elaine cries aloud, what is this misery?

Abruptly, she tears her eyes from her cell window and
swivels in her chair, only to find the same view waiting for
her in the mirror that hangs on the opposite wall: East Hill,
with the campus buildings forming an uneven horizon. She
remembers how on the Fourth of July the fireworks set off on
Schoelkopf Field arced up into the ochreous sunset sky, and
they'd stood together with the O'Briens on their back porch
watching them, while the boys had *jumped and hollered . . .*

It radiates from her—the misery: pulses out, wave upon
wave, each one darker and more destructive than the last.
She sits, Elaine does, by the deep, cold lake, surrounded
by dark wooded hills, in between which are still darker
wooded valleys, down which rush ice-cold cataracts—and
she sees, out there in the wilderness, the heavy bear *that
walks with me—that is me . . .* An ugly and benighted
beast that walks and walks and walks, then every decade
or so squats down to give birth to another little cub . . .

. . . The bear went over the moun-tain, the bear went
over the moun-tain . . . Elaine sing-sobs, then cries more
concertedly when she thinks of the Billy-of-the-future,
an orphan, compelled to go on alone through these dark
woods, and bowed down by the burden of all the anxieties
he's inherited.

The aroma of her own cooking comes wafting cartoon-
ishly through the bedroom door: a visible ribbon of smell

that wavers beneath her quivering nostrils. What a dumb idea: trying to resolve this dreadful mess with a casserole. She's had pangs for the fellow for a while—is it any wonder John put on a tough front? Shouldn't I at the very least be gratified that he cares enough to try and stop me playing around, even if it means whopping the bejesus out of me? Would I prefer it if he showed the white feather?

Ach! The farce of this New Yorker cartoon! Which Elaine has been hiding and retrieving, and hiding once more, as if it were a love letter containing his passionate declarations, together with exact details of what he'd like to do to her, and have her do to him.

She turns back to the window—stands, peers out, then down and to the right. The roadway rears up at her— and it's only then that she at long last realizes what the devil's going on. Because it doesn't matter how dutifully she records the relevant dates . . . *it always catches me unawares*: clinging to the chimney stack, and quite obviously about *fall off the roof . . .*

At which point, the telephone, being *full of the sound of its own voice* . . . begins clamoring, and continues to for the time it takes Elaine to get halfway there, then half the remaining half, followed by the time it takes her to further bisect these successively diminishing intervals—moving *carefully* down the slippery wooden staircase, *carefully* placing each stockinged foot athwart the narrow treads, *carefully* balancing her desperation to reach it before it stops against her fear of falling—because if it does stop ringing, by that fact alone it will deprive her for all eternity of the *caring* lover she's waited an eternity for, and with whom she is destined to spend . . . *all eternity.*

She presses the receiver to her ear and hears the echo of . . . nothing—an absence she nevertheless is certain indicates Ted's presence on the end of the line. The seconds tick away, lengthy as eons of heartsickness, and she hears in near-soundless suspiration his sweet and gentle sympathy. One beat . . . a second . . . a third—she counts him in, then he speaks, using John's voice: Elaine?

Y-yes? she semi-coughs—close up, the smell of stewing meat and vegetables is utterly repugnant.

Elaine . . . *the kidder continues* . . . something pretty damn upsetting has happened.

# .5.

## March to July 1955

The hollow report of a car door slamming back at the trailhead—it's either that or the flat crack of some teenager's twenty-two rifle. Whichever it is, neither can be responsible for the showers of powdery snow that cascade from the bowed and nodding trees, as these occur at entirely random intervals.

I should be startled, Elaine thinks—because being jumpy is what I do best. That, and like the good little doggie I am, leaping into the comforting arms of whichever man is available.

Perplexed, she can feel her own brows knitting—and must've broken step, or otherwise communicated her confusion to him, because Ted stops, disengages his arm, and with his hands on her shoulders, turns Elaine gently to face him.

It's a perfect day in earliest spring. The sky above the gorge is so clear and the sun so bright that the occasional cloud—straying from *some other poetic vision*—is thrown into sharpest relief, so seems fanciful as . . . *a Loire chateau,* its creamy, bulging buttresses, balconies, and balustrades floating out over the Finger Lakes.

And now . . . every time he touches her—no matter how casually—she's compelled to rhapsodize his capable hands, their blunt, manicured nails that reach up to brush the snow from the bunches of brown hair escaping from the band of her tam. Headwear picked up from a discount bin at Rothschild's, and which she doubts is really that . . . *becoming*.

Nearby, there's another miniature avalanche—but they just stand, bowed . . . *and nodding*.

You're awfully sweet, Elaine says, and you've turned me into a dryad.

A dry what? He smiles down at her . . . *dear dimples*.

She smiles back: An ancient tree spirit—the whole way up here, every time the snow cascades from the trees . . . it's like they're alive—like they're dryads shaking the snow from their leafy locks.

Oh, my, he laughs, you've got enough poetry for the both of us, I guess.

They can hear the kids as they come up the valley behind them—and in silent accord, Elaine and Ted link arms once more, then carry on walking beside the river, swollen with meltwater, as it rushes in the opposite direction.

Ted says, I'm a pretty down-to-earth character—I admit it. I see a fallen tree—like the sequoia over there—and all I think is, I wonder whether there's too much rot in the trunk, or if I could chop it up . . . make some garden furniture out of it.

You could do that?

He laughs again . . . *'cause he's enjoying himself.* Well, it'd be pretty crude—but, yeah, I could put together some rustic-style chairs and benches . . . Or take those rocks over there—the smooth little boulders. I see those and I think, is this some Japanese-type ornamental garden in the making . . . ? I can see them cleaned off and set upright in patches of either pure-white or pure-black sand. You get the picture?

I do, Elaine ruminates bitterly: he has a practical use for everything in this goddamn wilderness, except for wanton me! But to her companion she simply says, You're so domestic—you want to take everything home to your nest.

Another momentary check to their progress—then he urges them on: Yes, he concedes, that's the trouble—and I want to do it with women, as well.

Is she using the unevenness of the path as an excuse so that every sharp turn, step up or step down, she can lean into him more, feel his body *more* . . . ? And is she experiencing the obvious and baser urge? When did she last screw al fresco? Not for so many years . . . She can dimly recall some weekends when John drove down to Penn State and took her out in the surrounding country. Courting, it might have been called in a more decorous era—but in this one it was fooling around, nothing more.

For all his vaunted poetry, he didn't run to a book of verses under the bough—while his jug was full of applejack, not wine. As for the loaf of bread: potato chips and some baloney. When it came to singing beside one another in the wilderness—well, it never seemed wilderness enough, and while Elaine may've been willing enough, she was always profoundly shocked by how much more naked her naked-ness appeared in broad daylight.

I—I don't know anything much about trees . . . plants . . . or animals for that matter, she confides. I have no excuse—we only moved to New York when I was eight or nine—before that we lived in various small towns around Ohio, and usually on the outskirts. Which was odd—'cause my parents never took any interest in the outdoors. My papa is a self-made man, entirely preoccupied by the world men have made. In particular, stuff—its buying and selling, and the places you go to do that . . .

. . . As for my mother, well, if she ever considered the countryside at all it was with a shudder—she thought it dirty, and if she got mud on her shoes, it was the same as anyone else getting shit on 'em.

It's a long speech—and a revealing one. As she says it, Elaine feels the heat rising up her neck. But he laughs again! A happy guffaw—and seeing his broad shoulders shake, she awards herself this accolade: I've done it! I've seduced him . . . Because what other explanation can there be for his happy abandon?

They continue on along the path, arm in arm, maneu-vering to avoid fallen boughs and slushy puddles. Fantasy has the better of Elaine now—and thinking, as she often does, of the sticky-backed celluloid figures Billy transfers with precise little pencil strokes onto cardboard panora-mas, she does the same: positioning her and Ted's naked bodies, wrapped discreetly in a travelling rug, up on that

ledge above the cascade—or over there beneath the snowy
trees.

This is the real excitement of the erotic, she thinks: the
violent contrast between a man and a woman, skin to skin,
tensed, sweaty—and this homely-looking chap, hopping
along beside her in galoshes and a camel-hair coat.

Then: Are we fleeing our spouses—or our children?

They wend their way between the last few trees and, at
last, are standing in this extraordinary arena, one formed
*over thousands of years . . .*

A single, hundred-foot-long white tongue, wagged a little by the wind, lolls over the still-icy lip of the precipice
and lashes at the pool below, sending out wavelet upon
wavelet to lap at their feet. They are the only people here
on this enchanting day—the only people to hear this sibi-
lant and babbling soliloquy.

So . . . they stand stock-still, and she realizes this: the
true theatricality of nature lies in the ceaseless contrasts
it stages between motion and stillness. In the woods, muffled by the moss and the thick carpet of fallen needles
underfoot, Elaine saw a tiny fleck of leaf mold, caught
on a single stretched strand of spiderweb, that agitated
furiously—while all else seemed stupefied: a sedated rather
than enchanted forest.

Taughannock is nature . . . *incarnate*, and she pulls
Ted's arm still closer, hoping he feels her breast through
all their stupid costume. Elaine knows she wouldn't appre-
ciate this if the kids were right there with them—John
and Betty, either. Anyway, they'd been so caught up in the

conversation they began back at the house that when the two families exited their respective autos after the five-minute drive, they resumed it immediately.

Which was ironical, given that neither of them had wanted to come for the walk in the first place—at least not initially.

The Troppmanns' invitation was for Sunday brunch—the kids could play together in the room specially appointed for this activity, while the adults would lounge over toast, coffee, scrambled eggs, and Bloody Marys as they leafed through the Sunday Times, reading out bits of scuttlebutt in between their own, more parochial gossiping.

The Troppmanns' place is high up on the bluffs immediately to the south of Taughannock, and Elaine thinks it's the loveliest house she's ever seen—so completely modern, there isn't a single picture or stick of furniture the Hancocks possess that wouldn't look cheap and shabby in this shining context. When they went for the first time, and Ted gave them the tour, he said the name of the architect—and it was one Elaine thought she recognized.

Ted actually called it the dernier cri—and from the way he said it, she guessed he didn't really know any French at all, and was simply parroting. In any other guy this would be a complete and utter turnoff, but with him it's simply *endearing* . . .

There are two two-story wings of the same size, joined together in a wide-open angle. There's so much window and so little of anything else—that when they arrived, at dusk, the house appeared to be a series of brightly lit and conjoined glass cubes, laid across a vast lawn. Cubes full of stylish objects, paintings, furniture, and the gadgets that amuse Ted: an electric carving knife—an inflatable transparent plastic cushion.

But the next time Elaine came she was alone, it was daylight, and she sat with Elizabeth sipping coffee, and marvelling at the way the trees and shrubs edging the property seemed to've upped roots and ushered each other forward, so as to join them in the opulent sitting room.

Obviously, it helps to have money behind you—and from the way they are with each other, Elaine rather suspects there's plenty on both sides of the Troppmanns' marital divide. Can it be this alone that accounts for Ted's air of worldliness and masculine assurance? He didn't go overseas —or even serve at all—yet beside him John seems gauche and unsophisticated. At least up to a point, because once Ted starts prattling away—and my, he can yakety-yak—sooner or later he'll say something so ingenuous the Hancocks will exchange conspiratorial glances. Dernier cri, indeed!

If the Troppmanns' house had been described to her, in detail, before she went there, Elaine would've hated it. On principled as well as phobic grounds: she dislikes, she believes, any ostentation—while she craves cosiness in all its forms. Until it becomes too claustrophobic, that is . . . At any rate, while their own house may feel exposed, standing as it does surrounded by vacant lots, it at least has proper walls, with which to shut out the very wide-open vistas of the lake and the surrounding hills.

The Troppmanns appear to revel in the very thing she cowers before. In Elizabeth's willingness to be exposed in this glass house, Elaine senses the pulse of the other

woman's desire: she's not as afraid of her husband's passionate nature as she might be . . . *because she shares it.*

It's Ted who makes the house truly beautiful, though,
Elaine concludes—just as he makes icy water, muddy
woods, and mucky boulders beautiful. When she's with
him, *the heavy bear that's me* ambles off to play somewhere
else, leaving the two of them alone to enjoy this romantic
scene. Their spouses also deserve credit for . . . *their decorous behavior.*

Nothing has been said out loud—not yet, but they're all
edging towards it, testing the path ahead with small confidences and shared jokes. Whatever else may be going on
with this quartet's lives, they all know something momentous is happening between Ted and Elaine—so much so
that every moment they spend together feels *heavily pregnant* with the possibility of their *imminent union* . . . Elaine
never wants this walk to end.

Since before Christmas the couples have been seeing each
other on a regular basis for the usual rotation of drinks,
movies, coffees, and suppers in, or dinners out at the faculty club. The kids have helped cement the relationship.
Billy is on the verge of girl-hating prepuberty—his mother
can sense a certain coarsening in him, his movements can
be abrupt and peremptory— *But he's not there yet* . . . and
in the meantime would be more than happy to play quietly
with little Karen and her dolls, if it weren't for her older
sister's terrible crush on him.

Stella stands just out of sight, and peeks around doors
at the overpowering object of her affections, where he sits,

cross-legged on the carpet. Sometimes Elaine worries she may be using him as . . . *live bait.*

Because if there's one thing Ted takes pleasure in besides reducing complex social phenomena to simple and apprehensible categories, it's fishing. He keeps what looks, even to Elaine's untutored eye, like a pretty swanky motorboat in a boathouse at the lakeshore—and although it's too early in the season, he's taken an admiring John out a couple of times already, preliminaries for the serious fishing trips he's planning for once the weather improves.

At an entirely notional level, Elaine likes the idea of being rocked by this vast body of water—rocked a bit, but not too much, since the captain of her soul would also be the master of the craft. However, if she thinks about actually stepping into the boat, the engine puttering to life, and the shoreline steadily retreating into a greenish streak, while all around them the *wind rises* . . . Well, such a thing is obviously quite impossible.

Ted, Betty—their girls, John and Billy, too. Everyone, in point of fact, is perfectly safe—until Elaine, that Jonah, comes aboard, whereupon the frailty of the vessel—which should've been perfectly obvious to . . . *everyone*—is spectacularly confirmed as it sets off, straight and unerring, for the *bottom of the goddamn lake* . . .

Yet when Ted told her, drunkenly, at a particularly bacchanalian party, he was considering buying a bigger boat, Elaine feigned interest so well that when she asked him what he was going to call it, he answered: Elaine.

Did it matter that immediately after this he'd gone and necked in the kitchen with Claire Beamish? Yes, of course it did. Ted couldn't be seriously attracted to Claire, but even so, Elaine burned with jealousy, as if some madman had doused her in gasoline, then set fire to her. She'd put up a good front, but only because of this childish reasoning: he loves his boat and wants to be in her . . . quod erat demonstrandum: he must want to be in Elaine, too.

The Hancocks and the Troppmanns meet about once a week as a quartet—and Elizabeth and Elaine have had coffee together a number of times. She's unclear exactly how many days a week Betty teaches at the College—but she isn't full-time. The couples have also been running into one another at parties or other gatherings most weekends. Elaine has begun to see this busy social life principally as a pretext for her and Ted to meet up safely, and in plain view of their respective spouses.

When she knows she's going to see him that day, Elaine awakes in a daze—and immediately admonishes herself: Get ahold of yourself—don't get too tight or otherwise make a horse's ass of yourself. She sits, staring out the window at the campus in the middle distance, and trying out dialogue for them in her hazy head. On a couple of shameful occasions, she wrote out their imaginary exchanges— then obliterated them with fierce doodles. Then wrote out some more.

And some more—angry sex-hunger jerking through the nib of her pen.

I'll be put away, she thinks, in some awful state institution . . . Alone in a room like a cell . . . paper pants suit . . . small table . . . smaller than this one . . . have to write on toilet paper . . . more and more . . . hair and feces . . . year upon year . . . peeing under the rug—shoving the toilet paper pages in the cracks in the walls . . . Only found years after my death—this extraordinary manuscript, a procession of the most vivid imaginings . . . All we could do— all any ape could ever do to . . . anybody. Taking mad joy imagining our every possible degradation, then setting it down, parallel with the perforations, on every leaf . . . *the bars of my own cage.*

John has been far more outgoing since his fortieth birthday—participating in any dancing or necking on offer —and seeming to enjoy it as well. Elaine thinks he must view the Ted-thing as just a part of their social renaissance —but she knows the reverse is the case: the only reason she's so keen to go out is the chance she'll see him. The other men she dances and necks with are nothing but . . . *alibis.*

None of them can compete.

The way Ted rubs together his thumb and fingers, as if assessing the feel of *the very air itself* . . . then flicks back his heavy black fringe . . . His shyly wolfish grin—that of a bashful predator . . . Even his rather dreadful ties are attractive to her, and never more so than when she jokingly calls their patterns an eggy mess, and he haughtily replies that they're abstract.

Abstract, indeed!

It's pretty Betty Troppmann who's the real abstract— Elaine's noticed her husband never addresses her by her first name. It's always you-this and you-that, will you?

and don't you? You-you-you-you: it doesn't matter what
the construction is, Elaine always hears the steady beat of
*blame-fixing* . . . But what for? Is it something to do with
the way Betty behaved in the aftermath of his affair with
Mona Voss? The Vosses are still conveniently away on
Caspar's sabbatical—but they can't stay gone forever, no
matter how fervently Elaine wishes they would.

How can she possibly compete—Mona is a beauty,
that's categorical. Truth is, Elaine can't compete with Betty,
either, who's not only attractive but slim, and with good
legs and breasts. One evening when they'd gone over for a
pre-party cocktail at the Troppmanns', Betty invited Elaine
to join her upstairs . . .

. . . where she quite casually undressed, then went and
sat at her rather practical-looking vanity table—no frills
or flounces for scientific Elizabeth!—doing her face in her
bra and panties.

Elaine had felt flattered by such intimacy—and enjoyed,
as she imagines a pervert might, the sight of this neat, well-
kept body, smearing itself more supple, patting itself paler,
and plucking its near-perfect skin . . . *Where's she hiding her
stretch marks?* None of which stopped her from trying to
finesse a confession of some kind from her hostess, using her
usual tactic: admitting to her own past sins—the full-blown
wartime affairs, as well as the more recent misdemeanors
—self-exposures that, when she recalled them later, made
her blush, not least because the other woman had revealed
so little in return: Betty had had, she claimed, *plenty of
opportunities*, but had exercised *self-control*.

Sometimes Elaine suspects it's the existence of the gossips—like Bobbie, and that old stager Carlotta Henty—that creates intimate secrets, rather than vice versa: that the public bourse in reputation is what drives the real economy of endearment . . . *and repulsion.* Curiosity is its lifeblood —and she has to know, will do just about anything to truly know how things stand between these others, so as to calculate her own angles.

Which is tailspinning after Ted—and flagrantly so— she gets that. You might've thought . . . *You might've!* she'd learned her lesson after how nuts everyone got during the last round of promotions—Elaine was effectively scapegoated for John's colleagues' frustration, *and their wives'.* What had Bobbie actually said? She vehemently denied repeating what Elaine told her . . . *Je est un autre*, so is she, quite possibly, to her homely, bread-kneading, boy-raising self—which would make this a self-betrayal, as much as one of a close friend.

Whatever the causes—the consequences had been a small disaster: a waterspout, travelling fast across the lake's surface—then engulfing the little house on Hemlock. Harry Lemesurier called John into his office ten days before the end of the semester, and announced it had come to light that his (John's) wife had told Caspar Voss that, whereas her husband was definitely going to be appointed full professor, he (Caspar) most definitely was not.

*Come to light!*

When John called home with this baleful news, Elaine had a small fit—first banging the receiver against the hall wall several times, then slamming it down several more onto the cradle of her own eye sockets.

She'd wailed.

She'd shrieked.

Each time, numbed, she'd let the handset fall into the safety net of her skirt, the dumb passivity of her surroundings overwhelmed her: they stared at her—she stared back at the perished, flesh-colored rubber of the old sneakers John wore to play ball in the yard with Billy, tripping each other up by the screen door . . . the rusting hinges of that door . . . and through the gap in the kitchen door, a dully shiny trivet crouching . . . *scarab-like* on the dark-orange oilskin cloth.

And each time she brought her husband, still yapping, back up to her ear, the mad awfulness of it all overwhelmed her anew, so much so, her subsiding sobs convulsed together, and soon enough she was wailing again.

Later on—calm enough to sit shakily and smoke, but not yet to fetch a sedative from the bathroom, Elaine had what Freudenberg might've called a breakthrough. There was a modus operandi to these crimes against her own person—usually her head, by banging things on it, or it on things. These assaults, too, implied voyeurism—but in this case, she needed to be on the receiving end.

Elaine demanded a witness, who, in principle, might *be on my side*—which was why when she was a child these crises were so prolonged: her parents and her brother had *always been there*. While John had the best seat in the house when she hammered her head on the wall, or merely shouted and hurled whatever was handy at him, before collapsing into sobs and taking to her bed for an hour or a day, where she'd lie in a miasma of nerves and ennui, her bruised knuckles clamped between her iron thighs . . .

Whatever the secret calibrations of her menstrual cycle and her attacks of migraine, there was a particular quality to these hysterical episodes that supervened still more: they are so very social—so in-the-round, it was as if all that should be most carefully guarded—all that's loathsome and dread—were suddenly to be everted: an internal organ, slathered in mucus, still pumping with blood, and lying there . . . *on the grass.*

The plaster in the hall is still dented from her blows. John said he'd fill them and retouch the paintwork. But he hasn't. Elaine supposes this is to punish her, insidiously, since normally he takes such joy in patching stuff up. But for what? She'd said nothing much to anyone—certainly not that jackass Voss. Flushed with excitement, his expression as goofily proud as she can ever remember having seen it, John blurted it out to Betty and Ted—and the following evening, following their second Thanksgiving dinner, Elaine admitted she'd told Bobbie.

But how did the fact of one man's promotion become a rumor concerning another's?

In the immediate aftermath of her husband's call, Elaine had sat with her ringing head in her stinging hands. But, however infuriated he was, however insufferably mimsy as he looked down on her from on high, he'd still been the one to propose a strategic alliance: they would both do all they could to discover who the real culprit, or culprits, had been.

Really, if only there were a clear policy of telling the men immediately what their position was, rather than dragging the whole affair out over weeks through all sorts of veiled meetings, ad hoc committees, and quasi-confirmations . . .

Well, none of it would've happened.

Back at the parking lot, Ted lifts first Stella then little Karen up and over into the back of the jeep, their muddy snow boots kicking. Off to one side, John and Betty are saying their goodbyes. Glancing over, Elaine catches the other woman looking at her—she can't understand her expression for a moment, but then she does.

It's only momentary—yet it's revelatory: Elaine had never considered this possibility before, that Ted is *using this thing with me to arouse her jealousy* . . .

There's been no proper rapprochement between them— how could there be? Mona Voss is about as close as Cornell gets to a femme fatale—which perhaps explains her husband's paranoia—she has red lipstick permanently slashed across her sultry face, and never carries a light. How could she in that itty-bitty patent leather evening clutch? So, the men she asks for one are obliged to look deep down into the milky ravine between her breasts . . . How they'd love to drop something . . . down there.

It's easy to see how Ted not only making love to, but actually screwing, Mona would bring the Troppmanns to a crisis point—Elaine, though? She can't flatter herself in this regard—besides, Elizabeth really is perfectly chic, all the more so for her eggheady ways: the scientifically serious skirts—the very simple, and quite likely very dear, jewelry.

She's the mother of his children as well—and Elaine cannot help having a deep respect for the institution of marriage, while having contempt for those petty fools who always *abide by the rules* . . .

She glances over at her again: the other woman stands in a sporting pose, Elaine thinks: hands on her slim hips—her neat triangle of a nose angled up towards John, her smile considered and . . . *elliptical*, as if she's wondering whether to *play this ball* . . . Ted's the sort, Elaine thinks, to respond powerfully to indifference—he has a little boy's constant need to be listened to—and here's his chilly spouse, standing in the mud, and ignoring him while she pretends to be enthralled by John's *prattle* . . .

It's so unlike her.

They may not be good friends—but they're fast ones: and Betty's neutral, Elaine thinks, by nature: all passion banked rather than spent, her man controlled with the most softly acidulous statements, combined with *sidelong looks* . . .

Whereas Elaine?

She wrenches the Buick's steering wheel around, stamps on the gas, and the squeaky old coupe bounces over the curb by the entrance to the parking lot.

Whoa! John says—while Billy, who's sitting between them in the front seat, falls across her lap.

Instead of parting, the two families are sticking together: *Come back and the kids can toast marshmallows and have some hot chocolate*, Ted suggested—which, in a way, was the last thing Elaine needed: the walk had been enough—the walk had been . . . *sublime*, and now she'd like to get away somewhere quiet and think about it: replay every moment, and when one particularly appeals to her for further analysis: freeze the film.

But Ted wants this—and unlike his self-contained spouse, Elaine can't help giving a man—almost any man— what he wants: I'm incontinent, she thinks, as, hunched forward, nose to the windshield, she scans the solid-seeming screen of greenery for the turnoff to the Troppmanns'. I try and stop myself—but I can't . . .

I'm a queer fish, alright—I went and peed under the rug in my bedroom . . . and when I'm getting a migraine . . . my mouth fills—like some goddamn magic cauldron in a Grimm fairy tale—with brackish saliva . . .

*Againannagain.*

What she'd feared most about the Voss debacle was that she'd be a laughingstock. As if she cares about these awful stiffs! But there is one man in whose eyes she'd like to appear as better than the Monas and Bobbies of this incestuous scene . . .

Another wrench—another yelp from Billy. John sits serene, a slight smile playing about his *still slighter* lips. The Buick is bouncing up the unpaved driveway, and its driver remembers the last time she and Ted danced together: her fingers spanning the back of his collar . . . I told him I wanted to buy him a tie—it was quite involuntary: he made me do it . . . He has this curious kinda *built-in orphan power* . . .

A stiff yank on the handbrake—the Hancocks, all three, sit still for a moment in the cooling auto, listening to the ticking and clicking of its hot and so recently agitated parts. Framed by the windshield, one wing of the Troppmanns' futuristic house appears *instructional* . . . An illustration of a family—kids in the living room, kneeling on the rug, plates and boxes of marshmallows before them, Mom and Pop bringing more stuff from the kitchen.

It's an odd moment, Elaine thinks, because in looking at them like this—coolly, objectively—we can't help judging ourselves on these terms, so necessarily finding ourselves . . . *wanting.*

It'd only taken a frank conversation between John and Caspar Voss to clear the matter up: Voss denied having told the Dean exactly who had told him about his non-promotion, but conceded it most definitely hadn't been Elaine— Harry Lemesurier must, her husband told her, have been confused.

Confused! The man's a manipulative lech—Elaine detected somewhere in all this the civet-scent of Mona Voss coming over all kittenish, but she didn't have the evidence, or the opportunity to cross-examine Lemesurier. While John, not being the forceful type, obviously made no use of his when they did, eventually, meet.

Seeing him a couple of weeks later, as she was leaving another faculty wives' gathering, Elaine had been tempted to have John's say for him. Why not? His promotion had been confirmed . . . but of course she hadn't.

There's an open fireplace in the Troppmanns' aquarium of a living room—a raised plinth, with a cast-iron dish surmounting it. Ted's setting fire to a bundle of kindling as they come in, and John says, I had no idea you guys belonged to the cult of Mithras . . .

Which is typical of him.

Billy goes to find the girls, who've abandoned their preparations—and by the time he returns, the adults have more drinks, and are sunk deep in the two couches facing Ted's sparking and crackling creation, with another Bloody Mary apiece to warm them up after the walk.

It's immediately clear things aren't going well: Stella's sulking, Billy announces, sounding half pleased, half disgusted about it. She says she doesn't care if she never sees another marshmallow again in her whole entire complete life . . .

Elaine wonders if the girl's taken umbrage at some unwitting slight of her son's . . . *or a witting one*, because he's made it perfectly clear several times now—and that's just within parental hearing—that he can't stand it when she looks at him like that. His mother knows precisely what sort of look he's referring to—she can't see it on her own avid features, but she senses it every time she looks at the girl's father.

Poor Stella! She has her mother's air of rectitude—but none of the poise that prevents Elizabeth from becoming a mere prude. She isn't a looker, either—the lopsided features and crooked grin are very attractive once animated by Ted's charm and self-assurance. But in the little-girl version they're simply ugly.

Then there's littler Karen—who's everything her sister isn't: a jolly sort of sprite, wreathed in smiles and ringlets, and precociously oozing feminine charms. Is it any surprise, seeing themselves so caricatured, that their parents cleave to one girl and recoil from her older sister? So, the situation continues to deteriorate—since like all unloved children, she retreats into herself, either playing with dolls—or, on those occasions she's compelled to be with other children, playing with them as if they *were dolls* . . .

Elaine, conscious she's overstepping all marks in all directions, thinks she's the ideal person to help—after all, hasn't she been semi-smothered by a charismatic father and rejected by a pretty mother? And doesn't she—condemned as she is to live in an all-male household—long for feminine company?

Watching Billy and Karen settle down contentedly in the next room to watch The Howdy Doody Show—which is what they do, in fact, *do-do*—Elaine appoints herself the elder Miss Troppmann's adult friend and mentor. No one need know—but, yes: she will keep a maternal eye on the girl, and quietly scheme to have her to stay over if her parents go away. Like some one-woman religious order, Elaine feels she maybe could mold Stella's sensibility, helping her to become a happier and more outgoing child. The unuttered—even to herself—consequence of which might well be . . .

Well! What father wouldn't be grateful to such an exemplary female friend of the . . . *family*? One who, were she to stay long enough, might well become part of it. Because all families have this in common, she believes: there comes a time when there's no excuse for not leaving.

\*    \*    \*

Clarabell comes with the Hancocks. A middle-aged and moon-faced man in clown's white makeup and a bald wig, who wears a striped one-piece costume. Rather than speaking, he sits in back with Billy, and makes conversation with the honks of a little motor horn rather than words.

Then, when they reach Hemlock Street, Billy shucks off the striped suit and reassumes his own sweet character—leaving this grotesque creature to accompany his mother, who, having made her excuses—as she has so many times before—disappears upstairs, and closes the bedroom door with an air of finality she wishes she could emphasize by locking it. But then that's another of their dumb progressive family rules, isn't it? We Hancocks have no secrets from one another—by which is meant what, precisely? That we all know we all have bowel movements? That we urinate? Because the sort of secrets we truly have from one another aren't such that removing all the keys and bolts from the internal doors of the house, jumbling them in a mason jar, and putting this on a shelf in the basement will result in any great honesty.

No, she concludes as she sits in her stocking feet on the side of the bed, uncomfortably bloated by their rich friends' largesse—the only result of this openness has been that their son is just as vigilant when it comes to his parents' ablutions as they are: he, too, is an expert in surveillance . . . and its evasion.

Clarabell sits down beside Elaine, smelling of stale cigarette smoke and flophouses. She silently says to him: Fine, if they're going to neglect her, I won't . . . a restatement then augmented by this further fantasy: the Troppmanns, of course, have a maid—a tall, thin, light-skinned colored woman called Mrs. Hoskins, and in Elaine's Fireside Theater this heartwarming scene will unfold: Mesdames Hancock and Hoskins becoming fast friends through their mutual interest in this dispirited child . . .

The unforeseen—yet entirely welcome—consequence being, in turn, the breaking down of all racial barriers. Not just between Stella's two guardian angels, but more generally—an enlightenment that cannot help but affect Ted deeply, making him fall utterly in—

Honk! Honk! Honk! To be mocked . . . to be incapable of suppressing her own self-mockery, which is undoubtedly what makes her—Honk! Honk!—susceptible to the mockery of others . . . We-ell, that has to be the logical fate of any puppet dumb enough to remain tethered to the delusion *she has no strings* . . . when the truth is, she's *thoroughly enmeshed*, while the real live humans surrounding—toying with her—are always making double entendres *I don't understand* . . .

Elaine listens.

No mocking laughter—the little wooden house is silent save for its characteristic . . . *deathwatch ticking.*

She pictures her husband and son—John sitting in the old overstuffed blue armchair he prefers, reading in a pool of light that grows warmer as the evening draws in, and Billy kneeling on the rug by his feet, deftly feeding little colored beads onto plastic threads. The old leather pouf is shared between them: half covered in papers, half in beads. A strange sort of craze, but then *aren't they all . . . ?*

There's no point in envying them—for as long as the one reads and notes while the other selects and threads, they've achieved a desirable state of being that always eludes Elaine: *unselfconsciousness* . . .

She goes, sliding over the floorboards on her stocking feet, to her current hiding place and, retrieving her diary, retreats once more to the bedroom, where she and Clarabell resume their Honk! Honk! positions. Leafing through the pages, she's anguished right away—so much self-indulgence! Page after page of it, all focussed on Ted Troppmann: his thoughts, his feelings, his intentions . . .

To any reader who stood outside their charmless circle, what would this seem like? Not just page after page of girlishly purple prose, but a pervasive current of paranoia—yes! Fears expressed in the form of asides about the Honk! Honk! hierarchy in the Cornell English department: who was invited—who dumped, who was liked—who reviled? And all of it festooned and garlanded with migrainous doodles—spirals, stars, polka dots, and rainbows that mingle, promiscuously, with the calendars she's created showing the dates of her migraines and menses, the purpose of which is to try to predict when these two maladies will Honk! Honk! converge.

All day long Elaine's been resisting this queer feeling—that she isn't merely an outsider to the faculty gang, or to the human race conceived of in its most general sense, but to herself—she stands outside herself once more, seeing all Mrs. Hancock does and says and thinks and feels, through the wrong end of some futuristic instrument, like Billy's View-Master, one capable of capturing a single moment in her life, including all her actions and thoughts, with the fidelity of a modern camera snapping Bowery bums . . . *or the boys taking Iwo Jima.*

Honk! Honk!

All day, she's been aware of there being something she's neglected—but only now, with the diary open in her lap, and the hobo clown beside her, does she realize what it is—no, not taking Karma to the vet to be neutered, and no, not buying this, mending that, or discarding the other. It's more that there was an attitude she should've been adopting today. One necessary to guard against a grave eventuality.

. . . At the Troppmanns' place, around ten thirty in the morning—there were streaks of yellowing old snow striping the browning lawn, and sequoias leaned into—and in some instances over—that marvellous house: a series of glass chambers, in which its inhabitants came and went and posed in plain view for their visitors, who, having pulled into the flagged parking circle, got out and started up the path towards the front door . . .

Started—but Elaine had been dismayed by the way that well-nigh mystic portal *kept its distance* . . . retreating from her—remaining representation, *not real* . . . For a brief, sickly, and haunting moment the crack between the two that's always there widened . . . and widened, while into Elaine's mouth came the sour taste of vertigo.

Each month, she speculates, my mechanism adjusts such that cogs, wheels, and levers *soaked in blood and bile* ratchet everything forward—the whole world, forward. Yet, despite the machinery, there's no regularity to this—despite the machinery: Nature plays it close to her skin vest. Sometimes it's the migraine that arrives a day or three earlier than expected—other times it's her period. Ye-es! she sobs aloud: this is what she was supposed to keep in mind every moment of this day of happy forgetfulness.

For if it's a commonplace that women's premenstrual tensions deceive them precisely as to what they betoken— less well known is that migraine sufferers are subject to exactly the same syndrome: ignoring all the evidence of their increasingly disordered senses until it's too late.

A great shame . . . *I never can get in gear*—and one that affronts Elaine, since what's the point of being plagued by anxiety if it doesn't forewarn. What she needs is a varia- tion on the JEW Line—a protective ring of doctors of all specializations, all of the highest ethical caliber, all ded- icated solely to her care, including warning her when *to take shelter . . .*

Elaine's mother still hones her own sharp tongue on her friends'. Or, to be strictly accurate: the three brittle fakers she plays gin rummy with two or three afternoons a week. Her prophecy is wholly concerned with others' imperson- ations: *You're too easy . . . and you won't be able to put anything over on her . . . She's flattering you 'cause she wants something from you . . .*

In Lily Rosenthal's world, women are the adepts of psy- war, who soften the enemy up in advance of that monstrous regiment of men—only problem being: they are that enemy, too. On her account, men's conflicts are heroically mano a mano: every Ted and John an Achilles and a Hector, locked in single combat beneath the walls of Troy. Whereas women's? Well, a civil war, and all the bloodier for its causes, which are to be found, she believes, in women's irredeemable physicality: their messy flux . . .

. . . Which isn't helpful at all—hateful, in fact: as it's always driven her daughter to shame . . . *the diaphragm, clawed from the mouth of my womb.* One Elaine sees in this sweaty stocking, this second unpeeled from her alien, white leg, and coiled to form another *flesh-colored appliance* . . .

. . . she's left lying on the rag rug beside the bed—she flies to the bathroom, where she dumps herself down on the can and pees copiously, all the while spitting between her parted thighs, mouthful upon mouthful of brackish saliva.

No.

Helpful mothering would've been to school her daughter in the arts of seduction, and infuse her with sex appeal: forewarned is less than useless if you aren't *forearmed* . . . Which they often are, moving awkwardly towards you, their penises erect, looking as if they were giving birth, breech, and this was *the baby's arm* . . .

Elaine spits *strings of liquid pearls, my only finery* . . . and has the gumption, at least, to acknowledge this: Right now, John is the only man who could stop me menstruating—I lack the nerve for any affair, let alone one that serious.

It's different with her migraines—on at least one occasion, a full-blown attack was averted by *vigorous screwing* . . . She stands, tears off two squares of toilet paper, wipes herself, turns to the sink, and thinks: what a silly little woman—and so far off *in the depths of mirror world* . . .

She rubs the flannel around her face and neck, intent on removing the *shmaltzy* coagulation of sweat and makeup from her *chicken skin* . . . On another occasion, it'd been aggressive housework: staring at the iridescent foam, banking up and up as the drum spun, she'd realized it was the beginning of a migraine, and, as soon as the washing and rinsing were done, she'd yanked out the dank skein of shirts and shorts, separated then fed a random garment into the wringer's rubber gums, thrown herself on its handle with a vengeance, and so by some occult mechanism . . . *eased off the pressure.*

Not now—it's too late now.

She hears the screech of the el on Jamaica Avenue—sees KOSHER BOSHER stencilled on a grimy window all cluttered up with *dead ducks* . . . and smells the smell from her childhood that doesn't so much induce nausea as it is *nausea itself!* pure and simple. In her chubby thirteen-year-old hand is a cardboard box of caramels bought from Gross Bros., the wholesale candy business on the corner of 113th Street.

Ha-ha! Is it a memory—or a bad joke: the fat siblings' candies melting in the box . . . in her hand . . . then running in sickly sweet rivulets down her throat until her tummy's *slopping with liquid sugar* . . . while no matter how many times she swallows, she can't rid herself of their residue.

It's too late, now, for painkillers—while Nembutal isn't advisable: on more than one occasion a stuporous Elaine has vomited in the bed.

She staggers back to her bed and—after yanking the shades down and snatching the muslin curtains shut— tears the covers off. She removes her glasses, and stands, swaying dangerously as she disrobes—first pulling then peeling, until she's naked enough to fling herself across the half-bared mattress. The bottom sheet has come away—she grinds her face in the blue-and-white ticking, and sees plotted on its lines all the ups and downs of her social life. What a rube! Imagining their stock was going to rise—when she's worthless . . . and John's nothing . . .

The O'Briens are a much more sophisticated proposition —for all that they affect down-home manners: organizing folksy get-togethers at their house, where innies and out-ies, hairy chins and hairier armpits congregate to scrape fiddles and washboards, and drink whiskey from the jar. Truth is, it's an act quite as much as it is when they play with their string quartet at Bradley Hall—which they did last year. A starry affair, attended by various of Cornell's luminaries, and after which there was a reception, group photographs—people had loved them.

Not that the Hancocks were in attendance—because then, as now, poor Mrs. Hancock had been *indisposed* . . .

Indisposed—or rather, *un-disposable*, because she's too horribly incarnated to be got rid of—a corpse in a dream sequence, propped up by the jardiniere, or pretending to be an ornate table decoration.

Elaine rolls heavily over onto her back.

She wishes she were a sexless old maid in some mimsy upper-class Englishwoman's mimsy novel—the kind who, if she ever did have a vagina, never made much use of it, and whose intimate secretions came in discrete packages from Harrods, *wrapped in brown paper with that distinctive velvety patina and tied with string* . . .

Her pulse pounds in her ears—some ghastly slave driver keeping the beat, while her heart labors, and saliva by the bitter bucketful is winched up her gullet and into her mouth, so she's forced to swallow and swallow . . .

. . . and swallow again.

A grim parody of drinking.

Shivering, she pulls the covers over her prone form to create a kind of wigwam or otherwise instinctive burrow . . . *Oh, I wish I were a mole in the ground—like a mole in the ground, I'd root that mountain down* . . . Call-and-response plaited then paid out in one agonized threnody that drops down, lank and wistful, from the old three-story tenement with the iron grille on its windows—the one that just got poorer and more derelict, patched up more and more with plywood and tar paper, until not even the poorest of Jews would live there and the Negro folk moved in instead. *La-azybones, sleepin' in the sun*—and was then slung from awning to hump-bellied awning all along Jamaica Avenue, such heat! There's no heat like the heat of adolescence.

If not a Camp Fire Girl—or a little beast *whose fur*, as Ted said by the falls, *needs wibbling*, then at least somewhere far from here, far from the faculty club, where the principal medicine woman of Cayuga Heights, Selma Lemesurier, is forever turning to her, in front of the hot buffet, the scoop of mashed potato that's just been swivelled into existence for her, white and round and as dully shiny as a *human hip joint* . . .

Forever turning—the steam from her plate a smoky cone in the downlights, her top lip puckering then *ruching up* into a *pelmet* of disapproval, her mouth giving this line: *Well, yes, Elaine . . . I've heard quite a number of things about you . . . from Bobbie O'Brien.*

Upsy-daisy—which is what Elaine used to say when she lifted Billy aloft: Upsy-daisy . . . The cat is in her burrow now, and purring as loudly as a car's engine idling . . . *in a garage—with the doors shut.* All at once—Elaine dreams.

A cab pulls over to pick her up from the corner of Geneva and Seneca—by her dentist's office, downtown. She leans into the passenger window and both her breasts fall from the scoop neck of her blouse—they are enormously elongated, and covered in black, scaly skin.

Elaine is unabashed: Could you please just drive me around the block a few times? she asks the shadowy cabbie. I've nowhere in particular to go . . .

In back, she arranges a number of small brown-paper-wrapped parcels on the seat beside her, then adjusts her fussy lace bodice.

The cabbie's eyes watch her from the top of the windshield—a slice of mouth below them says, We gotta get outta here, lady, 'fore all this fall clean on top of us . . .

He means the Gothic spire of the Catholic church and the Italianate belvedere of the Congregationalist, together with the great waves of brick and masonry surging beneath them. What does she know of these sects? Doodly-squat. Only that they're cold and implacable—exerting many pounds of chilly pressure on every square inch of her sallow skin, and when it's nicked or otherwise breached, pouring into the world, so displacing . . . everything.

Let's skedaddle, she says—and they do, this little tribe, driving out from the dark defile between God-given oppositions: Protestant and Catholic, man and woman, good and evil, gentile and Jew, West and East . . . What is there to be said of them, the goyim? She couldn't even peek in the dark doors of their gaunt people-barns until she and John were married, and then . . . ?

The same old erasure: an empty nook—a lot of expectancy. The Jews—even the liberal ones—took God's effigy out of the nook, put it back in: in-out, in-out, in-out . . . What was the gimmick? Presumably they thought this lightning substitution would translate from the symbolic to . . . what it symbolizes. The goyim didn't even bother with such mummery: if they were Catholics they just stared at their dead god, bemoaning His squalid fate—and if Protestants, they put an X in the boxes formed by their austere altars, because despite all the graft He *has their vote* . . .

. . . and when it comes to His message, it's clear: this is the spiritual arm of the Times—since it's all the Good News that's fit to print. Elaine took Journalism 208, so she's noted down in Pitman the who, what, when, where, and why of the ancient world—Moses in his basket wailing—Abraham in his tent, screwing. The Samaritan on the road to . . . Taughannock.

They drive fast—slowing down at intersections, but not stopping: Jee-zuss! Elaine exclaims the first time this happens, and then again: Jee-zuss! But the cabbie pays no attention. This lurching progress continues—to steady herself, Elaine focusses in between lurches on a single tree or stop sign up ahead. But then they're right upon it in a blur of greenery.

She lights up and sits back on the surprisingly plush upholstery. It's a gas, she thinks—a gasssss: bowling along like this, the trees screening the lake from the roadway flickering in the sunlight, the smoke from her cigarette first staggering in the draft from the cracked window, then diving through it.

All along the West Side Highway—or anywhere up the Hudson, for that matter—Elaine would feel the black waters rising up above the parapet wall or other embankment: the glossiness of the boils and quick-moving whirlpools disfiguring its convex bulk suggested not only the hardness and turgidity of the river, but its depth and turbulence. And now, someone has taken a great brushful of this black-brownness and spread it along the verges of this lakeside parkway for mile upon mile, so as to create a regular pattern of brownstones and intersections—

Stop!

They do so, abruptly—and Elaine is flung forward off the seat: Jee-zuss!

Where's that butt gone? It could, she thinks, have flown from my fingers and, as a result of a complex series of air currents, wormed under the self-unscrewing cap of the gas tank, so that BOOM!

It's soft and hatefully squidgy in the cab's footwell. Elaine is conscious of Claire Beamish being in it with her, together with two or three of her beloved and ever-bawling babies—Elaine feels the same lush upholstery here on the

floor as she did on the seats, and realizes it's the skin flayed
from Claire's breasts, ever engorged with milk . . . and
mastitis.

There's something of Selma Lemesurier's blousy superiority in the fetid air of this seraglio as well as trampled
underfoot—while Betty Troppmann, her ankles crossed,
her arms embracing her legs, and her perfectly manicured hands clutching her beautifully painted toes, is
nakedly present like an expensive jewel: Oh, Elaine . . . she
drawls . . . What're you. Doing. Here.

What a clubwomanish, stagey emphasis she puts on
Doing and Here, Elaine thinks—while at the same time
knowing perfectly well: the nude woman doesn't sound
like Betty at all. Not really. It's one thing to be naked in
the privacy of your own home—but in public? Why, she'd
be distrait.

Dames, eh?

Fake Betty's unbelting then unbuttoning Elaine's jacket,
then unbuttoning Elaine's blouse and hauling out her pro-
digious breasts—long, black, and oily as hawsers uncoiling across a wharf. Gathering hanks of breast up—while
grabbing yet more coils with a longshoreman's hook that's
providentially appeared—Elaine wonders at the way her
début is going—that, and the smell of Billy's wax crayons,
or is it ether?

Fake Betty's hands are quick and deft—Elaine's are
never that sure, much as she prides herself on being able to
do fine work: purl-stitching, embroidery, selvedge. Didn't
she crochet Fake Betty's chestnut pubic hair—and sew it on
so neatly you can hardly tell? Fake Betty presses her small

cold mouth against Elaine's—and Elaine feels her sharp and abrasive little tongue scraping at her lips—which is neither unpleasant—nor unarousing.

That'll be a dollar and two bits, says the cabbie—he's opened the back door of the cab and all of the day's brightness shoulders its way in.

Disentangling herself from Betty, Elaine rises upright. The cab is parked in the Troppmanns' flagged turning circle, and their help, Mrs. Hoskins, stands behind and to one side of the cabbie. She has a plain white linen napkin draped precisely over her arm.

Fake Betty is inclined to dispute this: It's never cost that much before . . .

Elaine thinks, Aha! At last, I've got her—she's cheap. And would make this characterological analysis public were it not that Fake Betty hasn't uttered a word, only sent meaning-beams through her eyeholes. Meanings that the cabbie is either unaware of or couldn't give a rat's ass about, as he repeats his demand, in a thick, but unplaceable European accent: That'll be a dollar and two bits.

May I, m'dear? he continues, handing Elaine out of the carriage.

She stands, fluttering her eyes at him, and rearranging her white silk and satin-tasselled stole so it lies just so, in the crooks of her elbows. Behind the cabbie, Betty and Mrs. Hoskins, having linked arms, are cavorting around one another. The white linen napkin lies spread out on the grass.

The cabbie looks around, and through his eyeholes Elaine sees the broad backyard, the barbecue area surrounded by

crazy paving, a canopy swing, a novelty lamp standard, one
of the girls' discarded bikes. In the middle ground, shaped
like . . . the eye of Horus, is a large flowerbed overflowing
with aggressively bright marigolds.

Haff you painted them yet? the cabbie asks.

I'm sorry?

Haff you? He's not being rhetorical—but insistent. He
means an actual depiction of an actual thing of some sort,
but what? She's at a loss—although she doesn't doubt for
a moment that he's right, and that she should've painted
them. But what sort of a painting? He can't be thinking of
something like her mother's watercolors of off-kilter flower
arrangements, or malformed female nudes. Maybe something less constrained.

Constrained? But then nothing's constrained—only
abject, bowed down before its fate. Elaine isn't nothing—
she's free and easy. If she wishes to stretch here, she can do
so. If she desires to leap right up, or crouch down entirely—
these actions, too, are entirely free and easy.

She knows she's awakened

the shreds of her dream lie about, as wrapping paper
does that's been hurriedly torn—yet she's in no hurry
to embrace, or even touch, this gift of a new existence.
Instead, she remains *spreadoutski*, wondering if it might
just be possible, by some shape-shifting feat, to regain
admission to this compelling realm of breakneck cab rides,
sapphic embraces, and peculiar mutations—Elaine's hands
go to her breasts, and she considers for the first time ever
the ethics of her favorite homiletic—*Let's not and say we
did*—which she employs, she now acknowledges,

to paralyze her small son, by

forever presenting him with a possibility of anarchic action. One that has been, preemptively, cancelled—and substituted for with rank hypocrisy . . .

These aren't her own sheets—and nor is this the odor of the Hemlock Street house, a compounding of tobacco smoke and wax polish during the winter months, that remains staling during the summer ones—then is compounded some more. This place smells sappy—and herbal at the same time: crewneck sweaters topped by square jaws are massing for eggnog . . . *I fucking abhor eggnog.*

Elaine revisits the very particular squeal of mechanical anguish the machinery gave as the Philadelphia train pulled into Penn Station. By no means her most familiar entrance to Manhattan—but the most storied, for her at least, were those occasions when she went up to the city from college the year after she'd transferred to Penn State, and was beset by a sense of losing the city, and with it the greater part of her childhood—the young are such consummate nostalgists, she knows now, because they have so little past to cherish.

Now she'd cheerfully jettison a year—maybe, three. But then, actively trading on her big-city upbringing for kudos with her new classmates, she'd made a fetish of this sojourn in Kew Gardens, which was really just as sleepy as small-town Ohio or Pennsylvania. But to hear her speak of it, there'd been a mystical union between her blood and New York's scarified soil: it hadn't been that heehawing ass Harry Greenwald who'd really had . . . *the heart to conceive, the understanding to direct*, and *the hand to execute* the tricky maneuver required to get . . . *inside my pants*, but in some strange manner *the city itself* . . .

The admittedly filthy and scabrous embrace of which, Elaine nonetheless felt, possessed great strength and betokened equal security: if these blacktop moats and poured-concrete donjons couldn't provide refuge, what would? Detraining and, unlike the teeming crowds, deliberately slowing her pace to enjoy the concourse's fantasia on the themes of glass and steel, Elaine would then step out onto Eighth Avenue, walk a hundred yards, and look back to see the station's façade: a mock-up of some long-gone Roman baths.

And think: If something this big can brazenly attempt such fakery . . . Well . . .

It never lasted, though, this hepped-up strut, hip out, head high, *worst foot forward*— Because the truth was that while she may've arrived at a womanly estate, had drinks at twenty-one, and danced at the Starlight Room, and although she may've clattered back and forth on the subway, zoomed up and down in elevators, even saying such things as: *I'll get you the file on the Hokusai set, Mr. Aaronson*, then . . . *sashayed away*, she'd never got far enough in any direction—social, cultural, intellectual, political, or *damn and damner* physical—to escape those curved and rolling avenues, lined with spindly, unnameable trees and foursquare apartment blocks, brick-built, each dwelling mortaring its inhabitants into the general mass of humanity, that, while they had once seemed to her a world apart, she came to understand—in her jolted bones, her gritty pores—were, far from being separated by the East River, in such close proximity to Manhattan that the soured sweetness of her adolescence—its painful pangs for prettier girls, its often seedy and lubricious interludes with uglier boys, its utter and inevitable disaffection from parents who, by the time Elaine was sixteen, and no longer a virgin, had no more real significance for her than *their listing in Polk's*—and in particular, its crushing ennui—had gone there with her. Kew Gardens lumbers after her still, such that no matter how far she does end up travelling, upon her return it will await her: a rainy, chill afternoon in early winter, the drops, already sullied, falling a long way beside the streaked and saturated brickwork, before joining the rusty rivulets that twine down the iron stairs and balustrades of the fire escapes.

No. Inasmuch as the city excites Elaine—it enervates her. Besides, on this much John and she had always been in full agreement: it's no place to raise a kid.

Her head remains heavy, pressed deep down into the haven of a strange pillow.

In that expansive state, between sleep and waking, where it's as hard to distinguish between reverie and its reflection as it is to trace the join between a perfectly fitted carpet and a floor-to-ceiling textured wall covering, she remains capable, still, of admitting to this, her greatest and most faithless dereliction: that she'd truly desired to skip it all—the flirting, petting, screwing, marrying, and birthing—and be some place and time like this instead: this honeyed and slow moment, in which she awakes from a refreshing afternoon nap to find herself in her beautifully appointed contemporary home.

Alone—and delighted to be so.

True, she's married to a screwy, intelligent guy, who's an overpoweringly sensual lover—he'll appear at the door, and it will feel as if his Braille cheek is buried in her lap and he's *moving his lips* as he reads her. True, too, that they have two poised and already accomplished daughters, but the point is, it's so much more rewarding to enjoy all this in its absence—and to stay, secure in the knowledge of loving and being loved in these ways, as she rises, casts the coverlet aside, and advances on bare soles towards the ensuite, pees, returns to the hushed bedroom, lit only by the single right-angled triangle of light that's fallen through the gap between the floor-length drapes, where, caught by it—and so, shining in an unearthly manner—she sees a skirt draped over the back of a scoop-backed Danish modern chair, one which—since both style and size are appropriate—she decides may as well be *my own*.

A golden glass cube poised in a recessed shelf—its interior a honeycomb of glowing cells. A canvas depicting a single magenta dot on a cyan ground beneath a yellow sky—which she digs. The wide bed has a fitted headboard with bedside tables and reading lamps. The color scheme is muted—tawny, blond-wood, beige. She knows that there are no personal effects in those no doubt smooth-opening drawers—that this is a spare room.

Although the rest of the place is no more cluttered—and everywhere Elaine pads, still with her soles bared, she finds the same restraint and harmony, while what ornaments

there are gleam in the beams of sunlight lancing between
louvres that, she knows, are part of the house's unique
design. Every time she's been here order has prevailed—
maybe that's why, despite every sign this was an appalling
idea, *after frantic placation on my part*, she got John to
bring her.

Why ruin his afternoon and everyone else's as well over
this? It would only be to prolong the emergency—and turn
what she prefers to label a minor collapse into a fair- to
middling-sized breakdown.

He'd been in his office correcting the proofs of a review
article. He still did this: told her precisely which of the
word games he'd be playing when he abandoned her and
their child. Especially if it was on a weekend—and this
Saturday there'd been a plan to take Billy to Flat Rock to
swim—maybe Frank could come, too? But then Ted called
and offered the prospect of the sainted bloody boat—a
powerful attractor for John.

There was quite a lot of toing and froing about these
arrangements, with kids being canvassed during calls such
that reedy voices piped I don't wanna! in the background.
Elaine felt as she often did—that while many possible combinations of personnel, timings, and entertainments might
be considered, it wasn't so much that her wishes weren't
factored in as that she no longer possessed the will required
to give them any form—let alone substance.

This had enraged her—there'd been a sharp exchange in
the kitchen, and the next thing she knew John had gone,
with Billy, his objective being to dump him at the O'Briens'
for a couple of hours while he went to his office and graded

papers. In the afternoon, he'd pick him up—if he wanted—
and take him out to the boathouse, to join whichever of the
Troppmanns were going out on the lake.

As for Elaine, well, there's always nothing, isn't there—
nothing to do, and nowhere to go as well: that's an option,
and one which looks palatable enough when you can't bear
the thought of another second beneath the sympathetic,
appraising, and, in the end, always belittling gaze of Bobbie
O'Brien, let alone its reality.

Padding, her feet still bare, along the main corridor of
the house—the pale polished parquet of which processes
along the partition wall, and spreads through the arches
and doorways she passes, which give glimpses into Ted's
study, the dining room, the living one—each a more or less
perfect tableau of what the modern and affluent interior
should be, because there's a sense of stricture about the
Troppmann ménage—for all his ease and her poise.

The air is close—the heat comes in from all angles.

Ted inveighs against air-conditioning, and talks up the
house's revolutionary design: exterior louvres and under-
floor ventilation—but it doesn't appear to work: there's
a tightness in her chest—she feels at once alone, and
watched.

Across the wide angle between the two wings of the
house, she can see the kitchen. Mrs. Hoskins is sitting on a
stool at the breakfast counter, a soda bottle on the smooth
surface before her. Or maybe not—the figure is so angular,
its dress so plain, its limbs so structural: forming an assemblage of girders—Elaine doubts, quite suddenly, it's her at
all, rather a shadow thrown down by those revolutionary

louvres, or, if it is a figure, it's that of a robot, one which can simulate not just human appearance, human emotion as well.

Puffy-eyed still from the *Asphodel Meadows* . . . Elaine freezes and feels the sweat-dampened curls ungumming from the back of her neck. She's slept so long—through a revolution, no less—that while she knows the world of yesterday to've been a humdrum, servile sort of existence, the new one transfixes her as well.

The motionless figure in the kitchen is unsettling Elaine more and more—if that isn't a soda bottle, what else could it be, *skin, the coverall we're all . . . in*? The clammy cotton peels away from her armpits and the small of her back. She has an impulse to stride down the dog-legged corridor into the kitchen, and *pounce on Mrs. Hoskins . . .* Already, she sees them, their hearts drumming against each other's chests, as they stand, embracing, on the black-and-white checkerboard linoleum.

In April, she was standing in front of Bailey Hall when a tour bus pulled up and the MJQ got out: all tall, thin, elegant men—the word Nilotic came to Elaine from somewhere the violet hour had sustained, muddied and languid, for millennia. All manic grins, the kids from the entertainment committee hurried down the steps to welcome them, and ushered them up. She recognized Milt Jackson, who acted polite enough, if suitably remote. The group had brought a kid of their own with them, who had a red polo shirt on and very new and stiff jeans: Mind it! the vibraphonist snapped back at him as he pivoted on the top step, before disappearing between the imposing columns and into the building.

Elaine had crossed the road and walked around the tour bus—the kid hadn't registered any threat to the leather-covered instrument cases piled up in the back seats: flaring cones, slabs, and drum shapes that put her in mind of the basic geometric models she'd got for Billy when he was small.

She'd been on campus more than an hour early for the concert. The sitter had arrived prematurely, and rather than hang around in this alien environment—an intimacy she both hoped they might share and speculatively envied— she left her and Billy to it. But when she'd got there, she couldn't decide whether to go and find Ted in his office, or her husband in his, so wandered over to the venue.

She noticed the slab-shaped instrument case in particular because she loves the way Jackson plays the vibraphone: each stroke so soft, sending each liquid note flowing into the next. She understands little of how the group animates John Lewis's theories about marrying Baroque counter-point with the rhythms and melodies of the modern era, but her husband's only half joking when he condemns all such innovators, describing these particular ones as *the door chimes that welcome in the barbarians*. Reason enough to get the tickets.

It'd been, Elaine considers—one palm now lightly in contact with the window, so half obscuring the figure in the kitchen—the evening when whatever it was that was going on between the Hancocks and the Troppmanns became a whole lot more complicated. From her perspective it was all about rapport—she and Ted have it, which leads them to exchange criticism as lightly as they do confidences . . .

OK, perhaps she shouldn't've sniped at him—but for Christ's sake, surely it's nothing to've made him feel small, and to want to apologize? He does this with alacrity every time—he's always sorry, and wanting to be forgiven—

The figure in the kitchen resolves its own enigma by standing up into Mrs. Hoskins. Having forgotten her earlier sense of profound uncanniness, Elaine recoils—the last thing she wants to do is talk to this woman, who, on the couple occasions she's tried raising with her—in a roundabout, probing way—the matter of Stella's very obvious unhappiness, and its possible causes, has responded with such studied neutrality that Elaine's been arrested, minutes or hours later, by the intimidating realization *I've been told* . . . An admonition far more effective, when it comes to coaxing from her embarrassingly formative memories —*I used to pee under the rug* . . . —than any stratagem Freudenberg ever employed.

The audience in Bailey Hall gave the jazz group a standing ovation—and went on applauding and whistling for so long, Elaine had thought the contrast with their earlier rapt attention little short of demonic: *Those faces!*—a ruddy, shaking jelly, devoid of any individuality. The MJQ were the conservative cultists of cool—the Cornell students and faculty their angst-ridden adepts, whose intense nervosity resulted in them foot-tapping and head-nodding their way into a sort of wobbling inanition.

Looking from the mohair sweaters and lank bangs back to the stage, where the musicians, dressed as bankers,

manipulated their instruments with actuarial detachment—
calculating the life expectancy of a note well in advance
of its birth and subsequent development—it occurred to
Elaine for the first time that *we need them*, by which she
at last understood this: that what enabled her, despite her
dark-sallow skin and caricatural nose, to pass, was them
and their persecution.

At the faculty club the only table was right beside the
ridiculous ferny feature wall, down which trickled a urin-
ous stream—they laughed about it to the colored kid waiting on them, who Elaine recognized from the Lemesuriers'
the previous November, and whose presence she took as an
omen. A good one.

She and Ted shared the chateaubriand.

Right before her nap she'd been standing at the head of the
short flight leading down to the flagged turning circle, feeling like the lady of the house, and saying goodbye to John
and Betty, when she noticed that Betty was wearing the
pin he'd bought her for her birthday: a small asymmetric
jade lozenge, set on a slightly larger silver one. She nearly
said something about it—because a boat trip is the kind of
activity that potentially involves losses.

John got it for her on the trip they took to New York—
which, in turn, was a plan hatched after the MJQ concert,
so, in a way, Elaine felt it'd all been her doing, and if it
was any kind of a success, credit was due to her. It had
been a bold venture—one they wouldn't have undertaken
with any of their other Ithaca friends. The pin, with other
and curiouser brooches, was attached to a velvet-covered

display frame, set up in the cluttered window of an antique shop just south of Union Square.

It was a place she and John had mooched around when they were first together. The old Jew who runs it is from Baghdad, or somewhere equally caricatural. He sports ridiculous silver rings on his pudgy fingers—one in the shape of a naked woman, bending backwards and grasping her own ankles. He sells Persian carpets and bits of old furniture as well as jewelry and other ethnic clutter.

The Troppmanns had stayed at the Waldorf—the Hancocks at the Roosevelt, which Elaine chose to present to Betty as an amusing eccentricity on their part. Elaine recalled the big, slightly gloomy function rooms, with their vast electroliers dangling from their gilded ceilings, from a classmate's wedding she attended when she was at Queen's College. Bevvies of puce-faced girls and young women, close to fainting away as their tight bodices squeezed them into their voluminous skirts—the ladies' a dressing station for dealing with their half-contrived clothing disasters. The groom a redhead who burned so much under the lights his kippah *levitated*, and looking at him, and through him to his resemblances, the guests, pessimists to a fault, thought . . . *whichever direction a relative comes from, he's always trouble . . .*

Anyway, Elaine had said, isn't it kinda weird staying in a hotel in your hometown?

Said it—because she's felt it herself on the rare occasions she's done so: pulling her nightie over her head, or removing the cellophane from the water glass—felt that the real Elaine was back home in Ithaca, a distant location, but one from which she can nevertheless be clearly seen by her wandering other half.

Seen—and seen right through. A sensation of powerful estrangement: *Nowhere is home!*—and when it comes to what Freudenberg calls dissociation, way up there with her most flamboyant crises.

But Betty said they'd lived too far out of town when she was a kid, besides, they never went into Manhattan much, so the city still seemed like somewhere else to her . . .

A semblance the others, including Elaine and John, had vicariously enjoyed: they behaved like total out-of-towners, not scrupling to enjoy the most plebian pleasures—such as a cone of caramelized peanuts, on a brisk and gritty walk across the Brooklyn Bridge. She can't say—or doesn't want to, even in the privacy of her own head—whose idea it had been to go to the strip club, but it'd been hers, or Ted's, and it'd been a swell one—*about as far as it went* . . . which was a shell-backed booth covered in green vinyl, a gin rickey, four more, lots of nervous hee-hawing and guffawing and *so said all of us* . . . and an ice bucket with tinsel glued around it, and a little dais the same: all details retrieved from the evening's mania, which had begun there, when, despite being pretty stinking already, Elaine had been so struck by the first girl: so vulnerable as to shock her into sober awareness . . . *of my own.*

The six or seven who'd followed her hadn't effaced this with their own confidence in their hefty and heavily powdered nudity. Their faces hadn't been just defiant, as the single roving spotlight fingered them, and the hack trio in the minuscule pit fingered their instruments—but triumphant:

their mouths were all shapely, their noses all small—their breasts quite firm and proud, which might, Elaine thought, be occupational. But the first girl had been thin—so thin, there was a gap between the tops of her meagre thighs *the size and shape of a mailbox slot*, while the pasties stuck to her nipples shimmied as she shivered with embarrassment.

Age would definitely wither her. It already had.

In the corridor, on the way to the can, there was his dark shadow, and Elaine's nipples had burned—she'd been more ardent than ever, *shameless, really* . . . drawing him to her, hard, grinding her thigh between his, *hard* . . . and pushing her tongue into his mouth, hard, so she could feel his heart trip-hammering against her ribs, even as his penis pulsed against her hip, and she realized that tonight was one of those nights of his, the ones when he urges his listeners to Step in my rocket and don't be late, Baby, we're pullin' out 'round half past eight, Goin' round the corner to get our fill, Everybody in my car's gonna take a little pill . . .

Which Elizabeth, understandably, doesn't find funny at all.

It'd been one of those nights for Elaine, too, who'd taken the benny Ted had offered—and the others, wisely, declined.

Which was why her heart hammered quite as much as his—when they broke the clinch, falling away from each other to lie against the peeling paintwork, faces ghoulish in the sickly light of the caged bulb, b-b-b-b-boom-boom-boom! And went on hammering, as the cab bucketed back downtown, its snout snaffling up the genies of the man-holes, one after the next.

So drunk by then—but they'd wished to be drunker: as if this were the *earnest of our affection*! So they'd sat up 'til dawn in the grandiose gloom of the Roosevelt's silently echoing first-story salon, where the speckled mirrors recessed to infinity, and when, for the twentieth time, or so, Elaine took the exciting trek to the ladies' restrooms, along maroon-carpeted trails, she was amazed all over again by her own crazy clarity: every single little black or white tile shone lustrously and discretely, while she didn't so much pee as painstakingly *wring out* the sponge of her bladder with some system of internal *cranks, chains, cogs, and rollers* . . .

Her own face in the gilt-framed mirrors over the sinks appeared yet more stylized each time she apprehended it: an assemblage of planes and shapes, deeply shadowed. Her saliva came in tiny white tacky balls—and when she eventually made it back to Ted with this frontline dispatch, he told her this was called *spitting cotton* . . .

She'd brought with her the afterimages of those lights and mirrors, which hung, heavily brocading the sumptuous darkness, while they watched the old nightman. He groped his way towards them, the small leather satchel strapped to his belt, which must've contained all the keys, thud-tinkling against his thigh as he bumped into club armchairs and fleshy ottomans.

He brought ice, to freshen their drinks, and preserve their mood.

Then brought it again, and again.

Elaine believes they carry with them still all the complicity of that wild night. Only a week or so ago, Ted had mentioned the episode again, saying the tip he gave the nightman was *the best sawbuck I ever laid on anyone . . .*

But that wasn't it.

Elaine hadn't awoken until early afternoon the following day. In the centuries-long moments before she prised open her gummy lids, she'd experienced an inversion of the usual uncanniness: the real Elaine wasn't back in Ithaca, going about her daily business, but was, rather, lying in her room out in Kew Gardens, in her bedroom in their old apartment, with the striped wallpaper and the picture of the circus big top hung above the dresser . . .

. . . lying there, in the apartment she'd always thought of as one shoebox stacked along with so many others, and imagining a life ahead—one in which she was all grown up, married and with a child, although still enjoying wild nights out in Manhattan, one of which she lies recuperating from in her midtown hotel room, where . . .

. . . she'd lain until John arrived back to take her to the train. Lain, feeding quarters into the cumbersome contraption mounted on the radio, then switching from one preselected station to the next, all of them Puerto Rican, all broadcasting mambo after samba. The brittle rhythms shook her frantically, so dry little pellets of awareness rattled around in her head: sure, the complicity she and Ted now shared was deeper than ever. Confidences? There'd been plenty of those: boyhood had dallied with girlhood and begotten plenty of pleasing reminiscences—but inasmuch as they'd really *gotten to know each other better*, what it was Elaine knew now with certainty was that Ted would never, ever make love to her.

Moreover—which was quite possibly part of the same ghastly revelation—John had had enough of her. He wasn't angry anymore, hunching about the hushed bedroom, retrieving his clothes then dressing in the bathroom. It hadn't bothered him—as he eased open the faucet, moistened his hands, and damped down the creases sleep had ironed into his face—which was quite possibly part of the problem: he was indifferent to the situation . . .

. . . which made it, self-evidently, one to be dispensed with.

Late on the Sunday afternoon, the four shell-shocked survivors were winched up from the depths of the devastated city. Before the train surfaced at 125th Street, Ted went in search of a restorative—knowing full well it was hopeless. Elaine supposes they were all grateful for the alibi their hangovers provided: John told how, once he'd taken Betty back uptown and returned to the Roosevelt for a final nightcap with the night owls, he'd reeled to their room, and was so drunk he'd left the door open then collapsed across the bed in his clothes, remaining that way until Elaine arrived back, long past dawn.

Betty's story was complementary: she'd lost her way in the Waldorf and eventually had to return to the front desk. Then, having been escorted to her room by a page, she somehow managed to leave it again, mostly naked, and find herself locked out. She'd rifled a bedsheet toga from a linen cupboard, then loitered by the housephone until her own Shakespearean night porter arrived.

Sunlight flickering across Betty's face, Elaine was struck—as so often—by the peculiar lack of emotion the other woman displayed: if this was funny or embarrassing, she didn't give any indication, but rather recounted it, so to speak, as a pro forma: what an ideally amusing, self-deprecating story ought to be like, *if by any chance she were to tell one . . .*

She must have resented Elaine deeply then—and must resent her yet more now.

Everything that's happened between her and Ted could still—at a stretch—be passed off as drunken necking, even if it got a little rough on occasion. But behind Elaine's *scrawny, ardent* figure stands the distinctly more alluring Mona Voss—and once a man such as Ted has a past, well . . . he'll always have a future as well.

As to the necking itself. It had surely been a proof of the enduring closeness between her and John—a masochistic intimacy, formed over many years, by precisely these shared exposures and humiliations—that immediately after the New York debacle, as they drove home from the station, the Hancocks were already discussing a subject they would, surely, have rigorously avoided otherwise.

Queasily, Elaine had laughed, Ted's a slobberer: Sweet, but a slobberer.

While John riposted that *his wife would eat no lean*, her lips being parched, and her tongue—as Elaine had suspected—feline to the point of roughness.

How they'd laughed.

Now Elaine hears it for what it was: an echoing sort of cachinnation—as of caged apes—whose antics are only the deception of self and others. Because debacle the New York trip had most definitely been, given *no one had got what he wanted* . . . and it introduced a dangerous sort of oscillation into the mechanics of their involvement with the Troppmanns: they now regretted their friendship with this devil-may-care and charismatic couple in direct proportion to their own strengthening attraction.

If, that is, you could describe chilly Elizabeth as charismatic—let alone devil-may-care. It's more a negative capability she has, one expressed by the seeds of contempt with which she *sows her silences*.

Mrs. Hoskins is moving about in the kitchen—picking one thing up, putting another down, wiping a third with a cloth *as we do*. She must've switched on a radio, because the Man from Libertyville's voice nasals its way through the hot afternoon hush of the glasshouse. Elaine hears snippets: the New America . . . the Age of Abundance . . . What does it mean to you? Automation . . . a Second Industrial Revolution . . . the Power of the Atom . . . Terrible and Gnawing Anxieties . . . Want of Clothing and Food . . .

She thinks it a little odd the other woman's working on a Saturday afternoon, but perhaps it's something to do with the girls' schedule.

At any rate, after New York everything had been different between her boss and Elaine.

Through late spring and into early summer they'd kept to the same pattern of suppers and outings—adult, child, and combinations thereof. If anything, there'd been more impromptu cups of coffee and premature sundowners—but the atmosphere at all these events was . . . poor . . .

. . . *tainted*.

There'd been a midweek supper at the faculty club in early June. Although Elaine looked frantically forward to it for days, as they arrived, and she saw Ted standing by the lobby doors, legs spread, fists thrust deep in his pockets in a way he imagines to be . . . *folksy*, and laughing and chatting with some colleague or other, she felt sick to her stomach with the yearning that was for him, and yet not, perhaps . . . *for him at all*.

She tried passing it off later as no more than her fair share of the mayhem that often ensues when three dry martinis meet an empty stomach. Except that Elizabeth Troppmann never descends to mayhem, she's always calm and contained—which is why she makes Elaine feel inept, awkward, and bumbling. If she does have moments of abandonment, she probably announces them well in advance, which somehow counts against their being considered as such at all.

By contrast
Elaine
had shredded
her bread roll
conspicuously,
under all their eyes.
Worse still, those of the waiter as well—
the same colored kid
who'd handed Elaine her coat,
on the evening it'd all
begun.
The jade pin on Betty's lapel winked at Elaine as it rose and fell on her *heaving bosom*.

Is it envy I feel, Elaine thinks again, rather than jealousy? Is it that I covet that elusive, but for all that enjoyably
cool, state of being Elizabeth—she never falls off the roof,
only *wafts down in the elevator*—rather than any of the
benefits it's endowed her with, such as wealth, position,
fertility, and, of course, Ted?

At any rate, she'd shredded the bread rather than giving any thanks—shredded it, and at the same time keened:
a high-pitched whine the others chose to ignore, as if it
were an electrical appliance that's so very essential it's been
entirely forgotten and hence become a void into which
*everything disappears* . . . She knew from that moment—
the soup was pea and ham—that henceforth it would be a
matter of her . . . *and them.*

To them, her looks were indeed *laughable* . . . while
it counted against her, perversely, that her peccadillos—
being for the most part crimes of presumption rather than
passion—were *unphotographable* . . .

It shouldn't've gone on after that supper, which ended
with Elizabeth standing on the other side of the stall door
in the faculty club ladies' and suggesting that Elaine pull
herself together, so calmly and authoritatively that she
immediately did just this.

It *shoobee-doobee-doobee-doouldn't've gone on*—it
couldn't've gone on.

It did go on.

Stella Troppmann came to stay at Hemlock Street for a
long weekend while her parents went back to Chicago, for
the inauguration of some sort of institute Ted had had a
hand in setting up at his alma mater. Carefree Karen was

with Betty's sister in Tarrytown—the Hancocks didn't feel
as if they were having a child to stay at all, but rather as
if an eight-year-old sociologist had arrived to complete a
study of their family organization.

Conclusions of which included that 1. mealtimes were
too lax, 2. bedtimes too chaotic, and 3. overall household
management . . . Well, if Stella had known the word slut,
Elaine feels pretty sure she would've used it. Instead, this
little martinet set up office in the spare room: her doll,
Christine, arranged with her accoutrements on the windowsill, while Stella's own small suitcase rested, open, on
top of the bureau.

When Elaine had asked if it wouldn't be more convenient if she unpacked her things and put them in its drawers, her guest's reply was firm: It's more efficient if I leave
everything like this—you never know when you may have
to leave somewhere with only a few minutes' notice.

An answer that *speaks to my condition* . . . Elaine
thinks, still standing and watching Mrs. Hoskins move
about in the Troppmanns' kitchen, since she, too, is a
would-be escape artist. And a line delivered with a censo-
riousness that may well originate with maid, Elaine thinks,
rather than mother.

After all, Mrs. Hoskins is . . . *Stella's Prudence.*

Elaine had told John about Stella Troppmann's
three-minute warning—and he, too, dug it. For the duration
of the child's stay, it became their catchphrase for whenever
she was being particularly prissy: *You never know when
you may have to leave somewhere with only a few minutes'
notice* . . . Why would a kid get how rude this might appear

to her hosts—let alone the use they'd made of it to taunt each other with the possibility of . . . *abandonment*?

What had struck the Hancocks most about their young visitor, though, was how her behavior, her manner, and her very words blended together all her parents' most salient characteristics in such a way as to suggest this world-weary eight-year-old was Ted and Betty's progenitor rather than their progeny. Elaine had said as much to John and Billy when, after what seemed like days of notice—at roll call every morning Stella announced to her jailers the time she had left to serve—she packed Christine away in her suitcase, and the two of them were packed off back to Trumansburg.

The Hancocks waved goodbye from their front window: a perfectly disingenuous little triangle—and, while she acknowledges this probably isn't the straightforward, healthy way of raising a child, it's at these times, when they find themselves united in condemnation, that Elaine thinks them most perfectly a family—and one of equals, rather than Mosaic grown-ups commanding their kid.

Nevertheless, when Elaine said Stella would have to come again, she meant it. She'd put up with the dreadful little beast criticizing the way she opens a *can of goddamn beans*, just as she'd make a tethered goat of her beloved son . . . *again*, because no matter how captious the girl might be, she's a flesh-and-blood link to her father that's *quite unbreakable* . . .

What's more, is . . . more: riding in the Buick, with Billy and Stella bickering in the back seat, or, better still, rattling a shopping cart along the aisles at Loblaw's, with the pair of them *bickering along behind me* . . . Elaine felt that silly smile of brute, sensual satisfaction snaking across her face—the one she'd seen on the faces of other women who take great pride in being the human equivalent of a few square yards of *fertile topsoil* . . .

Yes: It's a party, after all, for YOU, not just for the FEW—and while Elaine *likes Ike* quite as much as the next proud specimen of American womanhood, there comes a time when *real change becomes unstoppable.*

But the biggest benefit of all that's accrued to Elaine as a result of her palling up with Stella Troppmann is, as the summer's worn on—its mature heat throbbing through the very earth, such that the trees became firecrackers-in-waiting—her own well-demonstrated capacity for putting up with the symptoms of this troubled girl's lovesickness means she, in turn, has also been tolerated when she whines at the dinner table, or takes a roll from the basket and slowly . . . *shreds it.*

What now?

Mrs. Hoskins is still moving about in the kitchen. We're in the same house, Elaine thinks, but there's the outside in between us.

The colored woman has high hips, and holds herself proudly— Does she feel my admiring eyes on her?

Stella had said, I do think there are more efficient ways of organizing your icebox, Mrs. Hancock, because Elaine was on her hands and knees, with quart cartons and grapefruit halves around her on the linoleum . . . *blobs of dried paint along the baseboard . . . egg-and-dart . . . cowrie shell . . . smooth prepubescent pubis . . . cleft mons . . .*

*Organizing the icebox* is how Elaine's come to think of this summer's activities—Billy tried day camp for all of a week, but that much boyish rowdiness intimidated him, and he's retreated into long, crystal-clear days at Flat Rock, with Frank O'Brien, Cal Williams, or one or both of the Troppmann girls. Here, the broad reach of river slides, gently roaring and loudly chuckling, over the stones, and the kids can slip in and out of its chilly silkiness, either dabbling in pools or letting themselves be tossed from one small cataract to the next.

A blue haze shimmers over it all.

Elaine, sat on her own rock, keeps a close eye first on the kids and secondly on whichever novel it is that day. Because she's been reading voraciously—anything rather than suffer the relentless progress of her own thoughts, which *slide, loudly roaring . . . maniacally chuckling . . .* through her mind.

Yes. It wasn't the vexed matter of her and Ted anymore—it was the positively gay affair of these three: if it wasn't Ted and John who were heading off for an afternoon's fishing in the boat, then, as now, it was Ted wrangling all the kids, while Betty took John for a spin in *the drowning pool . . .*

Stuck at Hemlock Street in the late morning—chagrined at the manner in which her Saturday had been *spirited away . . .* Elaine had, to begin with, thought it was a migrainous wavering in her visual field—then realized it was smoke from a fire that must be moving rapidly along the old fence line, through the parched brush and dried-out grasses. No sooner had she identified this pressing threat than she also noticed wisps of smoke trailing from the bushes on the slopes above the house—then, a second fire on the other side of it, also moving along the fence line.

She'd been inattentive for at most a few moments—now here she was: in the eye of a firestorm!

Or so she'd sobbed, when at last she got through to John on the phone, followed by: Where the hell've you been?

Where had he been? Certainly not in his office, which has a line that gets routed through the switchboard automatically at weekends. The fire trucks—an impressive total of three in the end, plus the Chief's patrol car—were there before him. He'd found Elaine chatting happily with the volunteer firemen, a couple of whom were neighbors who lived directly up the hill from the Hancocks' place.

Everyone was saying it was a little early in the season—and Herman Gower, the irascible emeritus professor of German who lived in the big house at the very top of the rise, was complaining about careless barbecue chefs, not that there was any evidence this had been the cause.

The Chief, a big Canuck fellow, who Elaine recognized from McLure's, a slightly seedy bar downtown, where, on one or two particularly desperate occasions, she'd taken a little mid-afternoon snort, laughingly told her that since her little wooden house was sitting right at the intersection of these three fire paths, all the pesky little critters who might otherwise have waited 'til fall would soon be taking shelter inside.

Slipping off to sleep in one of Betty and Ted's spare bedrooms, Elaine saw herself as she had so often before in these badlands of her imagination: the wooded hills, unrolling between wakefulness and sleeping, all the way to the Canadian border. Saw herself as a shaved kind of a bear—a vast, shambolic creature, shockingly pale and vulnerable, and with a Hamelin-like horde of vermin scuttling, crawling, slithering, and downright running towards the gaping lips of her sad, raddled . . . *snatch.*

Which was not only terrifying—but profoundly unjust, given she's already fully gravid with so very many other possums, chipmunks, squirrels, and . . . *rats.* She'd still been dryly sobbing—all tears being long spent—when they got to the Perisphere. Which is how, only semi-humorously, the Hancocks refer to their friends' house. Ted took her straight into the den—from his expression, it seemed to Elaine he was on the brink of giving her the kind of talking-to she's been expecting from him ever since they broke their clinch in the strip club's urine-smelling corridor.

But he only gave her one of his sedatives—stronger than her own—because he's such a nervy man, really, *too much of one.*

At last, Mrs. Hoskins has sensed Elaine's eyes on her. She does something so unexpected, Elaine is momentarily caught in this searchlight: the return of her own unthinking stare—she has become, for the other woman, an object of utterly impersonal scrutiny.

The words *dumb, crazy white woman* come to Elaine quite unbidden.

What did Ted call his new motorboat in the end—not Elaine, for sure, or Elizabeth, or Betty either. For the first few weeks of the season, as the early-bird launches and sailboats began crisscrossing the lake, he'd left the craft

unnamed. At Elaine's instigation, they all began referring
to it—her?—as No Name. Until one day, all six of them
were standing on the dock beside the boathouse, waiting
for Ted to return from some unspecified errand, when she
picked out first the distinctive, raked superstructure of his
vessel, then its prow cutting through the water. Then on
that prow, in neatly painted gold letters, the name Nemo.

It had been, Elaine felt, his beautifully understated way
of paying her a very great compliment indeed. Which is
presumably why John was riled enough to cross-examine
Ted concerning its derivation: Was this the Latin word,
with its associate meaning, or a reference to him who, at
long last, returned by water to Ithaca, and claimed his wife
for his own, against her suitors?

Ted, being Ted, showed no rancor—and was happy to be
informed in these matters. But henceforth, Elaine couldn't
look at the damn tub, or hear its dumb name pronounced,
without thinking something a little different: Nemesis.
Whether returning to its home port or setting out only to
return, given that Cayuga is a *goddamn lake*, whenever she
sees it, cutting through the wavelets, Elaine senses there's
something malevolent in every fiber of its polished timbers
and its shiny brass fittings.

Not generally—but specifically.

To her.

# .6.

## December 1955

There's an idiom for it, Elaine says.

An idiot? Billy grins up at her, his face lustrous with smears of brownie batter. He holds the equally smeary spatula in his fist . . . *like a spear.*

An idiom—a figure of speech: they say when a woman is pregnant that she has a bun in the oven—

But not a brownie?

She looks up quickly from the baking tin she's just about to put in her own oven—but his expression is perfectly guileless. We project onto others, Elaine thinks, every-thing . . . and all the time: No, not a brownie—a bun. The bun is the baby—

And the man puts it in there?

Exactly! She kicks the oven door neatly shut, and stands back, arms upraised, Voilà! Then turns to see how well it's gone down with her *audience* . . . Which, when Elaine looks upon her only beloved child's happy face, is how she often thinks of him, although *I probably shouldn't . . .*

On days such as these, it's hard for her not to revel in the very theatricality of their intimate life together. Because when it's like this—knowing they'll be alone, just the two of them, all through the day and the entire evening as well—their solitude becomes *densely populated*. They bathe in one another's limelight, while out in the darkness sit row upon row of Elaines and Billys, who, as the one-liners keep on zinging, roar with laughter. Hilarity redoubled by the corpsing performers, who can never quite get over how funny their dialogues and monologues are, especially when delivered in sweetly endearing baby talk: a *duolect* of diminutives and slushy suffixes that makes everything sound just . . . *cutesy*.

Scene after scene of the greatest complicity: *vrai bonheur*. The kind that stays with you when the curtain finally falls, the last handclaps scatter away, and you're more alone than you ever would've been if you'd never experienced it: this perfect circle, formed by your flesh and the flesh of your flesh.

The day began quietly—the winter dawn wheedling its way into a consciousness that, as soon as it was, half wished it wasn't.

It'd been like this for the past ten days or so: first, Elaine has awoken,—then the world, which, while it contains her, is somehow also entirely dependent on her—and which, in her most egomaniacal interludes, she assumes the baneful responsibility of having created—*wavers* into existence.

It's a world in which a Very Bad Thing has happened—one of those things that, while it may appear discrete,

nonetheless alters all aspects of everything. Each day, on
opening her eyes, and seeing how this irrevocably changed
world still has depth and breadth and height and color and
smell, together with shades and blends of these, Elaine
thinks, There is Before Thing and After Thing: BT and AT.

BT now appears to her ridiculous. A Hollywood wom-
en's picture, in which, following a good deal of hard work,
elbow grease, putting up with and getting down to it—the
eventual resolution is concocted quickly enough. Out on
the patio.

Yes, she'd been unhappy—upset, often, as well. But in
those far-off days of a fortnight ago, with her complaisant
old man, her girlish crush on his colleague, and her catty
best friend, Elaine had been a goddamn poster girl for the
Modern American Woman: posed in her kitchen, skirts stiff
as crinolines, smile plasticized, a penis in one hand . . . *a
spatula in the other.*

Billy must've crept into her bed shortly before dawn.

Because when she'd awoken in the pre-dawn darkness
and gone to pee, he'd still been in his own room. She certainly should be encouraging him to spend the whole night
in his own bed—if Frank O'Brien, or any of his other little
Boys Town pals got hold of it, he'd risk being ostracized.
But if it was going to be hard BT, how much more so it'll
be now that the exile can make the perfectly reasonable
objection *there's plenty of room!*

Besides, she ponders, as she moves about her gracile,
aristocratic son—who sits, erect, licking the spatula, then
running it in precise circles around the bowl, then licking it again—while there may be help and some guidance

from Dr. Burtt, she isn't there in that muffled, consanguineous-smelling darkness in which all of life's most desperate problems are posed.

Any more than Dr. Spock was.

It's almost certainly wrong—and quite possibly indecent —how much she enjoys these interludes: to lie there caressing the soft full bell of his hair, and feel his small body, warm and lithe against her flank.

Upon waking, though, his presence is still registered only after the Thing. First Thing—then its rightful antidote: her child—the Other Thing that makes the Thing of no consequence. Or should. But it's too late by then—Elaine's riven in two: cleaved by the division of before and after. Bang! Bang! Bang! A meaty arm descending—a bloodied cleaver ascending. Life's a goddamn butchery counter. *Bang! Bang! Bang!*

What was it Freudenberg said to her? Yes . . . after she'd given what she felt to be a bravura performance—fusing narrative, pacing, and vivid description to bring to life in all its strange pomp and delirium one of her more flamboyant migraines. He'd tartly remarked it sounded *like a parody of orgasm.*

Then added—so much worse, this—that he meant specifically a parody of the sort of orgasm *she would like to have.*

Well, by the same analysis, she supposes her and Billy's current situation isn't really that of an abandoned wife and child—but only a parody of separation. Because he's coming back.

Isn't he?

A return conceived—when Elaine's on an upswing—
in these terms: as being in order to frustrate, amend,
or otherwise do away with the way things are ordered
around here in his absence. There are a few more days
before the Christmas vacation—but even the martinet of
West Hill, Mrs. Hansen, the Deputy Principal, has given
up on corralling the kids. There are some ritualized gift
and card exchanges Billy will be loath to miss, but there's
no more pretence at education.

Elaine's always found the school relaxed to the point
of laxity anyway. Her son has always been *inclined to
agree* . . . He returned from his first day in first grade to
solemnly announce that the sign on the classroom door
read, COME ON IN EVERYONE AND LET'S HAVE FUN. The disgust with which Fun had been uttered was complete—the
reading was, of course, part of the problem.

Elaine began teaching Billy when he was just three.
What was the sense in holding off? He'd already been rec-
ognizing letters and occasional words—was trying making
them as well, with cutlery in soft food, with fingertip, con-
densation, and windowpane. He'd been a quick learner—
she wrote words clearly on file cards then held them up for
him to identify, or guided his hand as he marked the dense
burgundy-velvet pile of the small couch in the front room
with his finger. Then let him employ her own as an eraser.

Holding and held. Guiding and inscribed. One large
hand gloving the other, tiny one.

There's a thought here of some viability, Elaine thinks—
one that shouldn't just be left in the long grass for the flies:
in intimacy are the origins of all our meanings—the moves

we make on our very selves are crude and dismissive. We're always leading ourselves, via dreams and desire, to the point of some melting seduction, or fabulous endeavor.

Then fading away.

When Billy began at West Hill he could read—and he could write.

One of the first exercises had been to fill in the missing words—he squeezed entire possible sentences into the margins of the worksheet. Much to his chagrin, he was marked wrong accordingly. His chagrin—and his mother's anxiety. It isn't, Elaine keeps telling herself, a complete disaster: he has some friends among his classmates, and he certainly doesn't dread attending school. But there's a definite gulf between his social ambitions and their likely achievement.

Billy longs to be straightforwardly popular.

But he never will be, she tells him, he's too screwy and intelligent a guy. The popular guys are always glad-handers with open-prairie smiles and billion-buck handshakes, who, when you say boo to them, wet their pants anyway.

This doesn't seem to help.

Yesterday morning, he hadn't snuggled up on awaking, as he usually does—but instead lay beside her and mewled. Elaine had sensed, in the small hours, a clamminess in the atmosphere and the almost fecal smell of fresh sweat. Dismissing these as the lubrications of her own tossing and turning, she'd slept again. In the cold light of a day when the air temperature clearly wouldn't rise above nineteen degrees, a hand on his forehead was all that was required to justify fetching the thermometer from the bathroom—then, as soon as she'd withdrawn it from the charming, spiky-haired sprite's mouth, the customary negotiations ensued:

OK, suppose it's not above normal—but it is below. Everyone knows temperatures rise through the day, so it's probably best I stay home.

Yes, it is below normal, honey—but not very far below at all.

That means it hasn't got far to rise before it's above ninety-eight point six an' I'll have a fever!

I don't think it quite works like that . . .

The truth is, she doesn't really know how it works—the body. Does anyone? For most of the time—this much she can bear to acknowledge—it's a bitter struggle simply to keep it camouflaged in flesh and clothing, *and moving* . . . Some days the most minor of maladies are insupportable: only days before the Thing, Billy had a nosebleed and Elaine had to call John to come home early, because she couldn't face *d'aller avec lui au médecin*. Shameful.

That said, we're no malingerers, and we wouldn't want to exhibit the essence of Carmichaelism, now, would we?

Now, standing with her back to the sink, looking at Billy's face covered in chocolate, Elaine wonders at the morals of this wisecrack: the man had been uncouth, certainly—and, if it didn't sound ridiculous, somehow presumptuous: he knew the way he should behave—and simply *preferred not to* . . .

He'd knocked at the door, too loudly, two days after the Thing, when Elaine was still addled, and wondering whether she'd ever be able to face anyone she knew ever again: a tubby, moon-faced, very light-skinned Negro, who, without any of the usual niceties, demanded her old news-papers of her: *Gimme yer ol' papah bundles,* he'd ordered her: *I got so's I cain't work, see, an' they gimme five cents a bundle for 'em at the mill over in Virgil.*

Poking her head around the door, Elaine saw his beat-up old jalopy slumped in the roadway . . . *tell us about the fucking rabbits, George.* There was something at once pathetic and malevolent about the man—who, possibly by reason of his grift, smelled of mildew, and whose buoyant-looking paunch was cinched with a narrow belt that in Elaine's paranoid eyes assumed the still-narrower aspect of a . . . *garotte.*

Worse was his prescience: this was a well-informed character—the newspapers were, indeed, all bundled up and waiting on the back porch for the 4-H kids to come get them, as usual. Newspapers from which all the humor—in the form of the funnies, which Billy clips out and hoards—had been extracted. It was her pathetic fear and mistrust, as much as any real feeling, that made her damn him as a lazybones, and that impelled her—once she'd got rid of him, with a token bundle, cravenly offered up—towards Bobbie, who she'd phoned, ostensibly to warn her that this: *the essence of Carmichaelism,* was headed in her direction.

She came over later that day. They guzzled some bour-bon she'd brought with, and Bobbie commiserated with Elaine about John being away in Ann Arbor. Although, Elaine didn't tell her great friend and confidante, he was attending a preselection meeting with some prospective col-leagues, while neither of them mentioned the Thing: Elaine

didn't know yet who knew besides the four of them, and
Dr. Burtt, but clearly it *can only be a matter of time . . .*

She'd thought then—and continued doing so—about
her need for Bobbies and Bobbie-a-likes: women whose
confidence far surpassed her own, but whose wit quite
likely . . . *lagged.* It struck her at some point in her musing
that there were considerable similarities between the two
Bs in her life, beyond the obvious: they were both the
sort of fairer game men looked over Elaine's shoulder in
search of.

When, in early October, there were two concurrent polio
cases at West Hill, Elaine had panicked: the vaccination
wasn't available yet—was it even safe? Some of the other
mothers were talking about kids at a school in Hartford
who'd had very bad reactions. Caught between these two
invisible—therefore near-occult—phenomena, the virus
and the vaccine, she sought succor, first from Bobbie, and
then from a second sleek blonde, Betty, who'd joined her
one lunchtime at the Brush & Palette to discuss the evolv-
ing situation over a bowl of soup and a sandwich.

She'd said no, there was nothing to worry about with
the vaccine, she'd read the results of the relevant tests and
trials: it was as safe and effective as any medicine, so the
sooner it was rolled out nationwide, the better. As for
the situation at West Hill: one more case, and either the
authorities would close the school or they should keep their
own children at home, whatever the Principal's position.

This had, however, of course been Before Thing, when
Elaine, while perhaps aware of Betty Troppmann's potential for deviousness, had yet to experience the revelation

of her motives. Ha! BT! What an absurd era! Courtesy of the Walt Disney Corporation, the dinosaurs of desire had sported with the sea serpents of sexual frustration: and all this ancient while, Betty had been advancing her own cause with guile—ruthlessness, even. Although it's not in Elaine's character to be magnanimous—as against generous—she can't help but admire her rival's success, even as she despises her methods: Yassuh! She'd won! In the process, proving beyond doubt that whatever Dr. Burtt says on the matter—the counsel of women is to be trusted still less than that of men.

So, yesterday, in full Technicolor, A Patient Was Born! A charming couch one, with a whim of iron, who'd parlayed his degree-or-so-above-normal into quite abnormal extravagance: the housekeeping could, his mother said, go hang! What did it matter if she had to keep the furnace stoked herself while John was away, so costing him more of the beans he seems to feel he *shits on cue*, when truth is, every single one has to be squeezed out of him with *fanatic grunts*. The house would, at least, be warm.

As for Boston Charlie and the matter of *Nora freezing on the trolley* . . . Perhaps parody was part of the problem here, for the couch patient—for all of them. It was difficult to see the Hancocks in any kind of believable grouping anymore . . . *let alone the fucking Nativity*. The invalid is paradoxically a salve, because another of Elaine's inheritances is Lily's practical—if unknowing—application of Freud's theory that the mind's disorders are expressed by the body's malaises: for daughter as much as mother, whatever else illness might be, it's always a form of discourse—one between the sufferer and his symptoms, or between him and that numinous Other who tantalizes by either giving, or withholding, succor.

Elaine blames her mother for her own revulsion from perfectly normal bodily functions—eating, menstruation, defecation—quite as much as those rendered abnormal by illness and disease. Lily Rosenthal always seems to welcome illness—the worst has happened, which means Jack must compensate her with some treat or other. But nothing, her daughter knows, can compensate you for the fact of your own embodiment. If it was bad before, post-Thing it is almost unbearable—this dank fatigue, clinging to her goosebumps, dragging her down into the inexorability of her own dissolution: the water rushing past—the banks being *washed away into the gorges all tumultuous with brownyellow waters . . .*

*The macabre students, who know no better, call it gorging out.*

I'm not like that!

Elaine would so like to believe in a way out: she talks candidly to Mary Burtt—far more than she ever could to Freudenberg. It helps that the other woman is *homelier than thou . . .* and in turn, Elaine speaks candidly with her child: a commentary she believes explains—albeit with simplification—the actions she, for all this lucidity, cannot seem to forego: yesterday she'd been happier he was home *than he was . . .* and immediately planned an exhaustive program of recuperation *for us both.*

He would lie on the small couch in the front room reading and doing his beading—while she moved around him,

swaddling him in the happy sounds and smells of domes-
ticity as she did her chores—including changing his linen,
and generally sprucing up his room.

Because there's hardly any greater balm, is there, than
returning to bed—not going to it, but returning to one
tightly made with fresh sheets and smoothed blankets. A
bed you ease into the cool repose of, with all the languor to
be expected of someone *regaining their health* . . .

That's another paradox to be married with all the rest,
in the cozy little house by the big deep lake:—as the temperature continues to plummet outside, and the ice gathers
in evil gray nodules on the power cables: in sickness is their
health . . . *'til death us do part.*

Inconsiderate is not the word—what John's being, by
making this long trip only days before the holiday, is fool-
hardy: who knows if he'll make it back in time. He carried
on regardless of the forecast, though, and Elaine's perfectly
aware why—not that this makes it any easier to calm Billy,
who, since his father left, has been powerfully averse to his
mother doing the same, even for a few minutes. It was only
prolonged soothing and heartfelt reassurance that got her
out of the house yesterday—that and the promise of new
library books and either candy or store-bought cookies.
The same promise she's made to him today.

Because Christ! The kid can read— When they're alone
together, one in two mealtimes Elaine will declare dedicated to reading: eyes down, and no talking at the table
with this exception—which she thinks a stroke of peda-
gogic genius—you can either refer to, or tell your dining
companion about, anything in the book actually in hand.

That way—she's told him, only intermittently able to ignore her own sanctimony—we both get two books for the time it takes us to read one.

Or less, because when they're opposite one another, in a silence full of *chewing things over*, she can watch his eyes, limpid in their innermost liquid-crystal parts, flicker along one line, then flick to the next. Flicker-flick. Flicker-flick. She half expects the ting! of a carriage bell, implanted somewhere . . . *in his brain*, he reads so fast, and so mechanically.

When she gets back, as yesterday, they'll add this specialty to their luncheon: having it on a tray in his little room—which Billy likes welcoming her to with some ceremony: *You may sit on the straight-back chair, Mom . . .* So, she will, and hear the cats scratching at the door behind her for admission.

Karma and Maya—Elaine and Billy. Feline and human pairs have this in common, Elaine supposes: the parent unhappy, otherwise denied intimacy of the usual, adult kind, develops an unhealthy attachment to the child. Perhaps this wasn't a problem for Karma—she was only abusing Maya out of sheer malice, mere propinquity, or both. More disturbing is to consider that it may be the very contrivance of her own reproduction—and the disposal of most of its consequences—that's turned her against her own child.

If only such troubling speculation had been checked there, but the cat's mother's mother persisted: her own impregnation could hardly be said to've been freely undertaken, given this doleful eventuality: years later, in the wreckage of her and John's marriage, Elaine was still considering having another child. As late as the spring of this year, the idea of finally providing a little brother or sister for Billy, and some emotional glue to bind their frail familial barque together—if only for the passage to the children's adulthood—had been preoccupying her enough for baby names to appear, toddling along the narrow-ruled lines of her diary.

How pathetically delusional this all now appears, After Thing.

How violently demeaning it now seems, After Thing, that up until weeks, if not days, before it, she was still prepared to put out for him.

Yet any female, of any species, would consider this course of action—moreover, BT, the way humans and cats were mimicking each other had amused Elaine. Never more so than when she mentioned to Betty, she'd only allowed Karma her kittens because she wanted her neutered, and the ever-practical Dr. Troppmann had encouraged her, saying she'd taken their brindled old tom, Thaddeus, to have the equivalent procedure, and since then he'd been so much more docile, she'd suggested to Ed . . . *he have it done, too.*

A comment on his tomcatting in general—or specifically with Elaine?

Whichever, the fact is, Elaine's desire to be altogether rid of desire long precedes this bathetic, disastrous affair—and if cats' concupiscence can also be managed in this manner, why not that of humans? Anything is warranted, she believes, when it comes to protecting the mass of sensitive lacerated feelings she's acquired after twenty years of bitterness, pain, confusion, and sadness in the sightless, senseless, grimacing face of the act of love.

Now the Thing masks that face as well, with its treacherous, rubbery features—and if she pictures Ted Troppmann looming over her, it's as vile as being compelled to witness an atrocity, such as someone shooting a child in the head. Bang. Shooting a child in the head. Bang. Christ. How could anyone do that? Shoot a child in the head. *Shoot me in the head.*

*Bang.*

Mom. Billy holds the bowl out to her, continuing in a pretty good Brooklyn accent: Beddah—which she knows to be a one-word punchline, but to which she unthinkingly responds,

Are you, honey . . . ? I'm so pleased.

Men, they sully you with their desires, Elaine thinks, taking the bowl and depositing it in the sink. And they make you feel your own are dirty: there's no snow, as yet, and she recalls John telling Ted—all those eons ago, when they danced home through the rain from seeing Letter from an Unknown Woman—there seldom is, in the Finger Lakes, this side of New Year. The cold comes before it, though: a fist, punching from the north and concussing everything, rendering it *swollen* and somehow *sullied.*

Later, the block of brownies sits cooling on the rack, waiting to be divided—and the deceitful aroma sidles through the little half-saltbox house, *summoning remembrance of sweetmeats past* . . . Because there's a circularity to what happiness she may share with her son: it exists only as they feed it to each other. *Foo-ood, is Goo-ood . . . !* Or so the top-dollar pro punnyman on CBS declares. Elaine isn't so sure. Downtown, she'd crept back and forth across the Commons, from store to store, assembling her pathetic bundle of wares, while staring about her quite crazily, she suspects, on the lookout for anyone she might know, so as to avoid them.

Because she can't have that same conversation again, in which she gaily says John's away for a few days on a work matter—without cracking, then screaming to all and sundry the sordid little particulars of the great big Thing that's sundered their family so irrevocably.

I still want to try . . . Elaine sobs aloud—and hearing her from upstairs, Billy cries, Is that you, Mom?

From the rattan basket they bought at the Shaker village, she unloads animal crackers and chocolate milk for the invalid, a pint of bourbon for herself, and library books for both of them. She's finally taken a perverse liking to this sweetly oily liquor and, being a thoroughly modern woman, has no need of any mixer—let alone *a cherry on top*. She sits, these late afternoons of his absence, and projects onto the clock's minute hand her own shivery anticipation—it quivers, jerks.

Quivers.

To a halt.

It's allowably cocktail time.

Will she become a lush—or, worse, hopelessly addicted to the pills?

Or both?

Silly Lily says with authority Jews can't be dipso—
although she's never explained what this authority is. Elaine
certainly feels this within her: a capacity for *utter abandon*—
Mom!
I'll be there in a minute, Billy.
She picks up the library books—Chekhov stories and
some miscellany called The Spoor of Spooks for her, The
Children of Greene Knowe and Huckleberry Finn for him.
At just eight, is he perhaps too young for Twain's more
satiric passages? In a way sadly, she doubts it—besides,
she'll mostly read the novel to him herself, so can explain
its quirks and oddities. If it's at all possible, they find still
greater intimacy in this: the two of them, in a burrow of
lamplight, the cold kept at bay beyond it, and her tongue
bound to his ear by the thread of a tale. Sometimes, racing
to get undressed so they can enjoy this, she's struck by the
similarity between their behavior and that of—
When's Daddy gonna be back?
I told you, Billy: so long as the weather doesn't delay
him, he should be here by Saturday.
He hasn't gone forever, then?
No, of course not, baby doll—what makes you say such
things?
Or good . . .
What?
Or good—maybe it's: hasn't gone for good.
It's either—here, look what I got you.
Making light, disguising, repressing—these are the
weapons at Elaine's disposal, and she handles them better

than she ever imagined she would. Lying to an adult—even one you're married to? Ach! It's the world we're in—but a child? That's selling what's left of your conscience on the instalment plan. Which she duly did

accepting her son's trust, still, as her due. One thing Mary Burtt and Freudenberg are in complete accord about is Billy's unnatural closeness to his father. Great. What Elaine's new analyst has no settled opinions concerning are the disturbances in his sight and hearing he's been reporting recently: *Everything looked so far away and kinda little, like toys . . .*

Which sounded baleful to his mother—especially given this hallucination's rapid onset, and accompaniment by an auditory one: Mrs. Hansen had been talking to the class, and her voice went all high-pitched and squeaky, like this: *OK, children, now I want—*

*OK, Billy, ça suffit!*

She's been sick with anxiety—appointments had been hurriedly arranged, but the optometrist said there was nothing new to add: Billy's myopia would keep him out of the firing line, and off the pitcher's mound, but there was nothing drastically wrong with his eyes otherwise. As for the family physician, Dr. Thorogood, he was reassuring enough until you noticed his too-red nose and poor teeth, whereupon both his diagnoses and his treatments became suspect. Elaine's long since noticed them—and she only sticks with the man because he doesn't demur when it comes to prescribing, not because of his pediatrics. That, and his relaxed attitude to doing his billing.

John aphorizes him—and by extension, his profession—
as *Dr. Cursorily-Poor*.

Thorogood said: What about your migraine? It's a
highly heritable condition according to this paper I've read
in the New England Journal of Medicine.

This is his holy writ—and cited in this instance, she
understands, not to make the ostensible point, but rather
to support the general view of the heritability of all sorts
of mental disorders.

Billy has fetched a cool, damp washcloth from the bathroom and arranged it picturesquely on his forehead. Welcome back, honored mother, he says in a weird English
accent.

It's this very instant, his mother thinks, that the blanket
is tossed over the chairs, and the two of them are enclosed
once more in the warm den of their own precious intimacy,
around which revolves the cold and rotten world.

As you can see, Billy says, pointing to his forehead, I'm
above normal, now . . .

Really?

Feel.

Well, you've had the cloth on there, so my hand—no
matter how sensitive—won't be able to get an accurate
reading.

Above normal—or below. Dormant—or rising up: a
dangerously eruptive passion.

Elaine sits and looks at him, and thinks.

Billy reads the inside flaps and the backs of the books,
his *sweet lips* moving. There are two pictures above his bed:

One a framed watercolor of a martial-looking bunny rabbit banging a big bass drum strapped to his furry tummy. The other is of a character from one of the superhero comics he reads—he sent away for this: five cents and ten coupons, then got his mother to frame this image of a rubbery Übermensch, with mile-long legs and arms stretching out over a cityscape—as if this freak were bestowing some sort of benediction on Gotham.

Or is it Gomorrah?

When Billy was a baby, his mother hadn't so much read Spock—as communed with him: Spock said not to be worried by involuntary erections, or reports of the feelings that provoke them: these are perfectly natural.

Spock said that if the boy hasn't been circumcised, as he grows it's necessary to teach him to gently roll back his foreskin and clean the head of the penis, removing any of the white matter called smegma.

With very small children, getting an accurate thermometer reading in the mouth can be difficult. Elaine followed Spock's advice, and if she thought Billy was running a fever, she deftly inserted the thermometer into his rectum.

*Deftly, she inserted into his rectum the thermometer . . .*

No one, ever, she thinks, has ever considered my intimate parts with this combination of skill, and love. With the exception of Jimmy, her gentle wartime lover, who she'd alighted on by chance—falling into conversation over material remnants in the basement at the Fulton Street Market, discovering over coffee, quite quickly, that he was a graphic designer, while his wife was ill—bedbound, in point of fact—then taking him, in shortish order, *to my own* . . .

A man-child, really—classified 4F for a gimpy leg, but no problems with his hands—sensitive and deft enough to gently move his thumb inside her, while cupping her whole vulva in his palm, so his fingertips *softly wibbled* her pubic hair.

A golden moment, indeed—and one that's endured, making all other sex experiences seem tarnished, hence tawdry, in comparison. Jimmy will never leave his invalid wife—and over the years, meeting up for a fugitive embrace, it's quite possibly been the very intensity of his remorse that's sustained her repletion.

John has always wanted her to perform fellatio on him. *Perform!* Given his capacity for pedagogy—often to the point of boorishness—Elaine's faintly surprised he hasn't yet tried to persuade her by citing the relevant passages in goddamn Kinsey. What he doesn't understand—what no man ever seems to understand—is that a good place to begin with oral pleasure would be their own ability to practice cunnilingus, if not with worrying expertise, at least with some competence.

Billy has his father's pale-blue eyes—but with a hint of something more exotic in them . . . *amethyst?* He has his father's high-domed forehead and slightly square ears as well—but his white-blond cowlick is entirely his own—as is his sensualist's mouth, which at birth appeared to've had a thick coat of lipstick *only just applied* . . .

He has an adorable furrow between his finely arched brows.

Into it is going the dope about Huck and Jim.

Elaine sighs: she's going to have to have another of those conversations with her precocious son—about what can and can't be said, and to who—and who not. The Makers of New Rinso may bring you the Amos 'n Andy Show, but it doesn't matter how sudsy or soapy things get, fundamentals of the body cannot be washed away—whether one is blackened, or otherwise bemerded.

Elaine has *a hairball between my legs* . . .

And it prophesizes.

It had been in the late spring. Then, as now, Billy had inveigled his happily acquiescent mother, so was lounging about the house in his pyjamas. Betty Troppmann came by for coffee, and brought cannoli with her from the Italian deli. Elaine could tell the kid was struck forcibly by this manifestation: Stella's mom in her neat fawn work suit, sitting on the blue sofa with her knees neatly to one side, and eating her pastry with the side of her fork, so neatly not a smear of cream or a crumb was left on the plate.

When she'd gone, Billy struggled to express his impressions: She's . . . She's . . . She looked like a . . . lady.

A lady? A lady, indeed.

Lady-fucking-muck.

Did Elaine have a hunch, even then? Of course she did.

She'd snapped at her son: Yeah, a lady, alright—she thinks she shits chocolate ice cream.

Then instantly regretted it. Because henceforth, it hasn't mattered how many times, or how sincerely and thoughtfully she's admonished him, he'll still nod to some trim miss tripping along the aisles at Loblaw's, or musing over the accessories in Ladies Outfitting at Rothschild's, and hiss: I bet she thinks she shits chocolate ice cream . . .

I got maple syrup and the hickory-smoked bacon you like while I was out—how about some pancakes in a while?

His smile rises over this darkling plain: It is, Elaine thinks, what lightens my life—turns night to day and pain to joy. Whatever else the Thing may mean—for me, for him, for all three of us—to be deprived of this intimacy would be insupportable.

This intimacy—and, if she's perfectly honest, this collusion.

She shits shit—so does Dr. Elizabeth Troppmann. So does every live, real woman in the entire goddamn world. And her son—whose shit she's been wiping up his entire life—is going to grow up to be a man who has, at least, no illusions on this matter: she's suffered enough from male fantasy not to want to increase *its world supply*.

How many pancakes can I have, Mom?

Why, Billy . . . she can feel her rictus of indulgence . . . as many as you want.

Leadenly, Elaine rises and leaves the room. She leaves the volume of Chekhov's stories on her writing table, and leadenly she returns to the kitchen. All civilized existence is muffled by this: a blanket of repression thrown over carefully arranged chairs. It's claustrophobic in here—

Oh! So, claustrophobic.

Because what had incontrovertibly established the shittiness of Betty's shit? What had, so to speak, thrust her dear little nose in it? Only more social shenanigans—more gossip, more pecking, and more ordering that pecking. Standing at the sink, Elaine cannot prevent her eyes from rolling up the rise, and wonders what Bobbie O'Brien is doing this very second. It's tempting to think of her as some scheming Machiavel—a spider spinning her meticulously murderous web. But the truth is *she's like all the rest of us housewives*, for all her busyness, and her numerous activities, her life lacks the essential importance—let alone the habiliment of power—bestowed by male work, male careers.

Elaine considers John, out there in the world: a creature alien to her, pausing by a newsstand to adjust his hat brim, then slapping a nickel down and snatching up the Times. Men have so many places to go, people to see, interesting things to do! It makes things easier for them. I sit—Elaine thinks—and I brood.

I am, Elaine confidently proclaims in the echoing, empty hall of her mind, sick with loneliness now. All because Bobbie has a social disease, and couldn't prevent herself from palling up with the Troppmanns as well, and Elaine soon enough became aware of events in which the Hancocks were not included. It had been this—quite as much as the queer sort of standoff with Ted—that had put Elaine so hopelessly on edge.

Bobbie being Bobbie, she'd begun feeding Elaine the very dope on Ted and Betty that she'd so coveted three months previously: more on the aftermath of his dangerous entanglement with Mona Voss, plus up-to-the-minute bulletins on the Trumansburg ménage. John was fond of quipping that if they'd put in a party line with six subscribers, the Roman Empire would have fallen in weeks—and so it was with their own, far flimsier setup.

Bobbie had seen the Buick here, she said—and the Buick over there, parked in the lot in back of the College, which seemed a little strange. Bobbie had run into Betty driving her Chrysler on State—then John, right around the corner.

Which wasn't that great a coincidence—Ithaca's downtown amounting to no more than a five-block-by-five grid of streets.

Nor was it any particular surprise to see them together in the parking lot at the lakeshore in Stuart Park—it's an obvious rendezvous for Ithacans, and not anywhere you'd meet should you wish to be . . .

Clandestine.

Anyway, Bobbie, *the great artist*, was too busy with what she imagines to be *the wider picture* to connect the dots and see what had been staring them all in the face for months.

That was left to Ted.

The organization man.

When he called Elaine, it was with a fait accompli: he'd already had it out with Betty. Yet, as he'd begun to itemize all the instances when their spouses could have been alone together, undisturbed, not simply for the odd hour, here or there, but entire afternoons—!

Mom, if Dad likes the English department at Ann Arbor, will we all go to Michigan to live? And if we do, may I have a rabbit gun?

*May I—that's good . . . good diction . . .* Some of the faculty brats have elocution lessons to make them sound like little Lord and Lady Fauntleroys—clearly a crock of BS. A smart kid, Elaine's papa always says, will get an education in a plowed field. It follows, his daughter believes, that an instinctively refined one will acquire manners simply by being exposed to them.

She lights a cigarette before answering, I guess so, honey, but nothing's certain just now.

Nothing's certain—everything slip-slides over everything else, apparently solid walls bellying out into delicate traceries that collapse down into dust: an evanescent architecture—necessarily so, since it's home to *such things as dreams are made of* . . .

Ted and Betty are still setting off the day after Christmas for their long-planned winter break in Havana. Stella's coming to stay with the Hancocks again—while Bobbie's managed to glom Karen off her parents. And then there's the further coincidence of all this disruption—actual and potential—with the award of John's Fulbright, which they'd both long since considered dead in the water.

Funny how it's emerged, this possibility of a paradisical way out. Overseas! Europe, with all its profundity and strangeness, casts even the Thing in a different light. They order things differently there, Elaine thinks—perhaps a European woman wouldn't view what's happened to me in quite such a craven, self-annihilatory fashion.

Anyway, she also suspects John feels exactly as she does: like the survivor of a shipwreck who finds himself lashed to another, such that salvation is possible for either both of them . . . *or neither.* They've already demonstrated they're going to go, whatever the state of their marriage, by continuing to make arrangements throughout all the stifled sobs and muttered imprecations of the past two weeks. Another impetus is that they've told Billy about the trip—and that it means he'll be missing the fall semester, much to his delight.

Washing the mixing bowl—that's automatic. The spoons and the spatula, too. Cutting the brownies, and lining the storage tin with wax paper, these *come easily to me—would that they wouldn't!* These last few days, feeling more than ever she and her child are about to be engulfed by poverty, together with all its humiliations, Elaine's been casting about feverishly, trying yet again to alight on something she can do to earn money. Baking, perhaps? Or sewing . . . ?

What was it Ted had said, back at the dawn of time . . . ? Ah, yes: *When the man of the house goes, the household income goes with him . . .*

Indeed.

Leaving behind not just all the child-rearing and the housework—neither of which he took great pains over before—but more of the same, outside the home—or else another dull, stupid job, of the kind women in her straits are compelled to do, *and which I detest.*

Ma, I is goin' t'sit in de overstuffed armchair . . .

Another put-on accent, the kid's a joker, alright, but: Billy, what did we say about doing that kinda voice . . . ?

Yassuh!

Yes sir! He'd confronted her, in particular, with the night in New York. Mumbling to Elaine over the line, not wishing—especially now—to reveal intimate details of their life together, she nonetheless understood what must have happened: Betty's overnight absence had been correlated with some want or quirk in whatever physical relation survived between them. There had been a volley of accusations—and one of denials in response. Then for weeks and eventually months a troubled sort of armistice, during which the very daily working over of the marital soil eventually brought any undischarged ordnance back up to the surface.

A smart kid will indeed get an education in a plowed field.

And now?

I learned, Elaine thinks, not to tell in 1946—why couldn't John learn this lesson? As for Ted, that mannish boy, he confessed he'd said to Elizabeth, Would you despise me if I didn't do something to John?

Idiot! Buffoon! She despises you, Elaine thinks, precisely because you asked her what you should do. Men don't ask women what they should do—they do it. These kinds of men, these weak men, they carry on demanding the same rights associated with . . . well, with what? Being a heroic warrior? Or a caveman? Or perhaps the blind-bloody-poet, one of whose claims to fame is that three hundred years ago he wrote an infamous justification of ridding himself of his own termagant.

Yes . . . these weak men, they want to screw whoever they want, and take whatever there is at hand, and come and go as they please, while dispensing with any of the responsibilities that attain to these rights.

The rest of this century . . . Elaine ponders . . . and no doubt well into the next, people will be witnessing this:

the long, slow, and infinitely pained relinquishment of the patriarch's power, which he'll hang on to even as it's prized from his cold dead fingers. Ted Troppmann's a trendsetter in this, just as he is in architecture and the social sciences —a feminized man, who clings to his balls as if they were his pearls . . . *and vice versa!* He will, Elaine grimly predicts, turn himself inside out to keep her.

As for Elaine's feelings towards John—it's quite impossible to gauge these, as she meets Betty at every turn of the stair, bend in the road, and tendency of her own maddened thoughts: again and again, Elaine sees her rival take the lapel of her jacket between her dainty thumb and forefinger, just so, turning it this way and that, so as to regard the jade broach he gave her again . . . *and again.*

Obsessively running over the days, weeks, and eventually months since they'd met the Troppmanns at the Lemesuriers' party, Elaine recalls seeing them, even that very first time, coming together from the kitchen, and looking *conspiratorial.* It's the same with every dinner party, potluck supper, movie date, and informal gathering she cares to remember: John and Elizabeth, their cold, calculating, and oh-so-high brows in close proximity to one another. Only three weeks ago, Elaine had sat there . . . *the sap*, at the Hucksackers', and watched her husband come towards her, with his lover's lipstick on his cheek, and found it . . . *kinda cute.*

I am not what I seem, John had said to her, during just one of so many, many awkward and strained conversations: *I am not what I seem . . .* Nor was Maya, Elaine ruminates

bitterly: obviously the illusion was always going to be masculine, and when this one gets big enough, his bitch of a
mom better watch out. *Illusions . . . ha!* When she, the silly
girlish fool, was tripping up the Taughannock trail, imagining herself and Ted making al fresco love here, there, and
everywhere, John and Betty had been on the very brink of
getting right down to it. *Hard.*

John's pride in his ability to deceive her was, Elaine
believes, not unlike the pride he'd taken in belonging to a
subversive organization— He got bitter pleasure, she knew,
from concealing his activities from Authority, so getting
away with something . . . fooling the world . . . *and his
wife.*

Elaine surveys the little kitchen. All is tidied up, wiped,
cleaned, dried, and put away. It's not much, but there is
ground coffee in the can labelled COFFEE, and sugar in the
one labelled SUGAR. She listens, with a connoisseur's smirk,
to the light scattering of footfalls as her adored son, *who I
would die for*, goes happily upstairs to his sickbed.

It's she who was, is, and perhaps always will be the
Authority to him: his wife, to whom John Hancock (né
Johann Schitz) was too craven to tell the truth about himself. Is it simply that he's a coward, she wonders, and this
explains our whole sad mésalliance . . . ? Or is it that I am
frightening—objectively so? John could "protect" only the
sick part of me . . . The rest of me, my real self, laughs at
the idea that I need protecting—

That's enough! she cries aloud: E-nough!

Mom? Billy calls from upstairs.

Nothing, honey, she calls back.

She sees the rest of the day before them, growing warmer, glowing brighter, as the night outside falls, compacting layers of darkness thin as paper ash, as they sink down to the frozen earth. She sees them reading—she hears them laughing, she feels them gently cuddling. She sees her son, for once, not as her son, but only as a boy who'll grow, carrying whatever seed of germination or destruction he and John have planted within him.

And she sees herself, a young woman in slacks and a pullover, her hair a mess, no makeup, on her hands and knees in the basement, raking the coals over in the furnace, and beside her on the stone floor, the stack of buff-colored, spiral-bound, narrow-ruled notebooks that contain her diary.

We're all time travellers, Elaine thinks, setting off from the recent past, on a voyage of discovery to the near future: whose ghostly hands will glove mine this time, as once again I tear out page after page, then stuff them into the fire—as I destroy writing rather than create it?

Seven years earlier, she'd felt Genevieve Taggard's unquiet spirit goading her on—and now it is, perhaps, the younger woman she once was who's urging her to regard this intervening period as just another episode in her life, rather than that life itself. The old Russian émigré had said she should paint the bars of her cage— Could I instead, Elaine muses, burn them?